VINCENT
"AN OFF

NO JOKE

AND IT KEPT GETTING LESS FUNNY
ALL THE TIME.

Vincent Vespers didn't want to get involved with
the mob. He'd leave that to his brother Frank.

But Carmine Tucci wanted Vespers to do a job for
him. A job that would put Vincent very close
to the throne of power that Carmine Tucci had
occupied for so many years.

Dangerously close. To Tucci. To his wife. To his
daughter. To his secrets.

Hell was about to break loose—and Vincent Vespers was trapped in its searing center. . . .

BLOOD CONFESSION

"Remarkable . . . goes from one suspense
situation to another with astonishing
speed. . . . DiBartolomeo has an alluring
style all of his own that is refreshingly free
of stereotypes."
—Jerre Mangione, author of *Mount Allegro*

SPELLBINDING THRILLERS ...
TAUT SUSPENSE

- [ ] **A REASONABLE MADNESS by Fran Dorf.** Laura Wade was gorgeous and gentle, with a successful husband and three lovely children. She was also convinced her thoughts could kill ... "A riveting psychological thriller of murder and obsession." *Chicago Tribune*! (170407—$4.99)

- [ ] **THE HOUSE OF STAIRS by Ruth Rendell writing as Barbara Vine.** "Remarkable ... confirms (Barbara Vine's) reputation as one of the best novelists writing today."—P.D. James. Elizabeth Vetch moves into the grand, old house of her widowed aunt and plunges into a pit of murderous secrets 14 years old. "The best mystery writer anywhere." —Boston Globe (402111—$4.95)

- [ ] **GALLOWGLASS by Ruth Rendell writing as Barbara Vine.** In this stunning novel of erotic obsession, Barbara Vine illuminates the shadows of love cast by dark deeds. Her spell is gripping—and total. "Dazzling ... Barbara Vine's most penetrating foray yet into the dark mysteries of the heart's obsessions. (402561—$5.99)

- [ ] **SIGHT UNSEEN—by David Lorne.** Once Hollywood's top sound effects man, Spike Halleck has been forced to live in a world of darkness, after an accident took away his sight. And despite the odds, he sets out to save the life of a kidnapped little girl he loves.

    (165349—$4.50)

- [ ] **BLINDSIDE by William Bayer.** "A dark and sultry *noir* novel."—*The New York Times Book Review*. Burned-out photographer Geoffrey Barnett follows a stunning young actress into a world of savage secrets, blackmail, and murder. "Smashing ... unstoppable entertainment." —*Kirkus Reviews* (166647—$4.95)

Buy them at your local bookstore or use this convenient coupon for ordering.

NEW AMERICAN LIBRARY
P.O. Box 999, Bergenfield, New Jersey 07621

Please send me the books I have checked above.
I am enclosing $_____ (please add $2.00 to cover postage and handling). Send check or money order (no cash or C.O.D.'s) or charge by Mastercard or VISA (with a $15.00 minimum). Prices and numbers are subject to change without notice.

Card # _____ Exp. Date _____
Signature _____
Name _____
Address _____
City _____ State _____ Zip Code _____

For faster service when ordering by credit card call **1-800-253-6476**

Allow a minimum of 4-6 weeks for delivery. This offer is subject to change without notice.

BLOOD CONFESSIONS

A Novel
Albert DiBartolomeo

A SIGNET BOOK

SIGNET
Published by the Penguin Group
Penguin Books USA Inc., 375 Hudson Street,
New York, New York 10014, U.S.A.
Penguin Books Ltd, 27 Wrights Lane,
London W8 5TZ, England
Penguin Books Australia Ltd, Ringwood,
Victoria, Australia
Penguin Books Canada Ltd, 10 Alcorn Avenue,
Toronto, Ontario, Canada M4V 3B2
Penguin Books (N.Z.) Ltd, 182–190 Wairau Road,
Auckland 10, New Zealand

Penguin Books Ltd, Registered Offices:
Harmondsworth, Middlesex, England

Published by Signet, an imprint of New American Library, a division of Penguin Books USA Inc. This is an authorized reprint of a hardcover edition published by Walker and Company under the title *The Vespers Tapes*.

First Signet Printing, March, 1992
10 9 8 7 6 5 4 3 2 1

Copyright © Albert DiBartolomeo, 1991
All rights reserved

 REGISTERED TRADEMARK—MARCA REGISTRADA

PRINTED IN THE UNITED STATES OF AMERICA

Without limiting the rights under copyright reserved above, no part of this publication may be reproduced, stored in or introduced into a retrieval system, or transmitted, in any form, or by any means (electronic, mechanical, photocopying, recording, or otherwise), without the prior written permission of both the copyright owner and the above publisher of this book. For information, please address Walker and Company, 720 Fifth Avenue, New York, NY 10019.

PUBLISHER'S NOTE
This is a work of fiction. Names, characters, places, and incidents either are the product of the author's imagination or are used fictitiously, and any resemblance to actual persons, living or dead, events, or locales is entirely coincidental.

BOOKS ARE AVAILABLE AT QUANTITY DISCOUNTS WHEN USED TO PROMOTE PRODUCTS OR SERVICES. FOR INFORMATION PLEASE WRITE TO PREMIUM MARKETING DIVISION, PENGUIN BOOKS USA INC., 375 HUDSON STREET, NEW YORK, NEW YORK 10014.

If you purchased this book without a cover you should be aware that this book is stolen property. It was reported as "unsold and destroyed" to the publisher and neither the author nor the publisher has received any payment for this "stripped book."

To Susan

ACKNOWLEDGMENTS

I would like to acknowledge the assistance and support given to me, in one form or another, by the following people: Ron DeChristoforo, Irwin Hahn, Peter Rubie, Diana Finch, my family, all my excellent teachers at Temple University, and Sue Banka, who insisted for many years that somebody had to take the long shot.

ONE

I was sleeping when Frank called. A noise from far away grew louder and louder until finally it pierced my skull with a jolt and woke me. I lurched up from the mattress, blurted something, and glared around the room before realizing that the thing that had woken me was the telephone. Cursing, I groped for it in the liquid gray light and mumbled into the receiver while freeing myself from the sweaty sheets.

"It's seven-thirty on a Friday night and you're sleeping?" my brother said.

The hell with you, Frank, I wanted to say. "I was taking a nap."

"What, are you sick?"

"No, just tired."

I wasn't happy to hear from him. My brother never called for small talk or to hear about the rest of our scattered family. Even when he knew I had spoken to Jamie, his twin in Ohio, or to Ted, the youngest of us somewhere in the woods of upstate New York, he didn't ask about them. Frank only called for one reason: business.

"I want you to meet me at Charlie Shunk's in an hour."

"In an *hour*?" I sat up in the bed and turned on the table lamp. I didn't want to meet with anyone that night, least of all Frank to discuss his dirty finances, and I especially did not want to meet him or anyone at Charlie Shunk's. "Can't it wait, Frank? I have a date tonight." Another casino had opened in Atlantic City; after napping I meant to drive there with a girl I had been seeing.

"You can change it, or bring her along. Anyway, it's important, Vinnie, so don't be late." He hung up.

I slammed down the receiver, picked it up again, and dialed Frank's apartment. No one answered. I tried Shunk's, but Frank wasn't there. I dropped the receiver into the cradle, cursing and shaking my head.

I didn't know where else to call. Frank could have been in New Jersey with Carmine Tucci, his boss, laying out an extortion plan or something, but I wouldn't have called there even if I had to tell Frank that our father had risen from the dead. I would fool with Frank's money, but I wanted no contact with certain associates of his.

I rolled out of bed, muttering and cursing, and went through the house looking for something clean to wear. It was a row home on Jackson Street in South Philadelphia, a half block from the Church of the Epiphany, at Eleventh. We had all grown up there. After Alison and I divorced, I moved into the house because it seemed foolish to pay rent when there was an empty house I could live in for nothing. The house was empty because by then Frank had taken an apartment, Jamie had married, Teddy had begun travels that would not end until he settled in the cabin in the woods, and because we had placed my mother in the Home. I meant to stay in the house temporarily, six months at the most, but I had stayed years longer. Every week I told myself that I was going to put the house up for sale, move away from that part of the city, maybe move from the city entirely. I never did. I also did not keep up with the repairs, and as a result the house had a look of decay, both inside and out. The plaster ceilings were buckling, doors did not close, there were tiles missing from the bathroom walls. Every time Jamie returned for a visit, she scolded me for allowing the house to crumble.

"There's a damn crack up the front like the House of Usher," she said the last time.

It was too true. There were also cracks in the basement floor, the walls, and out front in the sidewalk. I imagined coming home one day and finding the house a pile of rubble.

In the shower, I thought of all the times Frank had called without warning, wanting me for something without considering what I might be doing or whether I wanted to see *him*. I always obliged my brother. It had been that way since we were kids. I felt helpless to do anything about it.

But it had to stop. I had obligations and priorities of my own to attend to without having to jump for Frank. I didn't care anymore how much money Frank had given me over the past few years. I was not comfortable with the idea of handling Frank's money to begin with, and I was no more comfortable with it now. Tonight, I would tell Frank, as I had tried to tell him before, that I no longer wanted to be involved in his financial affairs, which meant that I no longer would be involved with him period.

The front of Shunk's Tavern was brick, with seams of mortar so thin they looked compressed by age. The entrance door, painted the color of dried blood, was flat and solid except for a single diamond of bevelled glass. There were tiny bricks of glass to the sides of the door, but only occasionally and only at night did you see light flicker from within.

A red neon sign blinking "Shunk's Tavern," and below it, "Seafood" in blue, hung above the entrance door until a few years ago. A "couple of punks," as Charlie called them, had thrown rocks at the sign and shot at the door with a handgun. Luckily, it was late at night and no one was inside. Two bullets went through the window; one struck the wall above the cash register and the other passed into the kitchen where Charlie's wife Jemma prepared the food.

The bullet holes in the door were plugged with dowel and those in the wall were filled with plaster. But the sign was left hanging unrepaired, a single vowel and a few jagged consonants all that was left of its former message. The sign hung like that for years before a storm tore it entirely from its moorings and flung it into a parked Continental belonging to Tony "Buttons" Buttoni, the loanshark. The sign smashed the windshield and put a long gash in the hood of the car. Charlie Shunk purchased Buttons a new Lincoln, no questions asked.

By the time I reached Shunk's my entire body felt moist from the August heat, and when I entered the bar the frigid air from Charlie's mammoth air conditioners made me shiver. It was gloomy in the bar and the dense smell of beer had the quality of fumes. Mirrors ran behind the bar and along the opposite wall, so that looking in one I saw everything reflected into infinity. Stools with round, vinyl-covered seats sat in front of the bar, and across from them near the wall were small tables and bentwood café chairs. Candles burned in red glass holders on the tables, Charlie's attempt to add "class" to the place. A jukebox, glowing pink and white, squatted in the corner near the entrance door. The doorway at the rear led to the tiny bathroom and the small smokey room where my father had played gin rummy and pinochle for money. There were no women.

The bar was crowded. I nodded at the familiar faces, but Frank's was not one of them. He wasn't sitting at any of the tables and he was not at the bar. It wasn't the first time Frank had made me rush somewhere to meet him and then not be there.

Charlie Shunk caught my eye and motioned me toward an empty space at the bar.

"Looking for Frankie?" he asked when I came up.

"I'm supposed to meet him."

"He was here a few minutes ago, but he stepped out with Johnny Plum's brother. He told me to tell you to wait. You want a drink in the meantime?"

"Just some seltzer."

"Ok, have a seat." Before going away, Charlie

wiped the varnished bartop in front of me. His large arms, which looked too big for motion, moved swiftly and with a scary power, and his hands were so broad I imagined him cracking coconuts with them. A few months ago, I had watched Charlie use that linebacker body of his to break up a fight. He had grabbed the brawlers one by one and thrown them out the front door, actually putting them in brief, spastic flight. Charlie seemed to have been enjoying himself. One stubborn fighter had his nose broken when he tried to reenter the bar and ran into one of Charlie's fists. I had stood frozen all the while by the tilted pinball machine, afraid that in the confusion Shunk might mistake me for one of the troublemakers and toss me through the door like he had the others. He didn't, and I was able to watch the mayhem from start to finish.

"Still no Frankie?" Charlie said when he returned with my seltzer.

"Looks that way."

"While you're waiting, relax. You never look relaxed, Vinnie. You got a lot of stress?"

"No, I don't have a lot of stress."

"Well, you don't look so good anyway."

I looked over his shoulder at the mirror. I needed a haircut and had the weary look of an insomniac greedy for sleep, despite falling into bed that evening as if struck by a baseball bat. I had lain down with a magazine and, within minutes, the bottom dropped out of my consciousness. I slept deeply and did not dream. This had been going on for several weeks now and I had begun to wonder if planetary arrangements or the phases of the moon were affecting me, as my mother had claimed happened to her, or whether the syrups of my brain had begun to go out of balance from some bizarre affliction. But I wasn't worried. I even welcomed those deep naps because I usually had trouble sleeping, especially at night, when my mind refused to shut down. The not dreaming concerned me a little, because I had read somewhere that only psychotics and the profoundly depressed did not dream.

"I guess Frank's hung up with Plum's brother because of what happened," Charlie said.

"Something happened?" I said, only mildly curious.

"You didn't hear?"

"Hear what?"

Charlie leaned close to me and lowered his voice. "They found Johnny Plum last night upside down in a sewer on Tasker Street."

"What do you mean, dead?"

"Yeah, dead. Strangled."

"You're kidding me."

Charlie shook his head gravely. "The brother took it bad."

"I just saw Plum the other day on Broad Street, laughing with some guy."

"Well, he won't be laughing no more."

"They know who did it?"

Charlie shrugged. "It don't matter to Johnny Plum who did what; he's dead." He looked to the other end of the bar after someone down there called him. "Gotta go," and Charlie left me.

Johnny Plum had sat with Frank a number of times when I arrived at Shunk's Tavern to meet my brother. He did not always get up when Frank and I talked about money; and I sat with Plum alone now and then when Frank was called to the telephone. Plum seemed bright and laughed easily and often. He seemed to be interested in my job as a teacher and asked me why I had gone into it, what I liked about it, what I didn't like. He didn't offer to tell me what he did for a living and I didn't ask. I ran into him in Atlantic City once and we spent three pleasant hours playing blackjack together.

Thinking about Plum at the bar, I couldn't imagine what he had done to get himself killed.

The door flew open and banged against the wall as if blown by a gust of wind. I turned from the mirror along with everyone else and watched my brother come in. He paused just inside the entrance and looked quickly from one end of the bar to the other, his jaw rigid, his eyes hard. The silver light from the streetlamps seemed to cling to his tense and muscular body like St. Elmo's fire. I had seen Frank look that way many times before, rage like an aura about him, my brother not just ready to destroy, but to explode. When you saw him like that, it was smart to move aside or run.

The door banged shut. I thought Frank was looking for me, but his eyes slid past me without stopping and settled on someone at the end of the bar where it curved toward the wall. Frank sprang and rushed past without a look or a word in my direction.

The men at the end of the bar had been laughing and Tommy Green, who ran one of Frank's pizza shops, had been singing along with Sinatra on the jukebox. When they saw Frank slicing through the crowd toward them, they fell silent, and Tommy looked suddenly frightened.

"Jesus," I muttered, knowing what was going to happen.

Frank reached Tommy and grabbed his arm, jerking him off the stool. Green shrank backward, blinking rapidly. His friends took their drinks and moved away, as if obliging Frank with more room. A few of them averted their faces, embarrassed, it seemed, to watch. I looked away too, but only to the backbar mirror where I could still see a clear, though reflected view of my brother.

"What? What's wrong, Frank?" Tommy said, blinking.

"You know what's wrong," Frank said, pushing Green against the wall.

"I don't, honest. What?"

"Don't give me that shit." Frank had the front of Green's shirt in his fist and pushed so hard against Tommy's thin chest it appeared to cave in.

Charlie Shunk went up to them. "Take it easy, Frank," he said. "Do me a favor and take this outside."

"You want to go outside, Tommy?" Frank asked.

Tommy shook his head no in quick, nervous motions.

"Come on, Frank," Charlie said.

Frank looked at the bartender and let go of Green, not because of Charlie's large size, which meant nothing to someone like Frank, but because Charlie had known us since children and had nearly the same influence over us as our relatives.

Tommy appeared as if rescued; he stopped blinking and the blood returned to his face. Frank and the men around him seemed to relax as well. Tommy smiled. My brother smiled, too, without showing his teeth and ordered a drink. I knew that smile, and I knew not to trust it.

"The usual?" Charlie asked, eager to return things to normal.

"The usual," Frank said.

When Charlie turned his back and walked a few steps away toward the scotch, Frank turned to Green and, still smiling, punched him in the stomach. Tommy folded in half instantly and Frank punched him in the back of the neck, knocking Tommy out of sight behind the bar. Frank kicked him a few times, but I didn't see where the foot hit. My brother ducked down, grabbed Tommy from the floor and dragged him to the bathroom. Green looked dazed and sick. Frank shoved him into the little, smelly room and followed. The bathroom, with its single toilet and tiny sink, was barely big enough for one person, let alone two. Why Frank would want to take Tommy in there was beyond me.

When Charlie turned and saw that Frank and Tommy were gone, he looked to me for an explanation. I motioned with my head to the rear of the bar, but that wasn't enough for Charlie and he came over to me, Frank's scotch and water in his hand.

"They're in the bathroom," I said.

"The bathroom?" He looked that way. "Why?"

"Got me."

"I wish Frank wouldn't do this. Somebody gets hurt here and the place gets a bad reputation."

I nearly reminded Charlie that he was the one who, with the help of his sons, had abducted and thrown darts all night into the two guys who had vandalized his bar a little while back, and that he already had a reputation for lifting troublemakers over his head and throwing them across the sidewalk and into Passyunk Avenue.

"Nothing's going on," I said, as if wise about these things. For all I knew, Frank had Tommy's head in the stained toilet bowl, betting with him on how long Tommy could hold his breath.

"No, this is not good for business," Charlie said. But whatever Frank was doing, Charlie decided it was not serious enough to interrupt. He would have interrupted someone else, maybe even jumped over the bar to get at them, but Frank was a special case. You did not tangle with my brother, or some of his friends, without serious risk.

Charlie put down the drink and went to pull beer from the tap for some customers who had just come in and called their orders. As Shunk filled glasses, he kept taking nervous peeks toward the bathroom.

A minute later, Frank and Tommy stepped from the bathroom, Frank with his arm around Green's shoulders. Tommy, his face a little swollen on one side, looked like a contrite child. Frank sat him on a stool at the end of the bar and they took their drinks from Charlie, who watched them closely until he was satisfied that nobody's blood was going to spill on his floor.

That's over, I thought. Good. At least now Frank and I can get our business finished and I can go.

Frank said a few last words to Tommy, took his drink from the bar and sat next to me. We did not exchange greetings. We never did. All our conversations seemed extensions of a previous one that had been interrupted.

"You want to know what I did to him in there?" he asked.

"If you want to tell me."

"I took a dump and made him stand next to me."

I could only look at him at that.

"A birdbrain like Tommy, knocking them around doesn't always do any good because that's what they've been getting all their life; they're used to it. You have to try different things to get your point across."

"I don't get it."

"You're putting your smell on them, and you're making them think you're so sure you can kick their ass that you'll even make yourself defenseless by sitting on the toilet in front of them."

"Well, that's different, all right." I began to picture the scene, then almost immediately shoved it from my mind.

A man I did not know came up to us. "Excuse me, Frank," he said. "I was wondering if we could discuss that little matter now."

Frank looked at his watch. "Sure." Turning to me, he said, "It'll only take a few minutes. You don't mind, do you?"

I said no, but the hell I didn't mind. I didn't have all night to watch Frank assault people and hold court.

Frank led the man to "his" table while I stayed at the bar. Charlie came up after Frank had gone and asked if I wanted more seltzer.

I nodded. "It looks like I'll be here a while."

Charlie lingered in front of me, waiting expectantly for me to say more, then finally walked away.

I wanted to leave, but I knew if I did Frank would

send someone after me, probably Tommy, and I wanted to avoid that. I didn't want to appear like a flunky, one of Frank's boys, by having another flunky chase me down and bring me back to the bar. Anyway, if I slipped out without Frank seeing me, he would only get angry, which wouldn't bother me, but I would still have to see him sometime soon, which did. Leaving wouldn't do any good, I decided, so I stayed perched on my stool, chewed ice, and waited for Frank to finish.

I watched his reflection in the mirror. Of all of us, he was the best looking; he had entirely escaped my father's large nose and my mother's squat frame. His jaw was square and strong and so closely shaven it looked burnished. He had taken up weightlifting for the last several years and looked powerful in the tight knit shirt he wore. His hair and Jamie's was deep black, whereas my hair and Teddy's was diluted brown. I was as tall as Frank but lighter in the body; my nose was thicker in the bridge than his, my chin weaker, my teeth less straight. But over the telephone, we were told, we sounded alike.

Frank did not have an open face, one that encouraged confessions like Jamie's, but even if it seemed incapable of sympathy it did not look completely unkind. Despite his periodic flare-ups, people quickly warmed to him, and he was often so out-going and generous, it was easy to forget that strewn behind him were so many broken laws, broken heads, and broken hearts.

TWO

"Let's sit at the table," Frank said, finally coming over to me.

I slid off my stool without a word and followed Frank back to his table, which was vacant while Frank was in the bar. The men on each side of the table shifted away from us in their seats as we sat down. Frank sat facing the door. I sat with my back to it.

"Want a drink?"

"I have one." I lifted my glass of seltzer.

"Something stronger than that, I mean."

"No, I don't need anything stronger."

"Still have that date?"

"I cancelled it."

"Sorry to hear that."

"Me, too."

Frank didn't seem to be paying much attention to my answers, so I didn't bother too much with them.

I had the feeling I could have told him anything and his responses would be the same. He leaned forward, his arms on the table, his hands in the candle holder's ruby light, but he hardly looked at me. His eyes kept shifting around the bar and to the door every time someone came in. Locking eyes for a moment with Tommy Green across the room, Tommy smiled broadly and flashed an ok sign at Frank, as if his humiliation earlier by my brother was something for which he was grateful. For his part, Frank seemed not only unaffected by his performance with Tommy, but unconscious of it. If I had done the same thing, made myself a spectacle for a crowd, someone to be talked about, I would have carried something with me, an awareness that showed in my gestures and face. There was none of that in Frank, not even a shadow.

Frank glanced Tommy's way, smiling at him as Tommy tilted ice cubes into his gaping mouth and put one in each cheek.

"Look at that mongoloid," Frank said. "All he knows how to do is eat pills and make pizza. If I didn't give him a job, he wouldn't be working. And then he goes and helps himself to the cash register."

"So that's why you knocked him around?"

"Yeah. It's not the first time he stole from me. He steals a lot and I don't do anything. It's a fringe benefit. He probably even knows that I know. But sometimes he gets greedy."

"Is that what happened to Johnny Plum? He got greedy?"

Frank's head snapped away from the door. Whatever had been distracting him vanished. "I don't know anything about it. Anyway, it doesn't have nothing to do with you."

"You don't look too unhappy."

"Are *you* unhappy?"

"No, but he was your friend, not mine."

"Patty Leone was my only friend. Now let's shut up about it." He gulped his drink and left the table to get another.

I watched Frank's back as he crossed the room, sorry that I had mentioned Johnny Plum. Frank was right, these violent squabbles were none of my concern, even if they led to the death of someone I had chatted with about Caruso and the movie *Casablanca*. What I regretted most was that I had caused Frank to bring up Patty Leone, a subject I knew to be sore with him, and to which he always reacted with bitterness.

One of the photographs taped on the mirror around Charlie's cash register showed Frank standing outside the bar with Patty. He was the nephew of our neighbor, Mrs. Falcone, who raised him from infancy after his parents were killed in a car accident. Frank was friendlier with Patty than with any other person he knew, including his family. I never faulted my brother for that. Patty was so likable and generous-spirited that he seemed like part of the family.

There was another picture of Patty and my father, and one of Charlie Shunk and my father with Patty between them, all with their arms around each others shoulders. In all of the photographs of Pat, he is wearing his black leather jacket, which he wore even in the summer. When they were friends, before Patty disappeared, Frank had an identical leather jacket, so that occasionally, in poor light, they were mirrored images of themselves.

Frank returned from the bar and sat down. "Tell me what I'm worth," he said.

I looked at his dark eyes and the hard line of his jaw. I could see no more in that face now than what I always saw, a willfulness so blind and complete it was frightening.

"Ok," I said flatly. "You want me to figure in what you give me tonight?"

"I'm not giving you anything tonight," Frank said.

"I don't understand. You mean, you asked me here just for an update?"

"I wanted to know my position."

"But I could have given you that over the phone."

"I didn't want to talk on the phone. I thought we could have a drink."

"Frank, I had a date tonight, which I cancelled because—"

"Who with?"

"You don't know her, a medical transcriptionist, but—"

"A medical what?"

"It's not important. I just think you should realize what I gave up by meeting you here." After Frank called, I telephoned my date and said that I had developed a migraine headache and wouldn't be able to go out with her, at least not as planned. I told her that if I felt better in an hour, I would call. She said not to bother. I was certain she knew I had lied. I was also certain that I would never see her again.

"I appreciate it," Frank said.

"Sure."

"What do you want me to do? This?" He capped the flame in the red glass candle holder with his hand.

"What are you doing? Don't."

"It's my penance," Frank said, gritting his teeth against the burn.

I grabbed his wrist and pulled his hand off the holder. "Christ, are you crazy? Why do you do things like that?"

Frank set his glass of scotch and ice on his blackened palm. "The Hail Marys take too long," he said, glancing at the door as someone came in. He turned back to me. "Will you give me the numbers now, Vin?"

"I guess I better before you cut your wrists or something. You want just the liquid assets or everything?"

"I want to know how much cash I could get my hands on in a day or two, and then the rest."

I cleared my throat. "You have about twenty in cash in the safe deposit box and a little more than that in Krugerrands and silver. You could convert the gold and silver in an afternoon, maybe a day. The same to liquidate the CDs. The stocks would take a week, but they'd give you a check which you'd have to wait to clear. That would bring you up to about one-twenty. Then there are the municipals, which you could cash, but you'd take a bath on them because they're not mature."

"And the rest, the total package?"

"Counting the businesses, the triplexes, and that land near the Poconos, you're worth almost half a million."

Frank held his chin and worked on that awhile. Nothing could preoccupy him like his money. The worst part for me was sitting there while the figures churned around in his head.

Somebody put on more Sinatra at the jukebox and again a couple of men at the bar sang along, this time to "My Way." A large man at my back lit a cigar and sent a cloud of smoke over the table, then he coughed deeply and spat into a handkerchief. I wanted very much to leave.

"Ok?" I said. "That's your position."

"I want to be a millionaire in three years," Frank said, as if he didn't hear me. "Do you think I can make it?"

"At the rate you're going, you will."

"I don't ever want to be weak because I don't have money. How do you handle that nine-to-five shit, anyway?"

"Nine-to-three and summers off," I said, starting to fidget. "I'm a school teacher, remember?"

"What's the difference? You're still punching a clock, working for somebody, and you're never going to get rich because of it."

This was the part where Frank told me that, with a little guts, I could escape my humble position in life and "go places," "be somebody." He would help me, set me up in real estate, business, whatever I wanted. He made it sound so easy and appealing that at times I imagined myself making shrewd deals and raking in bundles of money. I saw myself in a speeding Porsche or playing hundred dollar blackjack, the pit bosses comping me tickets for the fights or the Lena Horne show. But I never took Frank up on any of his offers; I was resigned to my life the way it was, small and reasonably simple.

"Maybe I don't want to be rich," I said.

"Bullshit. Everybody wants to be rich, especially guys who grew up like we did, their old man unclogging somebody's toilet or putting in water heaters on Saturdays to make ends meet. I want a lot more and so do you. Why do you take the money from me if you don't want to be rich? You put it in the poor box at the church like Teddy used to do with my Christmas gifts?"

"Suppose I said I did?"

"Then I'd say you were kookier than mom."

"You shouldn't talk that way about her."

"No? Why not?"

Before I could say the obvious, that she was our mother, that it was bad enough she had lost some of her mind, Frank's attention went to the door behind me.

I looked over my shoulder and saw that two men had come in. They wore blazers and pastel-colored shirts. One wore a tie, but the other's shirt was open at the neck, showing a dense thatch of black hair in which gold nestled. The one with the tie walked straight to the back room, re-emerged, ducked into the bathroom, then went to the end of the bar near Tommy Green and stood there. Green edged away. The other man looked over the room with a sweep of his eyes and settled near the entrance. Both men were expressionless. I noticed that Frank had nodded to them.

"Who are they?"

"Guys I know. George and Leo."

"What are they doing?"

Frank didn't have to answer. His eyes went to the door again, and when I turned I saw two more men come in the bar. Even in the poor light I recognized Tony Buttons—that thick neck, the oiled hair, the gouge in his cheek. The other man was elderly, small, and he carried a cane for his limp. A tension came into the place as heads went their way. Someone in the back room, unaware of the change in the bar, said, "Gin!" Buttons looked toward the back at the sound, but the old man didn't seem to notice it. I realized, even before Frank stood up, that the old man was Carmine Tucci.

"I'll be leaving now," I said quickly, before Frank could move away from the table.

"No, you can't," Frank said. "How's it going to look if you walk out just as he walks in?"

"I don't care how it looks."

"Stay here a minute. I'll be right back."

"Frank," but he had started across the room.

I watched from the table, my stomach knotting, as Frank went to meet Tucci. I nearly followed him, in a panic now to leave, but Tucci and Buttons stood between me and the door. I would have had to go through them to get out. No, I could not do that, excuse myself, wedge my way through, risk Frank grabbing my arm and rooting me before those men. So I ground my teeth and waited for them to clear away.

Frank leaned close to his boss and spoke in his ear. Tony Buttons smiled down at them with only half of his mouth, then moved away toward the bar and motioned to Charlie for a drink. Because there were no empty tables and because Tucci would not sit at the bar, I knew Frank would bring his boss to our table. It had an inevitability about it that made me want to choke.

Frank held the old man by the elbow as they crossed the room. The men at the tables nearest us slid their seats away or left entirely. My face began to pulse, my armpits went cold, and when Frank arrived with Tucci I stood too abruptly and nearly knocked over my chair. I did not want to be in the same room with this man, let alone at the same table.

"My brother," Frank said, gesturing to me.

Tucci looked older than in the newspaper photographs or when he sometimes appeared on the television news. In the newspapers or on television, you did not see his wrinkled skin so clearly, his chapped, anemic lips, and the blotches that ran up from his forehead and over his shiny scalp. He did not look well.

Tucci extended his hand. I took it without hesitation, out of courtesy, but when I went to pull away after a moment Tucci held my hand more tightly than I would have expected from a man that looked as infirm as he did. As Tucci gripped me, he looked directly into my eyes, as though he were both plumbing my depths and transmitting a sort of force, through the circuit of his arm and eyes. It was a look both intense and probing, and it made me uncomfortable.

Tucci let go of my hand finally and sat across from me in the seat Frank had left, then asked Frank to bring him a glass of milk and me another drink.

"No, I don't want another drink," I said quickly. "I have to get going."

Frank turned sharply toward me. "You want lime with the soda?" he asked.

From his voice alone, I knew what he wanted me to say. "Uh, sure."

Frank said, "Lime's good. Charlie should have some. While I'm gone, why don't you have a seat?" He gestured to the chair behind me.

I looked dumbly around at the chair as if unaware that I had been standing. Frank nudged my arm and I sat. He smiled and walked toward the bar.

Tucci did not speak while Frank was gone, and neither did I, but he looked at me steadily with a calm gaze that I could not meet for longer than a moment or two. I kept waiting for him to say something, make a little idle talk at least. Maybe I'm ignorant of some mob protocol, I thought, and Tucci's waiting for me to speak. But that didn't matter. I couldn't think of anything to say, not even a comment about the weather. Instead, I sat there squirming beneath that steady gaze, unable to speak or to look at Tucci long.

I felt relieved when Frank returned with the drinks. He would have business to discuss with his boss and I could run. But as soon as Frank put down the glasses, Tucci dismissed him with a nod so slight it seemed like a tremor. I took that nod as my cue also and slid back from the table, preparing to stand.

"You stay," Tucci said.

"Huh?"

Frank put his hand on my shoulder and pressed down, wordlessly indicating that I was to remain with Tucci. After I sat, Frank walked back toward the bar. I watched him recede, feeling abandoned and confused. Charlie Shunk stood directly beyond him, leaning with his back to the cash register, but he wasn't looking at Frank coming his way. He had his eyes on me. With his arms folded across his stomach, he looked at me with bemusement and some other emotion he hadn't quite settled on.

I turned back to Tucci, flustered, a little afraid, and drew my chair slowly back to the table. What was going on? I chewed my lips, frantic to know. I almost asked him, the question nearly jumping from my tightened throat. But when I shot a look at Tucci, I felt his eyes on me like a weight and I said nothing. He sat with his knotty hands wrapped around his glass of milk, the blue veins so pronounced they seemed to run on the outside of his skin, and again he seemed to be waiting for *me* to speak.

"I've met you before," Tucci finally said, his sagging throat quivering.

I blinked, sat up in my chair. "You have? Where?"

"Your father put in some spigots for me a long time ago. A boy, ten, maybe eleven years old, was with him. That was you."

"It could have been Frank," I said quickly, almost urgently.

"No. I asked Frank. He said he never went with your father on any plumbing jobs. He said the other one, your youngest brother, never went either. It was always you."

What Frank had told him, for whatever reason, was true, and I didn't try to deny it further.

"Do you remember the house in Sewell?"

"I don't know where Sewell is."

"In Jersey, a half hour from the Walt Whitman Bridge."

"No, I'm sorry, I don't remember."

"You wouldn't eat anything for lunch."

"Excuse me?"

"You wouldn't touch a crumb. You wouldn't even drink anything. Only your father ate."

"I don't remember going to New Jersey with my father for a spigot job, or any job," I said. But even as I spoke, I saw us crossing the tall bridges on early Saturday mornings heading toward Cherry Hill or Pensauken or Deptford, my father's wrenches, pipe cutters, and acetylene torch rattling in the trunk.

"I remember," Tucci said. "Things keep coming back to me lately. Memories. Things I haven't thought about in years. Have you ever heard anything like that?"

"No." If I had, I wouldn't have told him.

He seemed disappointed. "Oh." He paused, and his blue eyes drifted away from me.

This was the man I had heard and read about, since I was old enough to be aware that there were men in my part of the world who had achieved power and influence from lives devoted entirely to crime. Evil men who maimed and killed, who ordered killings, who extorted, ran drug and prostitution rings, who paid off cops, who bribed politicians and judges. But close up, Carmine Tucci looked like an old man who had lived honestly and never harmed anyone. The thought did nothing to calm me.

Tucci's eyes came down from over my shoulder. "The spigots still don't leak."

"Excuse me? Oh. My father would be glad to hear it."

"I knew him when he was young, you know."

I nodded, not even thinking of asking, How? I

didn't want to hear any more stories that would connect me with Tucci, however slimly.

"He was a good man."

I cleared my throat. "Mr. Tucci," I said in a rush, my voice shaking. "I'm glad to have met you but I have to go now." I began to stand up.

Tucci touched my wrist. "I'll let you go soon." With his touch and piercing look, he froze me and made me understand that I was not going anywhere until he finished. "In the meantime, try to relax. Your knuckles are white from grabbing your glass, and you've been bouncing your knees."

I leaned back into my seat and put my hands under the table to steady my legs.

"I want you to tell me some things about yourself."

My knees started again and I dug my fingers into my thighs to stop them. "What do you want to know?"

"Frank says you're a teacher."

I nodded. My knees wouldn't quit.

"And you were married."

"I was married, yes."

"No children?"

"No, no children."

"You live on Jackson Street, you visit your sick mother once a month, your sister's married to a Jew?"

I hesitated a moment, my neck burning. It was as though he were reading my dossier. "Yes."

"If you're wondering how I know, Frank told me. He told me some other things and I wanted to meet you."

I forgot myself in my sudden anger and turned nearly all the way around to look at Frank. He had his back to me. I glared at the back of his skull and tried to transmit my anger into his Neanderthal brain. Frank didn't call me to Shunk's to give him the lowdown on his finances. Instead, he had gotten me there to meet his boss, who seemed to have some cockamamie idea that we might become friends.

"What's the matter?" Tucci asked.

I turned back to him. "Nothing."

"You didn't know I was coming?"

"Frank never said."

"Maybe you wouldn't have come."

I didn't say anything and looked at my hands.

Tucci fell silent again and seemed to mull something over. I looked away from him, as if that would make one of us disappear. It was still early but the crowd in Shunk's had thinned, and most of the men who remained were subdued. Only Tommy Green and a friend, shooting darts, seemed to have energy. The jukebox was silent. The candles on the tables burned in the gloom, it seemed to me, like votive candles at the marble feet of church saints. Frank's back still faced me; he was talking to Charlie Shunk, somberly polishing glasses behind the bar. The two men at my back, who had been talking boxing and baseball, had gone by the time Tucci began to talk. The men who had come in with Tucci stood together without speaking, looking our way, their faces unreadable, except for Tony Buttoni's. I saw hatred and anger in his eyes, and it seemed directed at me. He turned away before I could make sure.

"I have a favor to ask you," Tucci said, coming so far forward suddenly that the candle flame cast shadows upward from his nose, lips, and cheeks, turning him momentarily into a hobgoblin.

"Favor?" At the word, my spine went rigid and my stomach began to burn. Ever since Tucci came in, I realized then, a screw had been turning toward this. I had been stupid not to see it.

"You'll get paid, of course," Tucci went on. "This is what I want you to do. I want you to come out to my house. You'll come for as long as it takes, which shouldn't be longer than a month. For doing this, I'll give you twenty-five thousand dollars, half before you start, half at the end."

I stared at him, unable to comprehend what he was telling me, though when he said the figure I saw it in the air, dollar sign and everything. "I'm sorry, I don't understand."

"My life. My, what do they call them, memoirs."

"Memoirs?"

"I want to have them written. I want you to do it."

I sank back in my chair. I had lost control of my knees long ago and now they shook so violently I expected them any second to go flailing about beneath the table.

"I can't do that," I said.

"Why can't you?"

"I just can't."

"Give me a good reason."

"For one thing, I wouldn't know how to go about it."

"You come out to the house, you sit with me, I talk a few hours into a tape recorder, you go home. Later, you put it in order, do what you have to do, type it up. Simple."

"I'm just a school teacher." It sounded like pleading.

"But you should know how to do something like

this. How hard could it be, somebody with your brains?" He seemed annoyed. "Look, if you can give me a good reason for not helping me, I'll maybe forget about it."

"I just," but that's all I could say then. I lowered my eyes and stared into my seltzer. I didn't want to see Tucci after tonight, certainly did not want to go out to his house for any reason, but I could not bring myself to tell him that. "Why?" slipped out like a groan.

"Why you or why the memoirs?"

"Both."

"Would telling you make you agree?"

"I would only like to know."

Tucci said, "I've been thinking about this for a while. It started like an itch, but got bigger and bigger. It wouldn't let me alone. They write things about me in the papers. People assume things. They don't know who I am, where I been. Do you, even? Do you know who I am? So I want to set everybody straight, you know, before I die or something happens to me. But I don't have any experience in doing it, and I didn't have anybody to ask for advice. Then Frank mentioned you not long ago, I don't even know why, just out of the blue, and I started to think you could help me. After sitting here a little bit, I decided you could."

He let that sink in, keeping his calm gaze on me, which fell somewhere between infinite patience and heartlessness. I understood his impulse and did not question it, but I had no desire to act on it.

"I'm sorry, Mr. Tucci," I said, "but I'd be way out of my league."

"Thirty thousand?"

"You're generous, but the money doesn't matter."

"At least—" He winced suddenly and his hand went to his stomach.

"What is it?" I asked as he held himself and grimaced. "Are you all right?"

Tucci waved his other hand. "Ulcer," he said, breathing deeply. I saw pain in his eyes and around his taut mouth. Tucci reached into his jacket pocket and took out a white pill; he tossed the tablet into his mouth and swallowed it with my seltzer. "Thank you."

"Sure." I didn't want the seltzer anyway.

"At least think about it."

"All right. I will."

"Fine." Tucci stood, grimacing again as he did so. Before he left the table, he touched my shoulder and forced a smile. "You'll hear from me."

I stayed in my seat, barely nodding so-long.

Frank met Tucci halfway to the door and had a few words with the boss before he and his entourage headed out. I caught Buttoni's eyes again before he turned and in them still was the chilly anger and hatred I had seen earlier.

After the door closed behind Tucci, a wave of murmuring went through Shunk's as the tension in the air went with him.

"So what's up, Vinnie?" Frank asked, when he returned to the table.

"I hate that fucking name. Don't call me that anymore."

"Whoa, what are you getting crazy about?"

"You tricked me into coming here, Frank."

"He wanted to meet you, what could I do? You wouldn't come if I told you that."

"You should have told me anyway."

"What, so you would refuse to come and I'd look bad because I couldn't get you here?"

"So I had to suffer because you didn't want to look bad?"

"Suffer? You didn't look like you were suffering. I turned around and it looked like you two were making a deal."

"We didn't make any fucking deal."

"So what were you doing all that time?"

"You don't know?"

"How should I know? You think he tells me everything?"

"He's got this crazy idea about having his biography written, and he wants me to do it, which is even crazier."

"His what?"

"That's right, his memoirs."

Frank mouthed the word. "You mean, like presidents write?"

"That's it. He wants to do a fucking Ulysses S. Grant number."

"What's he going to do with them?"

"I don't know. Maybe he wants to get on the best-seller list."

"Come on. Did he offer you money?"

"Thirty thousand." I saw the figure again, as if in neon.

"Thirty thousand! Does he want you to clunk somebody?"

"I can see that: Schoolteacher turns hit man. No, no clunking involved."

I looked away from Frank, disgusted and confused. Before tonight, Tucci had occupied a very small part of my brain; he was a cliché, pictures in the media with no more personality or character than what little I got from Frank when he mentioned him. Now he had both; he had spoken my name, touched me, drunk my seltzer, and it made me feel peculiar.

"It's weird," Frank said after a pause, "but you have to do it."

"Why do I have to do it?"

"Because he asked you and because you're my brother."

"I'm not sure they're such great reasons."

"Ok, then think about the money."

"I don't care about that."

"You don't care about the money?"

"I don't care about the fucking money!" I jumped up from the table.

"Take it easy," Frank said, standing. "I mean you should consider the thing before you say no."

"I don't have to consider anything. I'll be seeing you." I started for the door.

"Hey, you need a lift?"

I made no sign that I had heard him and kept walking.

I hurried to my car and sped home. I left the car idling in the street as I ran in the house and took from beneath the carpet the four thousand dollars I had received from Frank over the last eight months. I hurried back to the car and sped away, the tires screeching as I went.

I drove to Broad Street three blocks away, made a left, and, a few minutes later, turned right onto the ramp that led to the Walt Whitman bridge. The Phillies were playing in Veteran's Stadium and above it was a giant mushroom of silver-blue light. I heard the crowd cheer briefly as I eased onto the highway.

The bridge loomed ahead and the usual dizziness and nausea started up. I reached the toll line in a minute, shivering with cold sweat and with my heart galloping. There was a lull in the traffic and I did not have to creep behind a long line of cars before dropping my exact change into the toll basket. I was thankful for that. Speeding away, I forced myself to breathe easily, and I fought the urge to stop and turn around as I crossed the entire one mile span of the bridge. Crossing the bridge, any bridge, was never easy, and this time was no different. But I made it across without glancing over the sides at the dark ships or the docklights reflected in the black river far below. And I didn't think except once, though that was enough, about the catastrophe on another bridge years before, and the screaming plunge into the water.

Coming off the bridge, feeling better and eager to get to the shore, I pushed the car up to sixty-five miles an hour. Later, as I rode through the Pinelands on the Atlantic City Expressway, smelling honeysuckle and sometimes pig manure on the inrushing wind, I did seventy and over. I wasn't afraid of having an accident. I didn't care if state troopers pulled me over for speeding. Nothing could touch me, not the humiliations or bad memories that kept me awake at night, not Tucci or Frank, not regret about the cancelled date, not even the poor woman Frank and I hit in the stolen car when we were teenagers. I was alone, in motion, beginning to feel lucky, and no one knew my whereabouts. Perfect.

THREE

On the return drive from Atlantic City, I tried not to think about the thirty-eight hundred dollars I had lost in four hours at the casinos. I tried not to think of all the stiff blackjack hands or the one string of seventeen straight losing hands that prompted the dealer himself to express *tsks* of disbelief. I tried not to think about the desperate attempts I made to recoup my losses by betting wildly at the craps tables and the roulette wheels, which only resulted in more losses. But driving through the black August night, the dreadful hours in the casinos kept playing themselves over and over in my head. I couldn't help it. No matter what other subject I tried to think about, the bad cards, bad dice, and my vanishing money kept flashing against the windshield. Thoughts of my ex-wife Alison would have shoved the images away, but that would leave her in my brain, which had an unpleasantness all its own.

I reached the city near five o'clock in the morning and parked at the end of the block. Jackson Street was quiet and dark, except for the light from the few streetlamps. I closed the door softly after getting out of the car. No one was on the street but me and the startled cockroaches speeding across the sidewalk. At least I thought so until I noticed the silhouette of a man standing motionless under the big sycamore tree outside my house. He appeared to be waiting for someone. Me? I slowed my walk and moved closer to the row homes, keeping my eyes on the figure. Then I saw the dog come out from behind the tree trunk and I realized who stood there.

"I know what I'm doing out here at this hour," my neighbor Lou Cocco said as I came up, his dog immediately sniffing me, "but what are you doing out?"

"I'm making sure nobody's dog pisses on my tree."

"He wasn't pissing. Anyway, since when is it your tree?"

"I carved my initials in it once."

"Who didn't?"

It was the only tree on the block and, with its green bloom and crude carvings, it was a freak. But I liked it.

"I never forgave you for painting the trunk red, white and blue during the Bicentennial celebration." I tried not to grin.

"I'm patriotic."

"It was a desecration."

"Get outta here, you meatball," Cocco said laughing. I laughed too.

Lou drove a city bus up and down Broad Street; when we stopped laughing, he told me that he was working a Saturday shift that week-end and had to be at the depot by seven o'clock. As he did every morning he worked, he was walking the dog while coffee brewed in his house across the street.

"So, are you coming home from a date?" Cocco asked.

"I don't want to tell you where I've been."

"That bad?"

"I was in Atlantic City."

"And you gambled and lost, right?"

"I lost, yes."

Now Cocco would chide me. Possibly, I wanted him to.

"Queenie," Lou said to his dog, "bite him. Bite him extra hard in a soft spot for maximum excruciation."

The dog wagged its tail.

"I know, you don't like the casinos."

"They're a blight," Cocco said. "What good do they serve? Tell me that."

"Well, they provide entertainment," I said, weakly.

"You think taking people's money and giving them nothing in return is entertaining them? Were you entertained by losing?"

"Not exactly, but—"

"They're selling a drug, is what they do. It's no different."

He was beginning to get excited, the way he always did when discussing some topic that offended either his sense of morality or decency. I didn't want him to start raising his voice and swinging his arms there on the sidewalk at five o'clock in the morning, bringing the neighbors to their windows to gawk at us, so I mumbled something that sounded like agreement, hoping that would calm him down.

"They're thieves," Lou went on, still agitated. "You're going to have crooks running things in Atlantic City, if they aren't already."

When Cocco mentioned "crooks," as he often did, I always became self-conscious; the back of my neck prickled and my face became warm. I never told Lou about my financial relationship with Frank, of course, and there was nothing visible about Frank's affairs that would make Cocco think my brother was anything more than a successful businessman. But Cocco held such high moral ground in all matters that my reaction to it was always that of uneasiness, as if he could see the dark things I hid. When that happened, I came up with some excuse to leave.

I faked a yawn and said that I'd better be going to bed.

But Cocco wasn't through. "Did you see where they got another one of those scum?"

"Who? What scum?"

"Yeah, some paperboy found this creep in the sewer. Death by strangulation, the news said. His name was Johnny Nunzio, with the alias of—what was it?—Johnny Plum."

I had forgotten about Plum. "No, I didn't hear that."

"Good riddance, I say. Let them wipe themselves out."

I grunted something and began to back up toward my house, pantomiming fatigue so Cocco would shut up and let me go.

"A few months ago, it was that guy they found in the trunk on Fitzwater Street, and a few weeks before that the guy at the Lakes with his face blown off. Something's going on, Vince. They're killing each other again."

"Yes, it's terrible," I said, reaching the steps. "Well, good night, Cocco."

"No more gambling!" he called.

"Never." I put the key in the door.

"Come on, Queenie. Want some breakfast?"

The dog barked.

I closed the door and leaned against it with my back for a while before trudging up the stairs to bed.

Late the next morning, just before noon, I went out to buy groceries at a corner store. The sky was hazy, the air thick, the sun already punishing. Mrs. Falcone, wearing a sleeveless house dress and running shoes, was washing down her sidewalk. She worked the jet of water from the hose back and forth across the sidewalk in slow arcs, pushing dirt and candy wrappers toward the gutter. When my brothers, Jamie and I were all very young, Mrs. Falcone would set her nozzle on spray, point the hose into the air so that the fine water came out against the sky, and create rainbows from the mist for us to see. She did the same thing for the children now; they would gather around her and squeal in excitement or stand in rapt wonder as the colors appeared.

"Good morning, Mrs. Falcone," I said, smelling wet pavement and cleanser.

She looked up and smiled.

"Need anything at the corner?"

She said no but that she could use a few things at Ninth Street. As always, she told me not to go out of my way and that I should only pick up the items if I was going to the open market on Ninth Street for myself. I never went there for myself.

"Yes, I'll be going there," I lied.

She said, "Good," and told me to stop by for her list before I went.

"Fine," I said, and headed for the grocery store.

Someone was getting married in the Church of the Epiphany. Clean cars were double-parked on Jackson Street, some with crepe paper streamers taped along their shiny flanks. Bridesmaids dressed in pink chiffon gowns with large matching hats, looking like flamingos against the church's gray stone, waited on the upper steps for the bride to arrive. Several ushers in black tuxedos milled around with them. I didn't recognize any of their faces.

A noise made me look to the other side of the street, where I saw a man taking pictures. It was the clicking of the shutter as the photographer snapped pictures of a couple getting out of a metallic blue Mercedes. Whoever was getting married, I thought, had enough money to hire several photographers, one just for outside shots of the guests arriving.

I turned the corner and nearly collided with Tony Buttons and Tommy Green. Tony wore a navy blue blazer and a tie; there was dried blood on his chin where he had nicked himself shaving. Tommy was dressed in khaki pants and a tee shirt, and he wore his simple-minded grin. I noticed a small bruise on his cheek bone where Frank's foot must have landed the night before.

"Hey, Vinnie," he said, glad to see me, "we were just going to your place."

I looked from him to Tony. "Mr. Tucci told me to knock on your door, see if you're in," Buttoni said.

He was just as unfriendly and dangerous-looking as last night.

"I was just going to run some errands," I said.

"I still gotta knock. Mr. Tucci says knock, I knock. I want to use your toilet anyway. They're waiting for the bride like an hour, and I'm ready to bust."

Tommy touched Buttoni's elbow. "Look, Tone, ain't that Philly Fats?"

Tony looked to where Green pointed to a man crossing the street. "Jeez, Maglio invited everybody to his son's wedding, even his fucking barber. Philly owes me eight hundred bucks, and if I find out he put more than a hundred in his envelope that'll piss me off."

"Tone, is the Maglio getting married the one they tried to nail a little while ago?"

Tony put his large hand on the back of Green's neck and squeezed; Tommy screwed up his eyes. "You a girl? You like to gab? If you do, get lost." Buttoni let him go and turned to me. "The door open?" he asked, walking toward my house.

"Open," I said, not knowing how to stop him.

In the house, Tommy sprawled on the sofa and watched cartoons on the television. Daffy Duck said, "Suffering succotash," as I walked by, and Tommy laughed and slapped his thighs. From the bathroom above my head came Buttoni's crooning.

The front door opened and Frank stepped in. Dressed for the wedding, I assumed, Frank wore a tan linen suit and a powder blue shirt. There was sunlight in the vestibule behind him and, with his black hair just right, his chiselled build, and his perfect clothes, he looked more beautiful almost than handsome.

"What the fuck are you doing here?" Frank asked Tommy.

"I'm with Tony," Green said, standing. "He's in the bathroom."

"Shouldn't you be at the pizza shop now, running lunch?"

"I wanted to talk to you about that, Frank."

"Talk? I don't have time for talk. Get going." Frank jerked his thumb over his shoulder.

"Frank," Tommy said, his head down, "I was thinking about making a change. Tony said he had a job for me."

Frank took a quick step toward Green. I thought there was going to be a repeat of the night before, only worse. If Frank hadn't been wearing a suit, I had no doubt that he would have roughed up Tommy a bit. "You want to be a bagboy for Tony, that's fine," he said, nearly seething. "But you give me two-weeks notice."

"Jeez, Frank, Tony says—"

"I don't give a fuck what Tony says. You don't get over to the shop now and put some pies in the air, I'm going to break your jaw."

Tommy groaned, hunched his shoulders, and walked out the door. Upstairs, the toilet flushed and the spigots came on in the sink.

"What, you're all buddies now?" Frank said, turning to me.

"I met them on the street. Your boss sent Tony to see if I was in."

"We talked about it. He wants to know what you decided."

"I didn't decide anything."

"But you're considering it now?"

"I didn't say that."

"What's the big deal? You sit with him for a few weeks and you get thirty thousand. When's that kind of money going to fall in your lap again?"

"You think I don't realize how much money that is? I do; I'm not a moron. But then I think about going out to Tucci's house and the numbers explode like balloons."

"I told him I could change your mind."

"I'm not surprised. But you shouldn't have done that."

"He asked me to, so I didn't have a choice."

"And if you don't, you'll look like a schmuck, right?"

"Right."

The bathroom door opened and Tony Buttons came thudding down the stairs. "Mr. Tucci didn't send you after me, did he, Frank?"

"No, but we better get going."

"Yeah, it's probably started by now." Buttoni hadn't looked at me when he came down and he didn't look at me as he went out the door.

"He doesn't like me very much," I said.

"Yeah, I know. But Tony doesn't like anybody."

"He likes you."

"You want to know why? Because after Dad died Tony came around to collect the money Dad owed him, and I paid Tony without asking a question."

"Dad owed *him* money?"

"Sure. So what." He glanced at his watch. "Look, I have to go." He put his hand on the doorknob but turned to me before going out. "Don't let me down, Vincent," he said and left.

"Did I ever, Francis?" I said. "Did I fucking ever?"

Mrs. Falcone's list consisted of zucchini, eggplant, dried lentils, oranges, fresh basil, and a fresh-killed capon. I did not want the chicken to bleed through the bottom of my shopping bag and maybe plop out onto the sidewalk, so I decided to buy it last.

I bought the spices and the lentils first in a shop near Carpenter Street, then I made my way back toward Wharton and picked up the fruit and vegetables. The crowds were thick and unyielding and reminded me of some spot in China or any other place where people converged in intense search for food. I couldn't walk three feet without rubbing shoulders with someone and I had a head-on collision with a large woman carrying full bags in each hand. She spit curses at me and continued on without stopping.

I didn't go to Ninth Street for myself because I couldn't bear the smells, the noise, or the rude vendors. The vacant-eyed fish stacked fin to fin on beds of gray ice nauseated me. Live crabs piled in bushel baskets made me depressed. The stupid clucks of chickens, the confused plaint of ducks, the chortle of pigeons—who ate those?—made me want to smash their cages and free them. Unsalable fruits and vegetables accumulated in the street between the stands, but the bums picked over the piles and happily ate mushy nectarines or bruised apples, the wet pulps clinging to their tangled beards. A diesel bus chugged carefully down the thin street every twenty minutes or so, spewing its dark gases, and the smell of the exhaust mingled with those of cheeses, fish, spices, poultry, and gasping blue crabs. It was all too much for me and I tried to get through Mrs. Falcone's shopping list as fast as I could. When finished, I fought my way through the crowds and back to my car.

Fifteen minutes later, I gave Mrs. Falcone her groceries and refused her money, which she tried to stuff into my pockets as I walked out of her house.

"Take it, take it," she said.

"No. No."

"Are you all right? You don't look so good."

"It's the heat." I said good-bye and walked out again into the hot sun.

Entering my house, I kicked something across the floor of the vestibule. Looking down, I saw that it was a thick envelope. I did not have to pick up the envelope to know what was inside, and I did not have to guess who had put it through my door or told someone to put it through. I stared at the envelope for a while before taking it from the floor and bringing it into the house. The envelope seemed to radiate heat, and I dropped it on the kitchen table as if to avoid being branded. I turned my back on the envelope and tried to go about my business, but I couldn't keep my mind from it no matter what I did to kill time. Finally, I gave up and sat down at the table.

I spun the envelope round and round for a while before suddenly tearing it open and dumping out the cash. It was all one hundred dollar bills, crisp and smelling newly printed. I counted them, putting the bills into piles of a thousand dollars each. There were fifteen of them. I thought of my father sitting at that same table with playing cards laid out in front of him. He had never had anywhere near that kind of money in his hands at one time. He thought a thousand dollars was an enormous sum of money.

I stacked the cash in a single pile and stared at it, hearing the conversations with Frank earlier and the night before. I saw my thirty-eight hundred dollars being stuffed into the cash slot at the gaming tables, and automatically calculated that I had in front of me nearly four times more than I had lost.

Frank was right about me. Like my brother, despite my refusals to allow him to set me up in business, I did not want to work as hard as our father had and receive so little for the effort.

I was stuffing the cash back into the envelope when the telephone rang.

"This is Carmine," the voice on the other end said. "Did you get the money?"

"I just counted it."

"So you'll come out to the house Monday?"

I didn't answer.

"Frank said you agreed."

"I guess I did."

"Good. I'll have somebody pick you up Monday night."

"All right, Mr. Tucci," I said.

FOUR

A little past seven o'clock on Monday night, a new model black Cadillac pulled up in front of the house. For the last half hour, I had been glancing through the window every few minutes for something like it. Because the sun reflected full off the windshield, I could not see into the car, but when Tommy Green stepped from the Cadillac I had a good idea who the driver would be.

Green seemed wound up and came toward the house in a quick walk. He leaped on the curb, threw a few punches at the air, and spit at the sycamore tree. I left the window and went to the door before Tommy could spot me through the crack between the curtains.

"You ready?" he asked when I answered his knock. He bounced on his toes and took quick looks up and down the street.

"I'll be out in a second."

"We're counting." He jumped off the steps and hurried back to the car.

Stepping outside into the moist evening heat, I saw Lou Cocco sitting on his stoop. He held a newspaper in his hands but instead of reading he watched me leave the house and cross the sidewalk to the black car.

"Ballgame," I called across the street.

"I thought you hated baseball," he called back.

"I had a change of heart. See you." I slid in the back seat of the Cadillac and closed the door without looking at Cocco again. I did not want to see the doubt in his eyes, and I did not want him to pick up the lie in mine.

Tony Buttons sat behind the wheel, giving off such a chilly air of brutal menace he seemed to be the source of the frigid temperature in the car. He pulled away from the curb without speaking to me or turning, or even glancing at me in the rearview mirror. I wasn't feeling cheerful myself and didn't say hello to him, either; instead, I settled quietly into the corner of the back seat, content to be ignored.

Green sat directly in front of me, his head and shoulders twitching. He or Tony, or both of them, wore enough cologne to nearly smother the new smell of the car. Looking at Buttoni's hands with the diamond pinky rings and the Cartier watch on his wrist, I imagined him buying a new car each time the smell of the one he'd just bought wore off.

At the corner, Buttons turned down Eleventh Street. He should have continued straight to Broad and made a left for the Walt Whitman Bridge. I had looked up in an atlas the town where Tùcci lived near, and it was closest to the Walt Whitman than to any other bridge you could take into New Jersey.

"I thought we were going to Sewell," I said.

"We are," Tony said.

"Isn't it faster to go over the Walt Whitman?"

"I don't know. Is it?"

I looked at the back of his head and imagined a crowbar striking there.

"Well, yes, it is," I said.

"Look, we have to make a stop before we go to Jersey. You don't mind, do you?"

I caught the irony in his voice. "No." If I did, I would not have said so.

"Just a little business, Vinnie," Green said. "It won't take long. Relax and enjoy the ride in this magnificent machine. Tone, what's one of these babies cost ya?" Tommy drummed on the dashboard so suddenly, it caused Buttons and me to jump.

"Cut it out, you imbecile, you'll knock off the statue."

"Sorry, boss."

"Don't call me boss."

"Sorry, Tone." A few moments later, Green took the statuette of the Virgin Mary from the dashboard, held there by Velcro on the bottom of her feet, and kissed it.

"The fuck are you doing?" Tony said, grabbing the statuette from Tommy. "You doing speed, Tommy? Coke?"

"What, I just kissed it to make up."

"You want to make up, say some Hail Marys. You don't touch the statue." He placed it back on the dashboard. "You nervous about tonight or something?"

"Why should I be nervous?"

"I'm taking a chance on you, Tommy, so don't fuck up."

"I won't, Tone."

"You do and that's where you're going back to."

We were passing Frank's pizza shop and Buttoni pointed to it. Tommy should have been working there now.

"No way! I'm done with that joint."

I saw Frank through the shop window, his back to the street; he seemed to be yelling at a young kid standing behind the counter. Frank had called me that morning wanting to know if I had changed my mind about the Tucci memoirs. I said that I didn't have to change my mind; he did it for me. When his boss called, I told Frank, I didn't have the guts to contradict what he had told Tucci, that I had accepted the old man's offer. Good, Frank had said, and then got off the phone before he had to listen to any of my resentment.

"You tell him?" Buttons asked.

"Why should I? No offense, Vin, but the way he jacked me up in Shunk's the other night, he don't deserve it." Green turned around to me. His pupils were so tiny he had to be on some drug. "You ever stand in front of a pizza oven for a few hours in the summer, Vinnie? The heat wipes you out. You bake. You lose the hairs on your arms." He turned forward. "I had enough of that sweat box. Tone, I'm working for you now, right? I'm on my way up." He twitched and jerked as he spoke.

"Yeah, like a rocket, Twitchy." Buttons said.

"Twitchy?"

"You're jerking around like you got a nervous disease."

"Ah, yo Tone, that's cruel."

"Just stop it, it's bugging me."

Tommy seemed hurt; he crossed his arms in front of his chest and appeared to sulk. This guy couldn't work a day without annoying Frank because of some foul up, I thought; what was he doing with Buttoni in much more dangerous work than making pizza? Why, for that matter, was Tony using him? I could only think Buttoni saw qualities in Tommy not apparent to Frank or me. What they could be, I couldn't guess. I didn't try too hard to make sense of it. I did wonder what Frank would do to Tommy for walking out on him so abruptly, but I pictured it as something less than what Buttoni would dish out if Tommy failed.

"Tone," Tommy Green said, as if he had been thinking about it awhile, "suppose I go up to one of these guys, right, and they tell me they don't have the money. They say they're short this week, you know, they got a car payment or they had to get braces for their kid, something like 'at. What do I do?"

Both Tommy and I looked to Buttoni for the answer.

"What do you do? I'll tell you what you do. You say, 'Look, you creepy bastard, I'm gonna take a baseball bat and by the time I get done with your car you won't have a car.' Or you say, 'Fuck I care about your kid's teeth? Let them stay crooked.'"

"Yeah? Ok, good. But what if they still give me an excuse?"

"Then you ask them how would they like to feel a pipe against their nose."

"But suppose one of these guys still begs me, says

his wife's in a wheelchair or something, he spent all the money on doctor bills?"

I looked at the hole in Buttoni's cheek as he answered, curious to know, too.

"That's when you whack him with your pipe wrench a few times. See if you don't get some money."

"I don't want to hit nobody," Tommy said, "but I will if I have to. Don't worry, Tone."

"Just get the money, I don't care how you do it. You don't get it, what do I need you for?"

We drove several blocks in silence, passing the house of my grandparents near Reed Street where my father grew up. My grandfather had died several years ago, but my grandmother still lived there. I passed by occasionally on Saturdays and saw my grandmother in a house dress fanatically scrubbing her marble front steps with a hard brush and cleanser to the whiteness of the Epiphany's statuary. It was her father who, at Ellis Island, *asked* that his name be changed from Vespucci to Vespers because he wanted to be more American.

Buttons stopped the car at Eleventh and Elsworth. A few years ago, two men had been shot to death almost exactly at the spot where we stopped. Lou Cocco had been outraged; he didn't stop talking about it for weeks. Several months later, Maglio's oldest son was shot at from a car while he was eating a steak sandwich on the sidewalk outside Pat's Steaks. None of the bullets hit him, and he finished his sandwich while the police questioned him. He hadn't seen a thing.

"Ok, Twitchy, get out and get to work. I'll give

you a call later. And don't get mugged on your way home."

"Ok, Tone." Green opened the car door and paused. "See you later, Vinnie V." He walked off down Elsworth Street, his shoulders and head still spastic.

"You want to sit up here so I don't feel like a cab driver," Buttons said.

"Oh." I hadn't realized he was waiting for me to move before driving away. I opened the door and stepped into the street. The humid air hit me like something solid; I smelled garbage, too, a common odor in the air lately, as though South Philly itself were rotting.

As soon as I closed the door, Buttoni pulled away from the curb and continued north on Eleventh Street. We didn't speak until stopping at a red light at Bainbridge Street some blocks later.

"All this used to be ghetto," Buttoni said, looking on either side of the street. "Now look at it. They got townhouses selling for a hundred and a half. South Street the same way. Used to be all spooks and cockroaches." He turned onto the street one block later on his way to Fifth, which would bring us to the Ben Franklin Bridge at Race. "Now look at it. Condos, more townhouses, these restaurants where you can get frog legs and some shit called gumbo. Would you eat a frog's legs?"

"I don't think so."

"Some heavy drug deals used to go down here. You'd see some hookers, too, a lot of hippies down at Third. Now everything's fixed up and the scum's gone. You see this place on a Friday or Saturday night, it's a mob scene. They got the kids with the purple hair and the safety pins through their ears, chicks wearing combat boots and chains for necklaces. It's nuts. There's the kids from downtown, too. And the yuppies are always here; they're the ones sitting at the sidewalk tables eating the frog legs. The mayonnaise face bluebloods."

He said the last few words with disgust, then quieted and resumed that cold indifference I met when I entered the car. All the while Buttoni spoke, I thought about the bridge five minutes away and did not pay too close attention to what Buttoni had said. The panic had begun at the Cajun restaurant. My underarms, despite the air conditioning, had begun to sweat, and I could feel my throat tightening.

Buttoni turned left at Fifth Street. Soon, the bridge loomed into view and my heart began to slam right against the inside of my rib cage. My forehead and the back of my neck burned, my insides ignited, and my brain began to swim. I gripped my knees, images of catastrophe swirling in my head. You're going to be all right, I said to myself. You're going to be all right.

"What?" Buttoni asked.

"Huh?"

"I thought you said something."

"No. But could you maybe turn down the air?"

He looked at me. "You sick? You look sick."

"I'm fine." I was shivering but trying not to show it. We were in the middle of the span now, and I sat rigid, with my face pointed straight ahead so as not to see anything over the sides of the bridge, especially the long distance we would plummet before crashing into the dead water.

Damn you, Frank, I thought.

Only when we neared the tolls on the Camden side of the Delaware River did I begin to feel some relief. I took deep breaths and let the air out slowly.

"What is it?" Buttoni asked, slowing down to pay the toll.

"What do you mean?"

"Back on the bridge. You looked like you were having a heart attack. I noticed."

"I just had a brief pain in my stomach, that's all," I said offhandedly. I wasn't about to tell him about my difficulty with crossing bridges. "So when will we get there?"

Buttoni paid the toll and sped away into New Jersey. "Twenty minutes," he said, after a pause.

We rode along the river for a few miles, heading south toward Sewell. I gazed out the window across the river at the twilight sky above Philadelphia, the skyscrapers there backlighted by the oranges and reds of the setting sun. Tony Buttons lit a cigarette and filled the car with blue smoke. After a few minutes, we joined the traffic on route 42. It was that familiar road to Atlantic City that I had driven so often, most recently Friday night when I lost close to four thousand dollars. There were only trees, exits, and overpasses to see until you took one of those exits to a small town or a mall and drove past the car dealerships, gas stations, building supply stores, Dairy Queens, and houses. But there was much open space, and, compared to my city, New Jersey seemed lush.

"I have a question that's been bugging me," Buttoni said after a time. "I want to know why after the Maglio wedding does Mr. Tucci give me a fat envelope of cash to stuff in your door, and then you come out to his house? You, a schoolteacher. What, you giving him English lessons?"

"No." That would have been easy compared to this other business.

"What then? Frank said you and Mr. Tucci were just talking friendly at Shunk's, which I could accept. But now I'm driving you to his house. Mr. Tucci didn't say why, and I want to know."

If Frank nor Tucci hadn't told Buttoni about the memoirs, they must have had good reason.

"I think Mr. Tucci should tell you."

Buttons pushed back into his seat. "You do, huh?"

I nodded.

"You mean you're not going to tell me anything?"

"It's not my position." I hated the way that sounded, but I couldn't think of anything else to say.

"Not your position? What the fuck is that?"

"I'm sorry."

"You're sorry? You look sorry." He ground his teeth and tightened his hands on the steering wheel. "Well, fuck it, it don't matter. You think I won't find out what's going on? Guarantee you I'll know what brand of underwear you got on before the week's out."

I did not doubt it.

A moment later, Buttoni suddenly rolled down the window, grabbed the statuette of the Virgin Mary from the dashboard and threw it out.

We stayed on the Black Horse Pike at the entrance to the Atlantic City Expressway and soon turned onto Greentree Road; a few minutes later, we made another turn. There were fewer and fewer houses; the open spaces enlarged. After several more turns, I became lost. Trees came up suddenly to the sides of the road and just as suddenly broke for a library and, a little farther down, a bowling alley and gas station. The trees closed in abruptly again, as if the buildings had fallen from the sky. A distance later, Buttoni swung the car roughly onto a side road and drove down that for a few hundred yards before coming to Tucci's house.

Tony got out of the car without a word and started up the walkway. I followed him.

The house was gigantic and made of the same gray stone as the Church of the Epiphany back in the city. A massive oak tree stood on the lawn, a rope swing hanging from a horizontal limb, but the tree was nearly leafless. Bushes went around the house like trinkets and shutters painted white flanked the windows. A movement in an upper window caught my eye but when I looked no one was there. As I drew closer, I saw that the bushes were rust-colored with blight.

Tucci's wife opened the front door just as we reached it and let us in.

Buttoni said, "Mrs. Tucci," and tipped his head.

"Tony, tell Carmine," she said.

"Yes, Mrs. Tucci."

She turned to me as Buttons walked away. Mrs. Tucci seemed suspicious of me and thoroughly looked me over in the hallway, as if trying to uncover any treachery I might have in mind. Though old and tiny, her hair evenly gray and in a tight bun, she seemed deadly, not to be fooled with. "Sit in here."

She showed me to a room off the hall. "A little Sambuca?"

"No, nothing. Thank you."

"I'll bring you some wine, no ice," she said. I watched her tight, steel-gray bun as she left the room; it looked like a stone instead of hair.

Dry-mouthed and anxious in that room, I thought of confessionals and the perfect loneliness inside them. What am I doing here? I instantly saw the stack of hundreds on the kitchen table, but that didn't feel like an answer. I looked in the mirror above the sofa to see what I could find in my looks, but all I saw were wide pupils and skin the pallor of fever. I sat down.

After a minute, I heard footsteps come my way. They were too quick for Mrs. Tucci's and too light for a man's. A woman stepped in the room without seeing me on the other side and picked up a stack of library books from an end table by the doorway. She wore blue jeans and a loose shirt that showed nothing underneath. Her hair was dull and limp and parted haphazardly.

"Hello," I said.

She gasped and dropped a book.

I stood up.

"No," she said, stooping to snatch the book from the floor before I took a step. She straightened up and hurried from the room without looking at me. I heard the front door open and close.

A little bewildered, I took a few steps after her and nearly collided with Mrs. Tucci returning with the wine.

"Where are you going?" If I startled her, she

didn't show it; even the wine, filling the glass, did not shake.

"Nowhere," I said nervously, as if guilty.

She looked at me with all the suspicion she had earlier. "Who went out?"

"I don't know. A girl, a woman."

She stared at my face. In hers, I thought I saw terrible secrets which, even under torture, would never leave her. There was coldness, too, a capacity to hurt. I looked away.

"Here, don't spill it." She handed me the glass.

I had to slurp off a half inch to keep the wine from spilling on the carpet.

"My husband's in the den. It's the door to the left. Go." She gave me a little shove and I started down the marble hall with my shaking wine.

A television played in the room to the right; on the outer rim of the television's glow Tony Buttons and the two other men, George and Leo, who had preceded Tucci into the bar the other night, sprawled in chairs. Tony did not stir as I walked past the doorway, but the heads of the other two men swiveled my way. They had the hollow eyes of mannequins.

Tucci was sitting in an easy chair as I entered the den. A single lamp on an end table to his left was all the light in the den and it cast dark shadows on his face and about the room. The air was still and warm. Tucci looked tired and did not stand when he saw me, but he leaned foward to offer me his hand. His grip was weaker than Friday night, his voice more weary; he seemed frail enough for a child to strangle.

Tucci motioned for me to sit in the chair across

from him, then he pulled a tape recorder and several cassettes from beneath the sofa.

"I saw my daughter go by," he said, placing the recorder and the cassettes on the coffee table between us. "Did you meet her?"

"The person with the books?"

"That's her. Marie."

"Briefly. We didn't get to talk."

"You're about the same age; maybe you have some things in common."

"Maybe."

"She reads a lot. That's about all she does."

"Does she live here?"

"You're thinking she seems old to still be at home."

"No." But I was.

"I'll tell you about that later. Let's get started with the other stuff. But first close the door."

The sound of the closing door seemed loud to me and almost to echo, as if the door had closed upon a crypt. The light from the hall was cut off and the room, already shadowed, became gloomier. I felt trapped with Tucci now, suffocated, entombed. I heard two clocks ticking on the mantle and the brittle sounds of the television from across the hall. Crossing the room to my chair, my legs felt suddenly wobbly.

Tucci motioned for me to set up the tape recorder. I tried to put a cassette into the recorder but my fingers trembled and I dropped it on the floor. I picked up the cassette but banged my hand on the edge of the coffee table and dropped it again.

"You want me to do it?"

"I have it," I said, tightening my lips and jamming the cassette into the recorder.

"Ready now?"

I nodded and sat back.

"Shouldn't you turn it on?"

"Oh, right." I lurched forward and turned on the recorder, then sat back again, wanting more than anything to be at home.

FIVE

"I was born on a little farm in Calabria," Tucci began in a weak voice. "The nearest town was called Nicastro. I never went there, not until years later when I went back. You could see mountains from our house; yeah, mountains. You ever see mountains? They were brown; sometimes they looked yellow, and they had snow on them at the tops. The sky was always very blue where I lived. So when I think of Calabria, I think of people squinting."

"Squinting?"

"From the bright sun."

"I see."

Tucci told me that a stream ran by the farmhouse; it was very clear and very cold. You could see little fish in the water and pebbles at the bottom, he said. He used to go to the stream and jump off the bank and sink a little bit into the mud on the edge. He would kneel by the stream, drink right from it, and it was so cold it hurt his teeth. "It was a beautiful place. I still dream about it. If you get a chance, go there. Mention my name. I still have relatives in the village."

"Thank you." I wouldn't be calling a travel agent soon.

His parents had lived in Calabria all their lives, he went on, and so did their parents and their parents and so on back. Maybe they were connected to the Romans. Who knows? His grandfather thought so. He lived with the family, the grandmother having died of a disease before Tucci was born. His grandfather said that he had the Romans in his blood. So little Tucci would think of tiny soldiers marching in the old man's veins. The grandfather had been part of Garibaldi's Thousand, The Red Shirts. "He would sit me in his lap and tell me war stories. How he killed men. How he had lost an ear fighting. 'Better than my whole head,' he used to say and laugh. I would bounce on his knee and look into the hole where his ear used to be. I would want to poke my finger in there."

I laughed slightly at that, but Tucci didn't seem to notice.

"He was my father's father. He had been a peasant farmer like my father, and he still took care of the goats. He gave them names. Nicolo. Teresa. He milked them and fed them." It was the boy's job to brush them with a curry comb. The family had a few olive and fig trees. But the soil was poor and they couldn't grow much. What they did grow, the government taxed. They taxed the goats, too, that's how crazy they were, Tucci said. They put a tax on the olive trees. Donkeys, they taxed. It was better, if you had goats, to slaughter them and sell the meat, which is what Tucci's father wanted to do once, but the grandfather wouldn't let him. The family just didn't pay the taxes.

"Things got so bad for us with the bad harvests and the taxes that my father had to become a day laborer. He dug ditches or cut down trees or cleared rocks from fields, put up fences, those things. Moron work. A day laborer was about as low as you could get in that country at the time. It meant that you were nothing, you had no skill, you had to do the work nobody else wanted to do. At least your people had a trade. They were cabinetmakers, isn't that what Frank told me?"

"My father's grandfather and uncles were, yes. My great-grandfather made his own coffin, I was told."

"It wasn't because he was cheap, was it?"

"It's possible he couldn't afford it," I said, never having thought of it before. "But I think it had something to do with craftsmanship. I don't think my great-grandfather wanted to spend eternity in a box somebody else made and which he knew he could make better."

"Pride."

"Yes, I guess so."

"But your father's father was a huckster?"

"First with a horse and wagon, then he had a stand on Ninth Street."

"Where he died of a heart attack."

"That's true." He had collapsed over his display of peaches.

"We all have to die," Tucci said, and then continued where he had left off.

One day, Tucci's father came in the house and announced that the family was going to America. Some people he knew had gone there, and there was often talk about America around the house. His father had pictures. There were tall buildings and crowded streets. All the people looked big. Tucci's father told him that there were fruits and bread on every corner, stores that sold meat and fish. The boy wanted to go just for that. He thought America was some magic place over the mountains where there was a lot of food and large people.

His grandfather did not want to go to America. No matter how much Tucci's father talked, the grandfather refused to change his mind. He wanted to die in the place where he was born and lived. He refused to pack any of his things. He had nowhere to go in Calabria, he couldn't manage on the farm by himself, so Tucci's parents thought he would come along, even though he didn't want to. His grandfather said that in America the country people like them were turned into animals because of the way you had to live. America didn't have enough air or light, he said. You had to live in small boxes like rats. He said he did not have his ear cut off for America. Tucci's mother packed his things anyway.

"On the day before we were to leave for this country, I found my grandfather hanging from the olive tree."

"Did you say that *you* found him?" I asked, having faded a little from Tucci's weary voice.

"I found him, yes. With a rope around his neck and the milk stool kicked over under his feet. I thought it was another one of his games. His twisted face would move and he'd wink at me, then laugh. But it wasn't a game."

Tucci paused there to sip tea. When he resumed, he told me about the train ride to the sea, the mass of people on the docks, the crowded ship, and the voyage across the ocean. He remembered the smell in the steerage of disinfectant mingled with that of sewage. He was often hungry and frightened at night. There was sickness and death on the ship; bodies wrapped in cloth were dumped overboard. Holding him in his arms one morning on the crowded deck, Tucci's father pointed over the rail at a school of dolphins. The trip seemed endless. Ellis Island eventually came into view. The family spent two days getting processed there. Little Tucci could see the tall buildings of New York City through the great arched windows. A ferry took the family to the city, where they were met by a brother of Tucci's father, who took them on a train to Camden. Tucci told about living in a tenement, picking rags with his mother, the entire family sitting around a table at night shelling hundred pound bags of walnuts for which they were paid a dollar. He told about crossing the Delaware River on the Camden ferry, a team of horses getting spooked, jumping over the side with their wagon, and sinking beneath the water in seconds.

Tucci paused again, this time clutching his stomach as he had Friday night at Shunk's Tavern.

"Your ulcer?" I asked.

He shook his head. "It's not an ulcer," he said, taking one of his white pills from his shirt pocket and swallowing it with tea. "It's cancer." Tucci said it without emotion, and I took it without feeling any, as though he had told me he had a cold. "I got a few months, maybe six. The pill's just a painkiller. I don't always use them. Some days I feel fine, other days I think I smell my insides." He sniffed. "Like now. You smell anything rotten?"

I shook my head no. All I smelled was camphor.

"You would tell me?"

I nodded. It seemed important to him.

"I guess it's my imagination. You think?"

"I think so, yes."

He put out his hand. "Help me up. I have to take a leak."

I lurched up from my chair and took Tucci's cold and clammy hand. He pulled himself to his feet. "Stay put. I'll be back." Tucci shuffled to the door, but before going out he stopped and turned. "You're the only one who knows it's not an ulcer," he said. "I want to keep it that way. All right?"

"If you want."

"I want." He left the door open after leaving and I listened to his slow doomed walk fade down the marble hall until the television and the ticking of the dual clocks at my back drowned out the shuffling steps altogether. Now I understood his urgency in the bar to get the memoirs done. Tucci was dying. It was a pity for those people who loved and depended on him. But I barely knew Tucci and so the news had no impact on me one way or the other. I also understood why he didn't want anyone to know. I, too, would want to keep a terminal illness to myself. People do not behave naturally around a dying man. By telling me, I figured Tucci assumed I stood at that same professional distance as his doctor or lawyer, someone with little or no emotional attachment to him. He was right, and he had to know it. So he must have told me about the cancer for practical reasons, I thought, to instill in me his need for urgency.

I turned off the tape recorder. Leaning back in the chair, I saw that Mrs. Tucci had noiselessly appeared in the doorway. Her eyes were fastened on the recorder, first in puzzlement, then alarm, but only for a moment. She looked at me, then back to the recorder, then slid her stoney eyes back to me again. In them, I saw that something had been confirmed for her, and she briefly grinned, but it was the malevolent grin of a gargoyle.

"More wine?" she asked.

"I didn't finish what I have. Thank you."

She nodded abstractly and, after another look at the tape recorder, left the doorway without a sound.

I didn't know whose company was worse, hers or Buttoni's.

"We had a cheap little funeral for my brother," Tucci was saying of a brother who had fallen from a roof. "He was put in a cheap little casket; the boards were rough and they had gaps between them, almost like a crate. The casket was closed because Antony was mangled from the fall. When I looked down from the roof that day, I saw Antony on the sidewalk; he reminded me of rags in a pile with blood around them. So I saw him in the coffin like that. My mother was out of her mind from the whole thing. She pulled out handfuls of her hair, she put dirt in her mouth from my brother's grave. My father took it ok. He was already dying of a lung disease. He was always weak, but he kept working at the hat factory in the shrinking room with the chemicals that he said were killing him."

"Was that Stetson in North Philly?"

"Fourth and Montgomery. My father would come home smelling of the place. There's just vacant lots there now."

After his father died, Tucci's mother married the uncle from Camden who had escorted them from New York City when they left Ellis Island. He moved into the Philadelphia house and got a job with the city. He was a streetsweeper, then an ash man; he collected the ashes from the coal furnaces. He also ran a crap game in the basement of a bar called Clem's. Tucci became a lookout for the games; his job was to watch the street for the cops who hadn't been paid off. If he saw the police, he'd ring a bell and the crap game would break up. He stood outside some nights in the rain and snow. Later, he became a dealer. He was good at it and was paid two percent of each pot. If he wasn't on lookout or dealing, he helped to unload the bootleg.

"Prohibition?" I asked.

"Sure. Anybody who was anybody had a hand in booze. My uncle was a nobody, but he worked for Erminio Gabba, who was small time himself but big enough to do a little bootleg. I was smart with figures and I wound up working for him in his warehouse on Bainbridge Street, keeping the books, how much booze came in, how much went out. I was an eighteen year old kid. I gave most of my money to my mother. She didn't ask questions."

Gabba, who had no children, liked him. He took Tucci to baseball games and to his house for dinners. Mrs. Gabba liked him, too, and made Tucci's favorite dishes. He worked for Gabba for about four years before somebody wanted to buy Gabba out and Gabba didn't want to sell. So they shot him at a flower stand on Eighth Street, a half block away from the warehouse. Tucci was in the warehouse when it happened. Somebody called him and he ran to the spot and saw Gabba on the ground. Gabba was still holding the flowers, yellow tulips. He was bleeding a lot but still conscious. He told Tucci to take the flowers to his wife and tell her what happened.

Tucci went to the house after Gabba was taken to the hospital. He was hoping Gabba's wife already knew about the shooting so he wouldn't have to tell her. He didn't want to say the words. He knocked on the door. She opened it and Tucci handed her the flowers. He realized then that the flowers had blood on them. Nobody had told her about the shooting but when Mrs. Gabba saw the flowers she knew.

Tucci quieted, his eyes fixed on the spinning centers of the cassette. He remained motionless, gazing at the tape recorder for so long that I shifted around in my seat and cleared my throat to rouse him. He looked up after a time, but he was still far away somewhere in his head. I said his name.

"Yes?"

"Do you want to quit now?"

"Quit?" He looked puzzled. "Oh, no. Where was I?"

"Gabba was killed," I said.

"Did I say he was killed?"

"I guess I assumed."

"No, Gabba wasn't killed. He had four bullets put

in him but he lived. I saw him in the hospital. His chest was wrapped up like a mummy. He was in a lot of pain and I felt sorry for him. He told me who shot him. It was the Spumoni brothers." Three nights later Tucci and his friend Al followed the brothers out of their house to their car, and when they reached it Tucci pointed a gun at them. He made them get in the car and then he and Al got in the back seat. Tucci told them to drive to the Lakes. It was a very cold night, maybe February, Tucci said. He made them drive around the area to make sure no one was around to see anything, then he made them turn off the headlights and pull up to the biggest and deepest lake. The lake was about fifty yards across. There was a full moon; it was low in the sky, and Tucci could see it in the lake, which was black like oil. He could see the lights of the ships at the docks. But everything else was dark. Tucci told the Spumoni brothers to get out of the car. They started to plead. They said they had a sick mother to support. Al told them to shut up. It was very quiet, and all they could hear was their feet on the frozen ground and one of the Spumoni brothers crying.

"Al kept looking at me for what to do, but I didn't know what to do. Nobody told us to do what we were doing. We didn't have a plan. We just thought we'd get these two guys in the car and see what happened. What happened was we were all standing on the bank of the lake and I was shaking. All I could think about was the sound the shots would make. I was afraid somebody would hear them and we'd get caught. 'Take off your clothes,' I said. I don't know why, it just came out, I wasn't even thinking about that, what I was going to do. They said, 'What?' and I said to strip. Even Al looked at me like I was crazy."

But Tucci pointed the gun at the brothers, and they started to remove their coats and then the rest until they stood in their underwear. They were shivering. The one brother kept crying. And then Tucci told them to swim across the lake. He said if they made it across they could go and they would not hear from him or Gabba again. They didn't know if Tucci was kidding or not, and they looked at each other. Al even looked at him, thinking he had something else in mind, maybe that he was going to shoot the brothers when they turned their backs. The brothers thought that too, Tucci said, because they backed down the bank and into the water while keeping an eye on the gun. When their feet hit the water, their faces showed the shock of the cold and they stopped. Tucci told them to keep going, lifting the gun at the same time. The brothers stepped back deeper and deeper into the lake until they could no longer touch bottom.

"They splashed a lot for a little bit, and one brother kept telling the other to come on, swim. But then they started to move slow, and then they didn't move at all. They just bobbed there, first one and then the other. They were about twenty yards away. I could see them in the moonlight. They called back to us a few times, asking if they could come back. They said they would pay us. One of them started praying but then his words got cut off by the water. Their arms stopped working and then their heads went under. We stood there awhile to make sure they weren't coming up."

"They drowned?"

"They drowned, yes."

"Then what?"

"Then we walked home. They found the bodies the next day. There was no evidence and no witnesses, except Al, and he didn't count."

"This the same Al who was on the roof with you and Antony when he fell?"

Tucci nodded.

"Whatever happened to him?"

"He was my best friend. We would have done anything for each other. After the thing at the lake, Gabba helped me out, and I helped Al out and we moved up pretty quick. We were doing good, going somewhere. We both married, we bought houses. We were partners in a few deals that made us some money. One day, I got a call saying Al was killed at a gas station. Somebody handcuffed him to his steering wheel, pumped gas into his lap, and threw in a match." Tucci stood up, went to a small desk and pulled something out. "This is us." He handed me a picture of himself and another man, both in their thirties I guessed, sitting at a table with plates in front of them. Al had his arm around Tucci's shoulders. Both men looked happy. "That was taken at my sister's wedding."

Tucci fell quiet for a spell as he gazed at the photo. He seemed again like just another old man.

"I pushed him," he said.

"I'm sorry?"

"Antony didn't fall from the roof; I pushed him. Me, Al and Antony used to go up on the roof of this abandoned factory and lay around. Antony and me had a fight about something stupid the way kids do. He beat me, made me say 'uncle.' After he got off of me, he went to the edge of the roof so he could spit and watch it fall. I got up quick, rushed him and pushed him over." Tucci gazed at the spinning centers of the cassette. "Al and me kept the secret."

Tucci went away again as if hypnotized by the turning wheels. I didn't try this time to bring him back. Let him stay wherever he had gone. I itched for the night to end but I wasn't anxious to hear any more tales of the sort he had just told. Not that I felt sorry for him in any way, nor that I cared if, right now, he was watching over and over his brother's plunge to the pavement four stories below, or if echoing in his head now was not the relentless ticking of the clocks but the sick thud of Antony's body. I wouldn't break that trance because I was afraid any further mention of his brother would take *me* to a place of mine, where my own brother waited, that I did not want to go. The stench of it, in the form of self-hatred and despair, clung to me still. I did not want to risk that. Yet, I was there already, fighting the images of Frank standing arrogantly against the stolen car in the late evening of that October day, taunting me. I could hear his mocking voice drowning out the ticking of the clocks. Soon, I was no more in that room than was Tucci.

I had tumbled back into the empty schoolyard where Frank, driving the stolen car, had spotted me shooting a basketball alone in the near dark. When I refused his offer to drive me home, our argument began and quickly became ugly as Frank called me those names—sissy, faggot, pussy—so inflammatory to boys of a certain age. Things became uglier still when, trying to start home, Frank blocked my path and said the names directly in my face while shoving his chest into mine for emphasis. We started to fight then. Frank beat me easily, as we both knew he would, but instead of walking away I stood up from the sidewalk and jumped into the car behind the wheel. Frank had just enough time to get in the passenger seat before I turned the key, threw the car into gear, and shot up the street. I had driven only once before, in New Jersey, when an uncle let us take turns driving his barge-like Pontiac up a sandy road that went nowhere. But that must have been enough of a lesson because, aside from going too fast and stopping too abruptly at traffic lights, I drove reasonably well.

Frank said to stay off the wide streets, so when we came to Broad I crossed it and, a few blocks later, swung the car north at Twentieth Street. I thumped across the railroad tracks of Washington Avenue, and continued north through the dilapidated black neighborhoods until we reached Lombard Street, where Frank told me to turn. He did not want me driving into Center City because cops were more likely to be there. I turned, not thinking about the police or, for that matter, anything at all. I didn't have a thought in my head, only rage and the compulsion to do what Frank said I could not do, and to do it with extremity and abandon so I would never again have to hear Frank's mockery or have to fight him.

I made the left onto Lombard and drove toward the river and the South Street Bridge a few minutes away. The traffic lights were sequenced and, catching all green ones, we went faster and faster past the row homes and all the way to the end of Lombard Street where it dead-ends and turns left to join South. Though moving too fast, I managed the turn, and was about to head toward home when the woman appeared from out of nowhere.

She froze in the headlights, her face terror-stricken, mouth agape, and, at the last instant, in her eyes a look of terrific sadness. Frank yelled, "Watch out!" and pulled the wheel sharply to the right, but I still hit her. She vanished with an ugly thud and the car jumped the curb and smashed into a telephone pole. We were not hurt.

"Get out!" Frank yelled at me, reaching across my lap to the door handle and shoving me out of the car. "Run, goddamn it! Run!" he shouted as he slid behind the wheel. But I stood unmoving in the lamplight, looking at the woman in the shadows until Frank jumped from the car and slapped me. "Don't you hear the siren?" he yelled, shoving me. "Run!" He kicked me. "Run!"

I did hear the siren now and, frightened by it, ran away from it and the woman on the ground as Frank sped away. The police car turned the corner, slowed only slightly where the woman lay, and sped after Frank. I had reached the middle of the bridge when I heard another siren coming from the other side of the river, and a moment later I saw the red flashing light in the distance. I stopped, took several hurried steps in the other direction, but heard sirens that way, too, and immediately watched light burst upon South Street as Frank, with two police cars speeding behind him, roared from the shadows. In trying to get away, Frank had doubled back and was heading for the bridge, me, and the other police car.

I panicked and scrambled over the walkway barrier. Holding tightly to the vertical bars, I crouched on the ledge out of view, sixty feet above the river. The sirens reached a crescendo directly in front of me, tires screeched, the policemen shouted, and in the red wobbling light of their cruisers they hauled Frank from the stolen car. He didn't say a word, not even when the cops beat my brother senseless, handcuffed him, and threw him into the back of a policecar. The police made some calls on their radios, drove Frank and the stolen car from the bridge, and then, laughing and joking, sped away themselves. I clung to the railing a while longer, listening to the water splash against the supports of the bridge, and shivered, sickened at the thought of the woman and Frank's bloodied face.

Making sure that no cars were coming over the bridge, I began to straighten up from my squat. But my legs had cramped, and my toes, bearing all my weight on the thin ledge those terrifying minutes, had gone numb, so that trying to stand while reaching for the top rail just above my head was a mistake. The pain in my legs as they uncoiled made me wince and my toes slipped from the ledge. Instead of grasping the rail, my fingertips only brushed it as I pitched backwards and down.

I seemed to smash into the cold water instantly. Only later would I remember the moments of dizzy wind in my face and the streaking lights as I fell. I struck the water head first and sunk, certain that I had split my skull and would die. The darkness of the water was absolute, a quality to it of oil. I thought I had blacked out. I tried to breath, gagged, then flailed against that palpable dark as much as against the water. I swallowed mouthfuls of the river before bursting through the surface, choking and sucking air. Chopping the water, I oriented myself, then swam frantically toward the west bank. I did not want to pass the spot where the paramedics had lifted the woman from the street.

I was a good swimmer and reached the bank without much difficulty until the end when my body began to give out. My arms and legs became leadened and my lungs ached for more air. I fought desperately against sinking those last ten yards, swallowing more water, but I had enough stamina to reach the bank. I clawed up the slope and flopped on my back, gasping and dizzy, stomach hurting from all the water in me, the sound of the cars whooshing by on the expressway filling my head. I lay in the weeds only long enough to catch my breath before crawling up the bank to the roadway and walking unsteadily back to South Street and toward home. If anyone noticed my wet clothes in the dark, they did not ask me how they had gotten that way. When I reached home, I was able to sneak in the house and up to my room without being seen or questioned. I had the first of many nightmares that night. A few weeks later, I learned that I could not cross a bridge without remembering too vividly the face of the woman I had killed and the plummet into the suffocating black river.

I escaped that night, both from drowning and the police, but it was Frank who kept me from having to pay for my crime. He could have saved his own neck by mentioning me, but he did not; Frank let the police assume that he had been driving the stolen car and that he had killed the woman.

Frank was later tried as an adult for manslaughter, but because he was a minor he was sentenced to five years in juvenile prison, of which he served three-and-a-half. I was convinced that any kind of incarceration and the humiliation that came with it would have killed me, and so I was grateful to Frank for what he had done. But I also put myself tremendously in his debt.

Tucci had killed his brother. I had enslaved myself to mine.

SIX

The phone rang the next morning and I shot out of bed as if from an explosion.

"Is this the Heinrich Himmler school of etiquette?"

"For Christ sake, Jamie," I said into the phone, blinking at the bright bar of sunlight that came in the room where the window shade did not meet the sill. "It's not even nine o'clock."

"I thought you would be up long ago. I called you about seven times last night but you weren't home. Or maybe you weren't answering the phone. Did you have a date?"

"No date. I went to a movie by myself."

"What happened to the hospital secretary? Or is that another one who bit the dust?"

"Another one."

"It would be nice if you met someone you could love."

"Love? What's that?"

"Be serious, Vincent. How long are you going to stay bitter about Alison?"

"I have to listen to this first thing in the morning?"

"Ok, we'll change the subject. I called to tell you two things. One, I'll be coming to the city at the end of the week. And two, I'm pregnant. I'm going to be a mother."

"That's terrific, Jamie," I said, meaning it. "So you don't have to adopt any Vietnamese kids after all."

"No, I'm going to hatch this one myself. Anyway, I wanted to see mom and tell her. I mean, try to tell her, hoping she understands that she's finally going to be a grandmother."

"She always wanted to be one."

"Plus, I spoke to Teddy on the telephone last night. He actually called me from a pay phone somewhere after getting my letter. He says that he'll come, too. Cyril and I will detour to his place, stay the night and bring him to Philadelphia with us the next day. So break down and clean the house some."

"I suppose you want me to change the sheets on the beds."

"That would be nice."

"I'll see what I can do."

After a little more chit chat, we hung up. I stayed in bed awhile, watching the dust motes floating through the shaft of sunlight and thinking about the night before.

Tucci had eventually come back from his reverie and begun another series of remembrances. I sat only half listening, plagued the rest of the night by images of the woman, Frank, and my fall from the South Street Bridge. A little before midnight, Tucci said that he was too tired to go on. He told me to turn off the recorder and to take the tapes. I put them in the inside of my jacket pockets while Tucci slid the recorder under the sofa. He told me he'd see me tomorrow, and walked me to the door. As we shook hands, he said he'd get Tony. I told him that I'd wait outside.

I stood just off the porch watching the drifting fireflies and the moths battling against the yellow light of the lamppost at the end of the walkway. It was a cool night and quiet, except for the chirping crickets, and I smelled mint and honeysuckle, but also some animal that must have died nearby; it gave off a putrid odor of decaying flesh.

Looking toward the oak tree, its branches skeletal and black against the sky, I noticed someone in the swing. There was just enough light from the lamppost to make out Tucci's daughter. Buttoni came out of the house before I could think about saying hello and walked past me without a word, his head so rigid he did not see Marie. I glanced toward the tree as I followed Tony down the walkway. Marie was staring straight ahead into the extreme darkness beyond the road and did not flinch when we passed.

I looked back at her when we reached the car. The swing seemed an odd place to be at midnight. I wondered why, of all places, she was there, and in that attitude of deep funk.

Buttoni and I drove without speaking over the dark, twisting roads leading away from Tucci's house, and still had nothing to say to each other when we joined the highway. His vapors of rage silenced us both. The only sound in the car was the hum of his new radial tires and the rush of air when some maniac, going faster than Buttoni's seventy, passed us. Because it was late on a Monday night, there was little traffic. We made good time through New Jersey, for which I was grateful, but with more cars around us I would not have felt so alone and nervous with Buttons.

"Tell me you didn't have a tape recorder in there tonight," he said suddenly, a few minutes before the bridge.

"Who told you that?"

"Never mind who told me. Did you or didn't you?"

"It wasn't mine," I said, seeing no reason to lie about what he already knew.

"Fuck I care whose it was? What was it doing there?"

"Isn't it obvious?"

"You being a smartass?"

"Not at all."

"If it was obvious, I wouldn't be asking you about it. Look," he said, pausing as if to control himself, "I know you're not stupid. You do Frank's money, you know some things. You know who Mr. Tucci is, how big, all that. Now, if all of a sudden he starts talking to a stranger—you—for three straight hours and with a tape recorder catching it all, it makes somebody like me nervous, which I don't have to tell you the reason for. All I'm asking is that you be a nice guy and tell me what's going on, so we both get saved a lot of trouble later on. Just tell me what Mr. Tucci talked about tonight."

"His boyhood, mostly."

"What?"

I began to summarize for Buttoni most of what

Tucci had related earlier in the den. Tony's mouth fell open and stayed open until I finished.

"He told you all that? What for?"

I told him.

"You're kidding me. That's what this is about?"

Through the windshield, I glimpsed the red beacons at the top of the Walt Whitman Bridge support towers. I nodded, distracted by the beginnings of panic.

"And this was his idea?"

"I didn't know anything about it until the other night," I said quickly, gulping air.

"I know he's old but I hope he's not getting soft in the head. A book?" Buttoni snorted and shook his head in disbelief. "I mean, why? Does he want to go on 'Phil Donahue'?"

"I don't know." We were seconds away from the bridge now and I could see the twin pair of massive supports and the great suspension cables looped between and away from them. I began to vibrate.

"What else did he tell you?"

"Just what I told you."

"Nothing else?"

"No." The road dropped away and the vertical cables, like gigantic harp strings, began to rush by as my stomach boiled.

"Nothing about me?"

"Nothing."

"You sure?"

"Yes." We were on the bridge now, hundreds of feet of black air and the languid oily river beneath us, the city glittering in front. I lost my ability to think.

"I still don't like this," Buttoni said. He ended our conversation there while I counted to myself.

I couldn't fall back to sleep after Jamie's phone call; the sun shone too brightly on the other side of the blinds and the noises from the street and the alley came in as if from the next room.

I rolled out of bed and went into the bathroom to shower. White dots clouded the mirror. Dense mildews and soap scum colored the shower curtain and the tiles, and wisps of hair clung along the walls and under the sink. As the water hit my back, I counted the tiles missing from the walls. Nine. I decided then to appease Jamie and clean the house.

I dressed, had a little breakfast, then went searching about the house for the weapons I would need against the filth I had allowed to accumulate. All I could find were a rusted steel wool pad and an empty box of Spic-n-Span hidden beneath the kitchen sink like artifacts. If I was to make the house a little presentable for Jamie and the others, I needed to buy the stuff to do it.

I went to the corner grocery and spent a few minutes with Purdy Grant, the owner, then returned to the house with two bags of cleaners and a mop.

First, I opened every window in the house that I could. Then I started on the bathroom. I had had some fun in there with my dates, and even with Alison. As I chisled built up soap like barnacle in the soap holder, scrubbed away hardy mildews, soap scum, and stains, I thought of lathering the naked bodies of the women I had known, their giggles, throaty moans, the way the soap ran down over their skin before the running water, revealing their wet nakedness. I missed that.

The first floor, except for the kitchen, was easier going. It was mostly a dust and vacuum job, and I decided to forget about the windows. The kitchen was another matter. I didn't remember the last time the range and the refrigerator had been cleaned. I sprayed the oven with Easy-Off, gagging as a cloud of chemicals billowed out, then attacked the rest of the range with Brillo pads.

I washed the several weeks of dishes, bagged the trash, and cleaned off the thick layer of grease and dust from the top of the refrigerator and the range hood. I used cleanser on the countertops and the sink. I buffed the chrome spigots until I could see distorted images of myself. I swept and mopped the floor. For the finishing touch, I sprayed the perimeter of the kitchen with roach and ant killer, which made the house smell toxic.

I began to clean the upstairs. I threw every scrap of clothing in sight in the hamper, having to stuff them in because there were so many. I stripped the beds of the old sheets and replaced them with new ones, still in cellophane, that Alison had bought just before she left. Over the clean sheets, I put a bedspread, another Alison purchase, taken from the blanket chest and smelling of cedar. I cleared the tops of the dressers; the dust was so thick, I could write on them with my finger. *Tucci*.

I scrubbed the windowsills, then worked on the windows with first the ammonia and water, for the worst of the grime, then Windex for the smears. Mrs. Falcone was washing her 1972 Nova in front of her house, and I called down to her. She looked around but could not find me.

"Up here!"

She looked up and waved, then frowned. This was the same window from which Jamie had tossed the dummy of herself that had caused my mother, sitting in a beach chair on the sidewalk, to pitch back and crack her skull. It was also the window from which Frank had thrown Teddy's telescope, smashing it on the concrete two stories below. My mother had ranted at passersby from that window in her final weeks with us. Judging by the way Mrs. Falcone looked at me, I suspected she must have feared that the unlucky window had claimed another of the Vespers.

"Jamie and Teddy are coming," I called down to her.

"Oh. Oh, that's nice." She sounded relieved and went back to the car.

I lugged the vacuum cleaner up from the basement and used it in the bedroom first. I moved the dressers and the bed to get at the dust balls underneath. These things hadn't been moved in years and there were deep dents in the carpet where the feet had stood, much dust, and something like a mine. I found coins, a fingernail clipper, hair clips, a postcard from Mexico that Teddy sent. "Went to a bullfight in Mex. City," he had written. "Had a 3rd row seat. Thus saw in vivid detail the slow and bloody deaths of the bulls by the matadors and other characters in the spectacle." There were magazines, condom wrappers, a wine glass, socks, a comb, and someone's pantyhose.

I went into the closet and cleaned out old clothes

I hadn't worn in years; they had either gone out of fashion or no longer fit. I put the stuff in a large plastic bag and would take it to the Salvation Army. From the shelf, I took a chess set, a half-assembled model airplane that Teddy had begun years ago, my highschool and college diplomas, a conch, boxes of old letters and photographs, a stack of *National Geographic* magazines and Frank's gun. I threw much of the stuff away. I put the gun and the letters back on the shelf without opening the box, but I chanced a look at the pictures.

I removed the lid from the shoebox and went through the layers of photographs as through strata and watched us leap through time. In group pictures, Jamie had circled her head in ballpoint or drawn bold arrows that pointed her out among the crowd. Teddy, except in the years before the loss of the telescope and the few days he was missing after running away, always wore the same look: a weak smile if he looked into the camera, nothing if he did not. Frank's looks were always impatient, cynical, or arrogant, and in none of the pictures did he seem to smile with real joy, except in one showing him and Patty Leone in a convertible.

There was a photo of Alison and me standing in front of the whitewashed beach house that first summer; we looked happy and eternal. I dropped the picture and buried it. Few pictures of my father were in the box, but there was one taken before he lost his eye; it was a grainy photograph, and in it his smile is fuller and more genuine than I had ever seen. His hair is thick and high, and he's wearing a suit with lapels that nearly touch his shoulders. His eyes stand out most in the picture; they are dark but luminous, glowing with youth and optimism. I stared and stared at them.

The pictures of my mother, from the brittle black and whites soon after her marriage up through the colorful Instamatic prints taken at parties and New Jersey cook-outs, show a history of fashion in hair and clothing. The later ones show changes in her face that seem to mark the confusions behind it; she is either staring dead into the camera, as if through the lens to see something, or she is looking away with a vigilant intensity, left, right, up, down, as if any moment she expected her enemies to appear.

I ran into a batch of photographs taken on the day of my wedding. I tried not to look at them but couldn't help myself. There we were, Alison and I, emerging from the Presbyterian church in Mays Landing, New Jersey, making our way down the steps beneath a hail of rice. The day had been as fine as this one. That it was a protestant church and not Catholic did not matter to me. I was a bad Catholic, no kind of Presbyterian, and I didn't want to get married in any kind of church. A Justice of the Peace would have been good enough for me. But I made a concession to Alison's parents, my gesture of good will. My own parents preferred to see us married in the Church of the Epiphany, but because Alison's father was paying the bills for the affair my parents did not insist.

Alison's parents disapproved of me from the beginning and did not want Alison marrying me at all. They saw a lack of ambition in me and had little faith that I would amount to much and be able to provide Alison with the material comforts they believed were her birthright.

About money, Alison's parents were correct. I had little potential, at least legally, for making the amounts of it they envisioned suitable for a child of theirs. My education had been in liberal arts; I had no interest in business and I thought being a teacher was fine, which would not make me wealthy. Why Alison ignored my financial shortcomings, I did not know. God knows, she wanted big money. She had grown up in a large house with fine antiques and a swimming pool in the back, and she was used to luxury and getting what she wanted. She had expensive tastes in clothing, jewelry, cars, everything. She had difficulty adjusting to apartment life, the year we lived in one, and hated more the time we lived in the row house on Jackson Street after my mother was placed in the Home.

The house had none of the modern conveniences Alison was used to, no dish washer, clothes dryer, or garbage disposal. The idea of hanging clothing on a line in the backyard or in the basement was something foreign and appalling to her. She refused to do it, so I hung them myself. I did have a garbage disposal put in a little before our first Christmas in the house and Alison seemed happy to have it. But a few weeks after the disposal was installed, Alison fed a dozen roses I had brought home for her, one after the other, into the churning machine. We had been arguing about money.

Alison disliked Philadelphia and the neighborhood we lived in so much that she often went home to Margate for the weekends. She returned late Sunday night or Monday morning, sullen and resentful. I went with her once but the tension between her parents and me was so unbearable I did not want to go again. The Saturday night we spent together, her parents went out and Alison and I, in some unspoken attempt to connect to the passion that had brought us together, cleared off her father's antique desk in the den and made love on it. But it wasn't the same; we grabbed and bit instead of caressed and our noises were more those of physical effort than of passion. We finished, dressed, and watched television the rest of the night. I knew then that no amount of money I could make would make Alison happy with me.

After a little more than a year of marriage, Alison began to complain that she felt "suffocated." She said she felt as though she were in a box and couldn't breathe. She said that she didn't want to wake up at thirty-five and still be in Philadelphia working as a secretary and making lunches for a couple of kids. She said that if she didn't "do something" it would be too late, she would be "immobilized" by children or stuck in a job she hated. Her "dreams" were dying, she said; she was losing sight of them and of herself. She said that already we were blurring into each other, that we weren't individuals anymore but a couple, an aggregate. Didn't I feel it? she would ask. "Look," she said, "you came into my life like a meteor, all fire and light, and those deep eyes of yours like you had two hundred years of wisdom or something. And, God, all that talk, that language. Where did you get it? Where did it come from? The things you could say, did say, almost poetry. You were pure then, you acted on impulses immediately, without considering, rationalizing, all that. And you made me want to be pure, to act that way, on impulse; and you made me feel that it was ok to have nothing in my head but passion for you, for things I liked, and to go through life at my own pace, to my own beat. You taught me that. For a while, it was beautiful and unreal; the more unreal the better. No concerns or worries. We were free. We were in a bubble. But bit by bit all that crumbled, and we wound up here. Look at our sex life, for instance . . ."

I had stopped listening. I did not have to hear what I already knew, knew perhaps better than Alison—that we were doomed from the start, that the extreme emotions and wild impulses working within me the summer we met had less to do with romance and love than with our own characters. Alison unlocked things in me and for a while it was all reckless speed and laughter. I worshipped her. I could stroke her for hours. She saw in me complete selflessness. For a while, we were in a cocoon, as she had said, suspended from the world. She was a dream. In her, I saw my ideal self. But I realized, as Alison did, that we had mistaken exuberance for love. When we had to live ordinary lives, we had nothing. It often seemed to me that, if my mother were right about these matters, Alison and I had met under a certain configuration of stars and planets, which eventually slid out of alignment, leaving us to face our true selves. We settled into numbing routines. Our sex became mechanical and spare. Speech between us shrank until, when Alison finally packed her things, she did it wordlessly and I made no effort to break the excruciating silence.

I was moving around the clutter in the basement, trying to reduce it enough so that someone could walk down there without tripping over an old toaster or a snow tire, when I heard the door open.

"Vince?" It was Frank.

"Down here."

He crossed the livingroom above my head, making the naked bulbs dance. "What are you doing?" he asked at the top of the stairs. "The place smells like a hospital."

"Jamie and Ted are coming this weekend," I said when he came down the wooden steps. Frank wore a cream-colored sport jacket over a knit shirt. "I thought I'd get rid of some of the crud, but I guess I got carried away." I moved boxes of books into the closet where Ted's second telescope nestled among old baseball bats. "Cyril's coming, too, of course."

"How are you going to see Tucci while they're here?"

"I don't know. I'll think of something."

"You don't want them finding out about that. They'd just get upset about nothing, like Tony."

"You spoke to him?"

"He came over to my place late last night, yelling about the tape recorder. He thinks his name'll wind up on the tapes. Has it?"

"Not yet. And not yours, either, if you were wondering."

"I wasn't wondering."

"Anyway, why's he so touchy about it? The tapes aren't going anywhere."

"Just the idea of his name on a tape makes Tony crazy. He hears it playing in a courtroom." Frank picked up a deflated football and tossed it to me. "How did he find out about the recorder?"

"I don't know exactly. Tucci went to the bathroom

once and left the door open, but I only saw his wife look in. Would she have told him?"

"She likes Tony a lot but that's stepping way out of line, telling him; she's supposed to pretend that den doesn't exist, except to clean it." Frank hoisted a full plastic trash bag of old clothes and heaved it my way, then brushed off his hands and trousers. "How 'bout giving me a ride to Seventh Street. I have to meet somebody in about ten minutes."

"Where's your car?"

"On Ritner Street. It conked out at a traffic light and wouldn't start. Lucky I was only a few blocks away."

"Yeah, lucky," I said, dusting off my hands, not at all happy to quit because I knew, once stopped, I would not want to continue and the basement would remain a deathtrap for another five years or so.

Stepping outside into the heat a few minutes later, Frank and I walked into Lou Cocco returning from work. Half moons of sweat marked his shirt under his arms and at his chest; he seemed to carry heat on his shoulders like a burden. We said hello but did not stop. I would have if alone.

"How was the game last night?" Lou called after me.

"It was fun," I said, turning and walking backwards. "I had a good time. See you later."

Frank and I walked to my car parked in front of the Church of the Epiphany. The church's carillon, as if waiting for us, started into *Ave Maria* just as we crossed the street. Something was wrong with the timing device and that and other tunes, which were supposed to be played around five o'clock, were launched into the neighborhood at all hours of the day or night. Some of the notes missed, and the number of dull bongs that the carillon belted out every hour never matched the time.

"What was that about a game?" Frank asked at the car.

"Nothing. I just told Lou that I was going to the Phillies game last night."

"I hate to tell you, but the Phillies were in Chicago last night."

SEVEN

I drove down Eleventh Street, thinking of what I could tell Cocco. Maybe, like me, he did not know that the Phillies were out of town, in which case I wouldn't have to correct myself when I saw Lou next. But if he had caught me in a lie, well, I'd make up something else.

Near McKean Street, Frank spotted a friend of his, Petie Bird, and had me honk the horn and pull over. Petie noticed Frank and came up to the car while Frank reached into his jacket and pulled out his wallet.

"Frankie V," Petie said, leaning on the car door. On the back of each finger was a tattoed letter spelling Petie, on his right hand, and Bird on the left. He glanced at me and nodded. We only knew each other by name.

"Want another job, Petie?" Frank asked as he gave him four one hundred dollar bills.

"You got one?" Petie said, pocketing the money.

"A regular job, I mean."

"How regular?"

"I need somebody to run the pizzeria at Tasker."

"I don't know from pizza, Frank."

"Don't worry," Frank said, giving him another hundred, "you could learn."

He studied the hundred before shoving it in his pocket with the others. "I guess I could give it a shot," he said.

"Good. See you tomorrow around lunch."

Petie said ok, and Frank told me to go.

"So Tommy told you," I said, pulling away from the curb.

"Not Tommy, but when he didn't show up I knew where he was, who he was with. Tony told me last night that Green was doing some collecting for him. Fine. Let Tony have that loony fuck for a headache."

"It was a career move. He expects to go places now."

"Yeah, he'll go places, but it won't be with his motorcycle. Tommy used to ride it to work and would spit-polish it on the sidewalk during his breaks. You passed his apartment on Broad Street, you'd see it chained to the railing. Well, the bike's scrap now."

"Petie?" I asked.

"Petie and a sledgehammer."

I imagined the sledgehammer coming down on the polished gas tank, the chrome exhaust pipes, the engine, the wire-spoke wheels, and Tommy coming out of the apartment house and seeing the mess. He would grab his head and moan.

"You wrecked his bike for not giving you two-weeks notice?"

"It wasn't that. He tapped the register every day, which amounted to a lot of money, and then quit cold like this. He treated me like a fool. The money's one thing; treating me like a chooch is another."

I knew that, aside from any other reason, Frank believed his behavior was necessary because of the circles he moved in.

Several blocks later, I stopped in front of the Villa on Seventh Street where Frank had asked me to take him. He left the car and walked through the cut-glass door of the restaurant.

I drove away and halfway back to the house before spotting Frank's wallet on the seat. He must not have returned it to his pocket after paying Petie Bird for smashing Tommy's motorcycle. I turned around at the next light, but immediately got stuck directly behind a trash truck. For ten minutes, I watched two men, their faces glistening with sweat, as they fed trash into the truck as it crawled down the street.

I turned at the nearest street and, a few minutes later, squeezed my car into a spot on Eighth near a tiny neighborhood park named after a local politician who had spent some years in jail for influence peddling. An old man sat on a bench under a tree and fed walnuts to a band of squirrels. He looked up at me with a sheepish look, as if I had caught him in a shameful act. Children played on the small street I walked down and the adults, sitting out in front of their houses, watched me with suspicion.

The restaurant was cool and smelled of basil and cheese, and the clatter of silverware and dishes came from the kitchen. Not yet five o'clock, only about a third of the tables were occupied. Frank was sitting with two men at a table by the wall. One man, his full head of black hair combed straight back, appeared to be in his fifties; he looked familiar but I couldn't place him. The other man was younger and larger.

Frank was turned just enough away from the entrance that he did not see me come in. But the younger man did. As I waved off the hostess and walked directly toward the table, Frank's wallet in my hand, the man watched me intently. When Frank noticed him reach into his jacket and begin to stand, his head snapped toward me, but just as quickly turned back to the table where he threw out his arm, keeping the man in his seat.

"A friend of mine," Frank said as I came up.

The two men looked annoyed, and I realized I had breached some etiquette.

Frank stood and I handed him the wallet. "You left it in the car."

"Excuse me," Frank said to the older man. He took me by the elbow and guided me out the door and onto the hot sidewalk.

I said, "I'm sorry I interrupted but—"

"You almost got yourself shot."

"*Shot?*"

"The way you came straight to the table like that with something, who knows what, in your hand, why are you surprised?"

"That's what he was going in his jacket for, a gun?"

"Why don't you say it a little louder?"

"But do I look like a hit man?" I asked in a lower voice.

"That goon thinks you do. Look, forget about it. I'll just tell them you're a little retarded."

"Oh, thanks."

"Don't you have to go to Jersey tonight?"

"Unfortunately."

"So you better get going."

Frank went back inside the restaurant, and I headed for the car. *Shot?* So the big man was a bodyguard, but who was the man he was there to protect? Walking through the gang of shrill children and the suspicious adults, I tried to remember where I had seen the man before.

At six-thirty, I opened the door at a knock, expecting to see Tommy Green with Buttoni's Cadillac behind him on the street, but Leo stood there. My surprise must have showed.

"Tony's busy, so I'm here to drive you. But call the house first. Mr. Tucci said to tell you when I got here."

"I don't know the number."

"Where's your phone? I'll do it."

I let him in and showed him the telephone in the kitchen. He jabbed at the buttons. "Mr. Tucci," Leo said after a few moments, "here's Vince Vespers for you." He handed me the receiver, then moved a few feet away to look at the calendar hanging on the wall.

"I changed the plans for tonight," Tucci said, after my hello. "Instead of coming straight to the house, I want you to meet Marie at the library first."

"I don't understand."

"She goes to that library almost every night and stays there until it closes. Then she comes home and sits in the tree swing out front. The mosquitoes love her. And if she doesn't go to the library or hang in the swing, she hides in her room. I want you to talk to her, Vincent, be friendly to her."

"Won't it seem odd, me showing up like that?"

"Make up something. But talk to her."

"All right." I was curious about his daughter anyway, and if spending a little time with her being "friendly" meant less time in the den, I wasn't going to argue against it.

"Leo will drop you off. Let me talk to him."

"Leo." I held out the receiver to him. He took it from me and held it against his ear.

"Yes, Mr. Tucci?" He listened. "Uh huh." Leo's head turned toward me. "Ok, sure. Bye-bye." He hung up. "He wants me to take you to the library," Leo said to me.

"I know."

"Well, ready when you are."

We left the house in a few minutes, I escaped running into Lou Cocco, and very shortly we were sealed off from the orange city heat by Leo's BMW and heading toward New Jersey. Leo did not have much to say but, whereas Tony Buttons radiated ill will, there was a cowlike quality about Leo, making him appear harmless. It made the ride over the bridge as bearable as it would ever be and the rest of the trip almost pleasant.

We reached the library in forty minutes. It was a squat building of sandstone and sat on the side of the road like a warehouse, separated from the other buildings by stretches of grass and a few trees. With

Leo waiting in the parking lot, the windows up and the engine running for the air conditioning, I filled my lungs with the New Jersey air and went through the door, hoping Marie would not be inside.

She was. I spotted her near the literature section, sitting by herself at a long wooden table with stacks of books in front of her like a barricade. Her head was propped up with one hand and with the other she twirled a length of hair that had fallen beside her cheek. Marie was round-shouldered, thin, and bent over, her hair shrouding her face and the book below; she seemed to be caving into herself. I remembered then seeing a photograph on the table in the alcove where I waited the night before that showed Tucci as a much younger man with a girl, Marie I realized, held up against his chest, her thin arms about his neck. In the photo, both of them are looking into the camera. Tucci is smiling, but Marie, even then, seemed to be staring into some unhealthy distance.

I tried to see what Marie was reading as I drew closer, hoping to discover something we had in common, but the spines of the books were turned away so that I could not make out the titles. I blindly grabbed a book from the nearest shelf before reaching her table.

"What are you reading?" I asked.

Marie looked up, recognized me, and instantly looked down. She began to bite her already shortened fingernails, tearing off a white sliver of nail so close to the skin that she bled.

"Mind if I sit down?"

She put her bleeding finger into her mouth and

moved her face closer to the book as if I were not there.

"I saw you in the swing last night," I said, sitting across from her and blundering on, "but I didn't have time to talk."

Marie hunkered lower over the book, her hair touching it now and her arms circling it like something she meant to protect.

"I thought here would be a good spot to, you know, get to know each other a little." I winced at that as soon as I heard how corny it sounded.

She glanced out from under her hair, and for a second I thought she was going to say something, but she went back to her book. Marie had my brother Ted's eyes, which seemed to hold some deep and unforgotten hurt.

"Well," I said, giving up, feeling like I had been rude, "I can see you'd rather not have company. I'll go." I began to move my chair away from the table.

"Did my father send you?" Marie's voice sounded weak, as if from too little use. She kept her head down, speaking into the book, and I strained to hear her.

"No. I've never been in a New Jersey library and I wanted to see this one."

"You like libraries?"

"I think libraries are wonderful."

Marie looked up. "My father sent you, didn't he?"

"Uh, yes." I felt ridiculous. "But I did really want to talk to you. I'm sorry I lied. I got flustered."

"Why did you want to talk to me?"

"Because you seem interesting."

Marie turned a page and looked at it for a while.

BLOOD CONFESSIONS

"This is one of the few places where I can get away from the hoodlums at the house."

"Do you think I'm a hoodlum?"

"Everybody who comes to the house is a hoodlum."

"Not me. I'm a teacher."

Marie moved from her book to look up a word in her pocket dictionary, ignoring or disregarding what I said. She found the word and went back to her book. "I know why you've been coming."

"Your father told you?"

"I don't talk to my father." Marie came out of her slouch a little and began to work on a fresh fingernail. "My bedroom's above the den. I came in through the back last night and while you two were down there, I heard him through the floor. I couldn't make out all he said but it was enough to get the idea."

"He's telling me his life." I told Marie about meeting her father at Shunk's Tavern when he brought me the idea.

She looked out the windows. "I suppose any person, no matter how much pain and havoc they've caused, has a right to tell his story."

"I guess so. I guess sometimes they can't help it."

Marie was silent after that and seemed to burrow into her book with a seriousness that dismissed me.

I felt lock-jawed again and stupid, without any idea what to say to her. Growing uncomfortable again, I was about to leave when Marie spoke.

"I saw you from the upstairs window when you came to the house last night," she said.

"Did you? I thought someone was there." I saw myself through her eyes, getting out of the big car below, making quick, nervous glances about the place.

"You looked afraid."

"I guess I was."

She fell quiet again and began to work on another fingernail. I could think of nothing else to say to her. I watched her bite the fingernail to the quick so that it, too, bled.

"I think I want to be alone now."

"Oh. Sure, ok." I started to stand. "I guess I'll see you at the house."

"You forgot your book," she said, reading the title before handing it to me. *"Sewing Basics?"*

It was what I had grabbed before following her across the room.

After we settled into the den, Tucci asked me how it went with Marie.

"There's not much to tell, really."

"You didn't like her?"

"No, I liked her fine."

"You know, a few years ago she tried to kill herself."

My eyebrows went up.

"She swallowed some pills. My wife found her, and they had to pump her stomach. I had her going to shrinks for a while, but they didn't do any good. She still mopes, still doesn't have any friends. Did she say anything about me?"

"No. She knows what I'm doing here, though."

"Yeah? And what does she think?"

"She didn't say."

"If she says, you let me know."

"All right."

"Keep talking to her."

"Sure, when I get the chance."

"Come on, turn on the machine. Let's get started."

I turned on the recorder and Tucci began. He brought his life up through his marriage, the birth of his daughter, his several affairs. It sounded like a soap opera to me until he began to tell about his career, the businesses he formed and ran, the people who worked in them, the troubles with the law, the violent deaths of relatives and friends, the violent retributions. He told about the politicians on the City Council he had bribed, the judges he had bought, the power brokers to whom he had lent money. There were the usual union connections. There was his close association with Maglio, then their falling out, and now the detente between them. He told of meeting my brother Frank, the many things Frank had done for him, and how he had long ago started grooming Frank as his eventual successor. Frank had what "it took." He had something inside that could not be described. "Not like Tony." Buttons was "coarse," a "hack man," a "dirty-worker," who was, nevertheless, loyal. Tucci rattled off a list of crimes that Tony Buttons had done directly or in which he had had a hand. Tucci told me of schemes that had netted him hundreds of thousands of dollars. He told me of the few years he spent in prison for tax evasion. He also told of his medical problems, his bouts with phlebitis, his polyps, cysts, blood disorders, and his cancer.

Frank was right not to be concerned about Tucci mentioning his name. Tucci referred to Frank only as "your brother." But he did use Tony's name, both Buttons and Buttoni.

Tucci went on straight for two hours, never tiring; his voice ran to the end of the tape and it was cut in the middle of a sentence. He waited for me to change the cassettes, and after I did he finished what he had been saying and began afresh. He went on for another hour, and I fought off sleep. He might have continued through the night, his will stronger than his illness that night, and I might have fallen asleep right there in front of him if his wife hadn't tapped on the door. She brought Tucci out into the hall and whispered something to him.

"That's it for tonight," Tucci said when he returned. "Go tell Tony to take you home."

"I'd rather not ride with Tony anymore."

"Why not? You don't like Tony?"

"I'd rather drive myself. I know how to get here now."

"You won't get lost?"

"No. And if I do, I'll call for directions."

"Ok. Tomorrow, you come yourself. But tonight, Tony'll take you."

I packed up the tapes and left the den. Tony was in the room across the hall, sprawled in the easy chair, sleeping, the side of his head in his palm and the television's odd light blanketing his large frame. His pants had risen up above his socks to show hairy bands of skin. Even in sleep, Buttoni looked threatening, and I gave no thought to waking him. I walked softly down the hall and out the door, thinking I'd wait outside for him to wake up or for somebody else to wake him.

I had walked halfway down the walkway when I noticed Marie sitting in the tree swing again. She faced the road, moving gently, as if stirred by the breeze.

The ropes jerked and Marie snapped around when I came near. I apologized for startling her.

"What are you doing out here at this hour?" I asked.

"I don't go to sleep until three, sometimes later."

"So you sit out here by yourself and kill time?"

"Something like that," she said, looking at the ground. "Or I stay in my room and read, or do crossword puzzles."

A three-quarter moon sent down weak light and it was enough, with the outer reach of the lamppost, to see Marie. The breeze stirred her hair. I had an urge to push her into motion, see her sail in gentle arcs at the end of the swing.

"I have trouble sleeping, too, but only at night," I said.

"I don't have trouble. I just don't get sleepy until past midnight. It's my inner clock."

"I think it's something else for me. Memory maybe."

"Memory can be a curse." She paused and dug her heel into the ground. "So can a name. Tucci."

"You mean for you, a curse."

She nodded, hammering her foot into the earth.

"It's only a name, and you can change it."

"You don't understand," Marie said.

"Then tell me."

She took a deep breath and seemed to gather herself. "Even if I changed it, I'd still know who my father is. You may not think it matters to be associated with him, but I do. My father spent my sixth grade year to my ninth in jail, and it seemed like everyone knew it. I got teased. Boys wouldn't go out with me. And if they did and then they found out who I was, I never heard from them again. Of course, I got come-ons from the men that showed up here over the years, but I hated them, they made me sick. I felt like I would be inbreeding if I dated them. Then I met a guy in the city, outside the Colonial Theater when I was seventeen."

"In South Philly?"

"Yes. He was there all by himself under the marquee, holding his arms around his waist in an odd way. And when I walked near, he said, 'Do you want a kitten?' and he opened his jacket and out pops this little head and looks at me. He said he had found it outside his house but that he couldn't keep it because he was allergic. He said he was on the corner asking people who passed by if they wanted the kitten. I said that I'd take it, but that I didn't want to take it on the bus, which is how I got to the city that day. He said he would take me home. I didn't hesitate at all. There was something very sweet and non-threatening about him. It was a windy day, with a perfect blue sky; as we drove over the bridge, even the river looked nice. He said he had seen me coming up the street and he knew that I would take the cat, that finding the cat in the first place was part of a destiny that led to our meeting. He talked like that. He said we were two of a kind; he said he could tell me my favorite colors, foods, painful things because he knew they would be the same as his. Then he told me what they were, and he was so right it frightened me. That's how it was with him. I was transparent. He dropped me off near the house and he asked me if it was all right if he could think about seeing me again. *Think* about seeing me? I said sure. And he just smiled and nodded. Then he drove off, his hand up on the seat in a wave as I stood there in the lane holding the kitten." She paused and turned to me. "I'm sorry. I'm babbling."

"No, it's all right. I'm interested. Did he find you?"

"I didn't see or hear from him for weeks," she continued, "and then one night he threw pebbles at my window, actually sneaked up to the house and did that. He could have been killed. I sneaked out of the house and we went for a drive in his convertible. I began to see him often. I would meet him in the lane away from the house and we would drive to the shore or go to out of the way places where it was quiet. He was smart. He read books, poetry, he read Shakespeare. We did a lot of talking. One thing led to another. Eventually, he met my parents. They didn't like him, especially my mother. They didn't want me to see him. I didn't care. He was the first person who made me feel wanted, needed, essential. I guess that's love. I would have eloped with him at the drop of a hat." She fell silent and stared into the darkness.

"What happened?"

"I don't know. He disappeared. I was supposed to meet him on the road one night, but he didn't show. It was November. All the leaves had fallen from the trees. It was a cool night but not enough to make me shiver. There were so many stars. I waited for hours, but he never came. I called his house but he wasn't there. The next day, he wasn't there either. I called his friends and relatives eventually, anybody I could think of. Nobody knew what had happened to him. I took the bus to the city and looked around his neighborhood. I finally went to the police. They didn't know anything; they never do. He just vanished. The last time I saw him was from this swing the night before he vanished. He had said so-long, he kissed me, and walked away slowly, so that, dressed as he was in his black leather jacket and dark pants, he sort of faded into the night, as if he just became part of it. Sometimes I sit here and I think I see him in the darkness, wearing the same black clothes he wore that night, as if he had only slipped into a time warp and just came back."

"Black leather jacket, you said? Convertible? And he was from South Philly?"

"Yes, that's right."

"Was his name Patty Leone?"

"Yes! Did you know him?"

"We were neighbors. He lived with his aunt, who I still see nearly every day. Mrs. Falcone."

"She's still alive? My God, what a coincidence."

"Frank was closer to him than I was. In fact, when Patty disappeared, I remember Frank doing the same thing you did; he looked around for him, talked to anyone who knew him to see if they knew what may have happened to him. No one knew anything."

"I know something bad happened to Patty. He wouldn't have gone to California or somewhere and not told me. I often wondered if my father had something to do with it. Him or Tony. Because Tony was jealous. I hate that man."

"I'm not so crazy about him either."

"Did I say that Patty wrote letters to me? I've got a shoebox full. It was the letters that my parents couldn't stand most of all. I know that they intercepted and read some of them. I can see my mother standing over a pot of boiling water, steaming the letters open, and then wracking her brains trying to read them with her limited vocabulary. Some of them I never received. I knew my parents had grabbed them, read them, and decided that I shouldn't. They never admitted it, of course, as they never admitted to reading my journals. I knew one of them did. It made me furious, but in the end Patty, who was always tolerant of my parents, would just re-write the letter and hand it to me."

I was about to ask her if she had any other male friends, past or present, when the front door of the house opened and Tony Buttoni came out and down the walkway. He came toward us quickly, and for a moment I thought he might slug me.

"What are you doing? I look in the den and you're gone. I look in the livingroom, you're not there. I check the bathrooms but I don't see you. I don't know what happened to you. You could be copping the silverware for all I know." His tone softened. "Hello, Marie."

"You were sleeping," I said. "I didn't want to wake you."

"I wasn't sleeping. I just had my eyes closed. He bothering you, Marie?"

"Not at all," she said.

"You, in the car," Buttons said to me.

"You'd better go," Marie said.

I nodded and walked to the Cadillac. Marie stayed in the swing, looking away, as Tony spoke to her.

I could not hear what he said. He joined me in a minute and gunned the engine when he started it. I looked past his nose and at Marie, still hanging from the tree like a pendulum. As we pulled away from the house, Marie lifted a finger from the rope in a tiny wave. She looked like she might hang there forever.

"You ever pull a stunt like that again, I'll rip your heart out and shove it up your ass."

"What did I do?"

"I look out the window and you're like two fucking parakeets chirping away. You got some idea about her or what?"

"I just went out and she was there, so we started talking. I couldn't ignore her."

"That's exactly what you should do." He turned out of the lane and onto the road. "You met her at the library, that was bad enough."

"I was told to go there."

"I don't give a shit. Let me tell you something, smartass. Mrs. Tucci is sweet on me, and there's nothing she would like better than if I married her daughter. You heard me. I'd be set up for life if I got in that family. I'm in line, and I wouldn't care if Marie was crazy as a bedbug, I'm taking my shot, and I don't need some shit like you fucking it up. Where the fuck do you get off, anyway, coming here the way you do, some jerk-off from the outside don't know his manners? You, a nobody, acting like a weasel and sneaking around."

"You're wrong about me," I said, still trying to explain.

"I'm not wrong. I know a thing or two about you. Now shut up, unless you want to walk to Philly."

What a goddamn maniac, I thought. Baboon. Moron. I looked out the side window at the dark countryside and thought what pleasure it would give me to be able to hold a gun to this man's face. I'd hold the barrel against the bastard's nose and watch him sweat. But maybe he wouldn't sweat at all. Go ahead and shoot, he might say. He might laugh, the truest of soldiers, as eager to die as to kill. Maybe I'd have to put the gun in his mouth, make him taste the metal, move it around in there and break some teeth, then maybe he'd have an opinion about dying.

The bridge arrived after fifteen minutes of tense silence, first the red beacons in the black sky, then the gigantic supports and the series of thick cables, finally the bridgeroad and the dark chasms to the sides. I squeezed my knees and shook.

Buttoni suddenly slammed on the brakes. Cars behind us screeched and honked. "Get outta my car."

"What!"

"You heard me. Out!"

"We're in the middle of the bridge, for God's sake. I can't get out here."

"The fuck you can't." He pushed a button on the dashboard and the door unlocked.

"It's a bridge. Nobody's allowed to walk on it."

"Get going before I get mad."

"But—"

"Out, fucker." He shoved me hard against the door.

"Ok, ok."

I left the car slowly, hoping Buttoni would burst into laughter and call me back. But he leaned over, pulled the door closed after me and sped away, releasing the cars that had piled up behind us. I stared after him, unable to move. I felt airy and light, afraid to lift my feet for fear of gusts getting beneath them and tossing me up and over the side for the long black flight down. I felt the bridge sway. It made a sound, too, not just of cars, but a metallic groaning as the bridge balanced itself against its own tremendous weight. I stood paralyzed, my eyes leaping from the glitter of the city to the pier lights to the underbellies of jets as they sunk toward the airport.

"Hey, you all right?" A car had stopped; two men in suits sat in the front seat.

I could not speak.

"You want a lift?"

"Uh, yes, please," I managed to say. But I could not move.

The men looked at each other.

"Well, get in," the driver said.

It took some effort but I finally took a step and shuffled toward the car without lifting my feet from the road, as though skimming on ice. I reached the car and grabbed the door handle, feeling instant relief. I climbed into the back seat and the men started toward the tolls.

"What were you doing out there?" the driver asked.

I did not answer, the feeling of being out on the immense structure with all that black air around me lingering on my skin.

"Anything wrong?"

I shook my head no.

"You looked like you were in trouble."

"I, my car broke down."

"We didn't see a car," the other man said.

"You must have missed it," I said, as we slowed for the toll booth. "Ah, you could let me off at the first exit. I don't live far from here."

"We're going in town. You want a lift that way?"

"If you know where Jackson Street is, I'd appreciate a ride to there."

The driver looked at me in the rearview mirror. "We know where it is, Carl?"

"Yes, we know."

It wasn't until later that I realized how peculiar that sounded.

EIGHT

Four days after being shoved out of Buttoni's car, and with three more sessions with Tucci completed, I sat in a booth in Frank's Pizzeria beside my brother Ted and across from Jamie and Cyril. They had arrived the day before. Cyril and Jamie, breathless and pink-cheeked, came through the door as if on wind, and the house seemed to swell with them. Ted walked in slightly behind, a cleansed look of the country and the odor of wood in his skin. His eyes had lost some of their long-standing hurt, but not so much that another deeper consciousness did not seem to lay hidden and untouchable behind them. I had missed him more than Jamie in many ways, and it felt good to sit beside him.

Jamie had wanted to go out to dinner that first night, but I told her I had a date and would not be able to join them. When Jamie suggested that I bring my date along, I said we had made previous plans which could not be broken. Jamie was not altogether disappointed because, to her, every new date I had was the potential woman who would provide me with the happy life she was convinced I lacked. My sister encouraged me to have fun. I said that I would try. I left the house at six-thirty and drove to Tucci's.

Like the previous nights since Buttoni forced me onto the bridge, after finishing with Tucci I hurried down the hall, past the room where Tony sat watching television and out the door. As I walked to my car, I only tipped my head toward Marie, dangling yet another night in the swing. I irritated myself for allowing Buttoni to intimidate me into not talking to Marie but, while he was in the house, I was not going to risk getting tossed onto the bridge again, or worse. For her part, Marie seemed unaffected by my not stopping.

Reaching home around midnight, I found Jamie awake and in the livingroom, reading one of my mother's fat novels she found somewhere. After relating my fictitious outing to her in the most general and unspecific way, we sat up talking for a couple hours about the family, old times, and our lives now. She was "very content" and would not change any of her life. She and Cyril had a "perfect marriage," and they could not wait to have their baby. She had no worries and looked forward to a bright future. The eternal optimist, I had said. When the talk came to me, I did not mention any of my entanglements with Frank, Tucci or Buttoni. I said nothing about how the disappointments and failures of my life had been plaguing me lately and ruining my sleep. I did not bring up my cowardice or weakness of will, my bad attitude or passivity. I confessed to living a monotonous life, saying that I preferred it that way. But that was a lie; I realized it as soon as the words came out of my mouth. I realized then, too, what kept me involved with Frank and caused me to fall in with Tucci. It wasn't just the money or whatever I had lost by allowing Frank to go to jail for me. In Frank and Tucci, I sought vitality; I sought consequence.

At two o'clock, Jamie kissed me goodnight and went to bed. I stayed downstairs and, in an effort to force from my mind all that had surfaced but which remained unexpressed, I opened the fat novel to a random page and read until my eyes became sticky.

I called Frank the next day to tell him that Jamie and Ted had come into town. Though he did not sound happy to hear it, he suggested we all stop for a late lunch at his pizza shop, where he said he would meet us. Jamie thought it was a good idea, but she first wanted to go to the cemetery where my father was buried. Asked to the cemetery with her, I claimed a queasy stomach while Ted, who said he wanted to go alone sometime during his visit, ran his daily seven miles. Jamie frowned at us but let it go at that.

"I didn't remember the cemetery being that big," she said when she returned. "There's a whole quarry of stone there. And all those names and dates. Some of the stones were over ten feet high, and the mausoleums remind you of miniature banks. I hadn't been there for so long that I didn't remember where Dad was buried. I felt bad about that. I tried to put myself back to the time of the funeral, but I couldn't remember the spot."

"Section B, plot 36," Teddy said.

We looked at him.

"It's just something I never forgot," he explained.

"He's right. Two ladies are in this little building like a bunker at the entrance to the place and they have file cabinets of who's buried where. They look up the name and give you a diagram of the cemetery and an X on the spot of the grave you're looking for. I found it in a few minutes. It's so strange seeing your name carved in stone. Vespers. And the dates below it. And Dad being under the ground, right there, so close."

I saw little purpose in visiting the dead. They were put in cemeteries as a comfort to ourselves, but it was a comfort I did not need.

"We'll bury Mom there," Jamie said.

"Don't bury me at all," I said. "I want to be cremated."

"So we'll have your ashes to hold when we miss you," Cyril said. "The fillings of your teeth, a few bits of vertibrae."

"Stop that," Jamie said. "Let's go to lunch."

She wanted to walk to Frank's, and none of us argued with her, even though I knew she could not resist making stops at Mrs. Falcone's and Purdy Gant's grocery to say hello. Luckily, Mrs. Falcone was not home and Purdy had a store full of customers; he could only hug Jamie and make her promise to stop back. She said that she would, and Purdy gave her a pack of chewing gum as he often did when we were children.

Petie Bird, Frank's new manager at the pizzeria, was standing in front of a large pot stirring tomato sauce when we came in. He looked over his shoulder at us in the slow, dullwitted manner of an ox, then turned back to the sauce before I could say hello. If he recognized me, it did not register in his face. I had the feeling anyone could walk in and Petie would look at them with the same dead eyes.

We sat in the booth nearest the wide front window, close enough to hear the snapping and buzzing of the neon sign that advertised the place, and almost directly under a slowly twirling fan in the ceiling. Two painters, speckled with blue dots, glumly ate a pizza in the rear booth. A kid of about seventeen worked the oven; as we sat, I watched him pull a steaming pizza out of the oven with his large wooden spatula and slide it neatly into a box, which he then quickly taped.

"Here's another one, Birdman. Half-pep, half-'rooms and ready to go. You people, what'll it be?" he asked.

"Nothing now. We're waiting for Frank," I said.

"Uh, oh. You hear that, Petie? The boss is coming. You relatives? Yeah, sure you are. Look at the resemblance. Petie, the family's here."

"Don't you have some hoagies to make?"

"You're right. Two with the works, the Frank Special. Good choice!" He went to work behind the counter; slicing rolls and stuffing them with everything he had. "Guy's here maybe four days and he already knows how to crack a whip," he said out of the corner of his mouth and in a low tone.

"What?" Petie said.

"Just talking to myself, boss." The kid winked at me.

"Well, stop it." Petie turned toward the window

to look in the street, and the kid pantomimed stabbing him in the back.

"Live entertainment," my brother-in-law said.

"At Frank's, you get treated like royalty," I said.

"We have a joke man and a Cro-Magnon man. I mean, a straight man. This is much more pleasant than that boot camp exercise I was on the other day."

"What boot camp exercise?" I asked.

"Getting to Ted's. Weren't you ever there?"

"No. I thought I'd let you reconnoiter for me."

"Well, I did. Here's the report: Teddy, bless his heart, sent us a map showing where a road gets you to about a mile from his cabin. The road dead ends, but does Ted tell us it quits at the face of a mountain? Noooo."

Ted smiled. "Mountain?"

"A very big hill, Mr. Davy Crockett, which my poor wife, gone with child I might add, and I trudged up, carrying sleeping bags, a snake bite kit and toilet paper. Just in case."

"Get out," I said.

"He's serious," Jamie said, laughing, enjoying the story.

"The humidity got to me," Cyril went on, "or the altitude, or maybe the claustrophobia from the trees, which were all around and thick, with the sunlight coming down in only bright shafts, just spots on the ground. I felt, anyway, exhausted and weird. Maybe from something I ate at the two-bit diner we stopped at on the highway. This was a place where you couldn't tell the waitresses from the truckers."

We all laughed at that.

"It wasn't that bad," Jamie said.

"Bad enough. But I felt lousy, worried about ticks and poison ivy; and it reminded me of one of those survival adventures where superhuman efforts and great sacrifices are called for. Like having to draw straws to see who gets eaten so that the others may live. I mean, it was quite possible we were making our way toward the bunker of some bizarre cult, weirdos, psychotics who indulge in human sacrifice, neo-Nazis, even. They would invite us into their odd-smelling cabin, offer us beef jerky and homemade cider, and the next thing you know we conk out and wake up tied to crude altars looking up at a figure in a black robe and holding a large knife. Strange markings are drawn on our chests with chicken blood. Somebody in the background says, 'I got dibs on the Jew's pancreas.'"

I howled. Ted gave up his quiet, breathy laugh. Jamie shook her head. "I don't know why I married you," she said.

"It could happen. You read about it in the newspapers. Anyway, I reached the cabin without having a coronary. But I was disappointed to see a water pump and an outhouse. I didn't expect that. Frontier chic? Ted here was out running, and so we went in. Vince, your brother's an ascetic. He's got a wood-burning stove, austere furniture, and a cot maybe wide enough for a broomstick. Ted, how do you live like that?"

"I'm used to it."

"Don't you ever get lonely?" Jamie asked. "I mean, day in and day out with no one to talk to."

"It's not so bad. I was looking forward to coming home, though, and seeing you all."

"You should do it more often," I said.

"Yes. But you know how I feel about the city."

"You've done a lot of travelling, I heard," Cyril said. "Where were your fondest places?"

Ted thought a few moments. "Greece, Montana, Nova Scotia. But I was on the Amazon once, at night, riding in a boat and lying on my back, looking at the stars. There were so many and so close-looking, the sky looked fake. That's hard to beat."

I pictured Ted on the Amazon, happy for him that he made it there. Beginning early on, hardly a teenager, Ted talked about leaving us. He spoke of travelling to far away places like China and Australia, and living there. He studied the world through library books with the same fervor he had studied the night sky back when he had a telescope. He wanted very much to visit the countries that girdled the Mediterranean Sea, but he also wanted to hack through the jungles of Borneo and Brazil. The Nile was on his "list." So were the Alps, Pantagonia, Iceland. As were tiny tropical islands he had uncovered. He said in a letter that he wanted to ride trains across the vast midriffs of entire continents. The Orient Express, he admitted, became a mania with him. He also wanted to hitchhike across America, and to drive long and solitary—always solitary—into the dense forests of northwestern Canada. Everywhere on the globe was a possibility.

After several stabs at college and several jobs, Ted announced that he was going to Mexico. He had somehow hooked up with a group of archeologists who were studying the Aztec sites. I took him to the Greyhound Bus Station where I watched him board a bus for Texas. He returned a year later, his skin a dark sienna and his hair lightened by the tropical sun. But he did not remain in the city long. When he left this time, he said he was heading "Anywhere," as if desperate to get away. He said he would write. He did not. Jamie made a few attempts to track Ted down after eight months of not hearing from him, but our brother had few friends and they had not heard from him either. Two years passed before we received a postcard from Ted with a Post Office box number for a return address. He had settled in his cabin and for the little money he needed he hand-carved bowls and other objects and sold them at craft fairs or to galleries.

Ted could only be coaxed back to the city after we told him that we were thinking of putting our mother in the Home. We wanted to share the guilt, Jamie told him. Our mother had been slipping rapidly over the last year, becoming too much for us. She had spells where she looked at everything, including us, with a look of bafflement. The neighbors became strangers to her, the neighborhood a foreign land. She wandered out into the cold. She began to talk to herself.

Ted came home and, shortly after coming through the door, he sat down on the bed beside my mother. Jamie took the wicker chair while I stood, arms folded across my chest. The air smelled of rotting fruit from the banana skins and apple cores that my mother had tossed under the bed. She wore my dead father's suit jacket and gazed at the television with that look of incomprehension she now wore so often. She seemed to be groping, trying to make connections, but much of her world had lost its logic, and she had not yet reached that point where it did not matter to her.

BLOOD CONFESSIONS

She looked from the television to Teddy. Her lips trembled.

"I was going to the corner store for milk," she said to Ted as if responding to a question. "I left my babies alone for only a minute, but when I came back the house was on fire. The flames were terrible, terrible very high flames. I heard the babies crying but I couldn't get close because of the fire. I couldn't save them." Her eyes had watered.

Ted looked at Jamie and me and motioned us to leave. We went downstairs and sat around for an hour with Frank, watching a football game. When Ted came down, we looked at him as if for his judgement.

"I don't think she knew who I was," he had said.

We began to make arrangements with the Home the following day, but Ted had gone back to the woods by the time my mother's admission date arrived. I saw him only once between then and now, at a crafts fair in Valley Forge.

"We were rummaging around in the cupboards like Goldilocks looking for something to eat," Cyril continued, "when Ted came in. He was wearing only running shoes. The noble savage."

"Shorts *and* running shoes," Ted corrected.

"Well, anyway, I was wondering what we were going to eat, when Ted says we have to go fish at the lake for dinner. So we hike to the lake. But, of course, when my lovely wife saw that lovely lake, she had to swim in it. Never mind that she didn't have a bathing suit. Never mind that quail hunters could be in the bushes with binoculars. No, Jamie *had* to swim."

"It's true. I couldn't resist."

Cyril told how Jamie had crossed to the other side of the lake so as not to scare the fish away from Ted's hook and how she stripped in the shrubbery and waded in the lake where she "frolicked" for twenty minutes. Ted caught several fish, a smallmouth bass and a few perch, they hiked back to the cabin, Ted cleaned and cooked the fish and they ate them along with canned peaches, peanut butter and flapjacks. That night, Jamie slept in the cot while Ted and Cyril slept on the floor in sleeping bags.

"I heard mice scampering all night," my brother-in-law said. "And the outhouse experience—"

"Forget the outhouse experience, darling."

"Nothing like modern plumbing and civilization."

"You can have your fill of civilization tomorrow when we visit New York." Jamie turned to me. "We're going up for a day to look at the museums and bookstores, and to shop Macy's."

Petie Bird called to us. "Yo, it's for you," he said to me. He held out the phone. It had rung a few times since we sat down; customers phoned in orders and, though I would not mention it to the others, with bets that I watched Petie write down in a black book.

"You're still there," Frank said, after I said hello.

"Yes, we've been waiting.

"I won't be able to make it. I'm hung up with some things."

"They were looking forward to seeing you."

"I bet. I'll get together with them tomorrow."

"Jamie and Cyril are going to New York tomorrow." A trolley rumbled by on Eleventh Street and I couldn't hear what Frank said in return. "What was that?"

"I thought they were going to the Home tomorrow."

"That's Monday."

"What time?"

"I don't know. Around one, I think. Why?"

"Just so I know when I could hook up with them. One piece of business before I go: start doing whatever you have to do to change all my paper into cash, the stocks, bonds, whatever. Make it so all I have to do is sign my name, ok?"

"I'll do it as soon as I can."

"Tell Petie to give you whatever you want on the house." He hung up.

I went back to the booth. "Frank can't make it."

"Why aren't I surprised?" Jamie said.

"But we can eat whatever we want, free."

"That's a big consolation."

"Mr. Bird," Cyril called across the room, "we are finally in need of your services."

Petie looked at Cyril as if he wanted to use his sledgehammer on him.

Early the next morning, with the sun at the end of Jackson Street not yet higher than the telephone poles but already something to dread, Ted and I drove Jamie and Cyril to 30th Street Station for their trip to New York City. We four hung around in the cavernous hall together until it was time to board the train. After Jamie and Cyril sunk out of sight on the escalator, Ted asked if he could use the car after we got home. There was a person who lived about an hour away from the city he had been writing to that he wanted to visit. Sure, I told him.

We left the station and crossed through the line

of taxicabs to the car. I told Ted to drive and to leave me off at Broad and Oregon.

"I feel like sitting in the park," I said. "I'll walk home from there." The walk would not take longer than twenty minutes. "If you could just be back by six o'clock, I'd appreciate it."

"Another date?"

"Yes. Same person."

Ted started the car and we swung around the station and onto Market Street, heading briefly toward City Hall before I had Ted turn onto the Schuylkill Expressway. In a few minutes, we were rushing past the oil refinery and its spherical holding tanks painted to resemble gigantic baseballs. A spectacular fire had erupted there several years ago that lit the night sky as orange as the setting sun. The refinery no longer gave off the choking reek of sulphur and gas you smelled when I was a kid, but there was still an odor, when you passed by, of some unnatural process going on beyond the fencing.

"Sure you don't want me to drive you all the way home?" Ted asked at Oregon Avenue.

"Yes. I want to walk."

"Ok." He put his hand lightly on my shoulder. "See you."

I left the car and walked to one of the park benches near the boccie court where, even at ten o'clock in the morning, a group of old men played a game while a larger group looked on. At a table near the court, four old men played a card game, periodically slapping down cards like vicious insults. I watched the boccie game for awhile and, to the left, boys accumulating in the baseball field for a game. When the water ice stand opened, I walked across the street and bought a dollar lemon and three pretzel sticks, then sat on the bench again, slurping and munching in the hot sun.

I felt bloated and drowsy when done, and fought a powerful urge to lay down right there on the bench and nap. I closed my eyes and would have fallen asleep if a car horn had not blasted in the street and jarred me out of my doze.

"Vinnie!" a girl not much older than one of my eleventh grade students called from the passenger side of a new Saab. "Vinnie!" She giggled all the while.

I did not know her, and tried to see past her to the driver.

The horn blatted again and the girl, enjoying herself, sang my name in a brittle falsetto, still giggling almost madly. The old men behind me cursed and shouted. Feeling conspicuous, I went over to the car, trying to place the girl.

"Hiya, Vinnie," the girl said as I came up. "Vinnie V."

I nodded, stooping slightly to look into the car.

"Yo, Vin!" It was Tommy Green behind the wheel. "What are you doing sleeping on a friggin' park bench? You been drinking?"

"I wasn't sleeping."

"Guy like you nodding out on a bench like a bum. We saw you. I said, 'Hey, I know that guy.' So I stop, I goose the horn, I tell Liz to call you."

Liz giggled. "Hi, Vinnie." I noticed a purple bruise on her neck, a passion mark.

"I only had my eyes closed. I was just about to walk home."

"You want a lift? Come on, get in. You don't want to walk in this heat."

It was hot, and I still felt drowsy. I wasn't keen on riding with Tommy but I wasn't up to the walk either anymore.

"Ok." I got in the car behind the girl.

Tommy pulled away. "Let me take Liz to Sixth Street, first."

"Ah, Tommy, I don't want to go home."

A few minutes later, she stepped out of the car, slammed the door and stalked off, not happy to leave Tommy. Tommy did a U-turn and made a right onto Seventh Street.

"How d'you like the car?" Tommy asked after a block. "Turbo charged, leather interior."

"It's nice."

"Tony set me up with a dealer. The guy's way behind on his loan, so he wanted to do Tony a favor. Low down payment, low monthlies."

"Convenient for you," I said.

"I wouldn't a had to buy anything if Frank didn't smash up my bike. You hear about that?"

"I didn't know you had a bike," I lied.

"I loved that bike. It wasn't right what Frank did. What, a guy can't quit a job? What's wrong with him?" He paused as if wanting me to answer.

"Even Tony says he's acting strange," Tommy said. "He's not right these days. And then I run into a friend of mine this morning who's a waiter at the Villa restaurant and he told me he saw Frank there the other night with you want to know who? Joe Maglio."

At the name, I remembered where I had seen the man with the straight black hair sitting with Frank.

His picture was in the newspapers a few years ago when he went on trial for bribery and extortion, which the prosecutor failed to prove.

"That doesn't mean anything," I said. "Frank did get invited to the wedding of Maglio's son."

"Vin, I know I'm not bright but, come on, even I know the difference between shaking somebody's hand at a wedding and meeting them at a restaurant."

I did too.

NINE

The doorbell rang late that afternoon. I thought I had locked the door by mistake and Ted could not get in. But when I opened the door, Carmine Tucci stood in front of me.

"Vincent," Tucci said, stepping in.

"Hello," I stuttered, a hot flash passing through my stomach.

"I'm happy you're in."

"What are you—?" but then I noticed that one of Tucci's front teeth was missing and that his jaw was bruised. Blood ringed one nostril and there was a smear of blood across his cheek and drops of it on his shirt. "Are you all right?"

"Just a little banged up," he said, walking past me and into the house. The right pocket of his trousers was ripped and there was a tear at the knee. "You have a glass of water?" He walked back to the kitchen and I followed him. "I was in my old neighborhood, Fifth Street near Passyunk. I got mugged by a couple of kids. They knocked me down and tore my wallet out. They took my watch."

"What were you doing down there by yourself?" I took a glass from the cabinet and poured him cold water from the pitcher in the refrigerator. "Where's your driver?"

"I wanted to see where I used to live, see how it changed. I grabbed Leo and walked out without telling anybody. I had him drive me to the neighborhood, then told him to get lost. After I was robbed, I looked up your name in the phone book for your address." He tilted back his head to drink the water and his whole body followed. He fell against the kitchen counter and would have fallen to the floor if I had not grabbed his arm.

"Sure you're all right?"

He waved me off. "I had worse than this. Let me just rest a little." He handed me the glass and walked back into the livingroom. "If I could just lay down for awhile, I'll be ok."

"Shouldn't you maybe call someone?"

"Call my daughter. Tell her where I am and to get me, but don't tell her what happened. If anybody asks you if you saw me, lie, say no." Tucci told me the telephone number, then removed his shoes and laid down on the sofa. "Look, when you're done, why don't we have a session." He sounded tired and his words whistled because of the missing tooth.

"Are you sure you're up to it?"

I imagined Tucci having a heart attack right there in my livingroom or suffering a hemorrhage in his cancerous stomach, vomiting blood, and me having to call an ambulance—the neighbors crowding around the front door, Tucci being carried out, the recognition, the surprise, the descent of the news media. I did not want him in my house longer than necessary.

"Are you trying to get rid of me?" he asked, as if reading my mind.

"No, not at all. It's just that you're not looking well."

"I'm fine. You have a tape recorder here?"

"No."

"All right. Then just take notes."

I went to the desk and took out a notepad and pen.

"Make the call, first, then if you have tea, can I have some? Make it weak, no sugar, a little milk."

"All right."

I went into the kitchen and called Tucci's house. His wife answered the phone. I asked to speak to Marie.

"Who is this?" Mrs. Tucci asked in a voice that made me think she was capable of the most brutal tortures.

I told her.

"Who?" she said, disbelief coming over the wire like static.

My neck went hot. I said my name again.

"Are you coming here tonight?"

"I'm not sure." I wasn't, because Tucci was in my livingroom with a swollen face and a missing tooth, about to share some more of his memory with me, which might excuse me from visiting his house later.

"This morning, he said you were to come."

"Then I guess I am." I was not going to argue with her.

"Is he with you there?"

"Excuse me?" But I had heard her.

"He is not here, and no one has seen him. I was wondering if he was there. Did he tell you to lie to me if anyone asked about him?"

"No, he didn't say that to me."

"What did he say?"

"He didn't say anything. I—"

"So he's there with you?"

"No."

"You can lie if he said to lie, but I would like to know if he is there. Say, 'He is not here,' which will be a lie, but I'll know where he is."

She made me dizzy. "He's not here."

"I'll get Marie." There was a sound of clattering, as if she dropped the receiver and it banged against the wall.

It took a while for Marie to come to the phone. I listened to a game show on the other end, while peeking into the livingroom every other second to check on Tucci. He was lying with his head on a pillow cushion, eyes closed. If I described that scene to Jamie, she would be astonished and shocked, unable to comprehend how such a thing had come about.

"Yes?" Marie's voice was tentative.

"Your father told me to call you. He's here at my house, and he wants you to pick him up."

"Me? Why can't Tony or one of the other goons get him?"

"He asked for you."

"My father has dozens of people he can call.

Doesn't he want you to take him, or don't you want the chore either?"

"A little of both, I think."

"I was just about to go to the library."

"What should I tell him?"

"That I won't be coming. I'm sorry." She said good-bye and hung up.

I was sorry too. Now Tucci would either make me call someone else or I would have to take him home. Going out to his house was one thing, but I preferred riding in the same car as Tony Buttons than with Tucci. His lying on my sofa was worse than riding with either of them. The sooner I fixed him his tea, I thought, the less he would hang around.

"Marie can't make it," I told him.

"No? Did she say why?"

"She was in the middle of something important."

"I'm disappointed, but it doesn't surprise me." He closed his eyes. "She probably won't come to my funeral."

"I'll get the tea," I said, hurrying away before he could launch into why Marie would not attend his funeral.

I turned on the spigot and let the water run into the sink, then I let it run into the teapot as I took a cup and a tea bag from the cupboards. I muttered to myself the entire time.

Turning off the water, I heard voices from the livingroom. I walked out there and saw Lou and Purdy standing just inside the door, with Tucci in front of them. They gazed at him as if at something rare and mysterious. He had apparently answered their knock, which the running water had blocked out.

"Uh, these are my friends," I said to Tucci. I hoped by some miracle they would not recognize him.

"We came to see Jamie and Teddy," Purdy said, nervously.

"Why are you staring at me?" Tucci asked. "Oh, the bruises, my tooth. I was mugged not far away. Since I knew Vincent, I came here."

Purdy and Cocco looked at me. I avoided their eyes.

"You're Carmine Tucci," Cocco said, turning back to him.

"And you're Lou Cocco."

"You know my name?"

"I used to live close to here," Tucci said, looking out the window. "So I know a lot of names. I know the name of that woman sweeping the sidewalk outside. Maybe if you called her, she would come in and sew my pants."

"Your pants don't look that bad," I said. At the knee, I saw dried blood and the skin of his leg, and at the torn pocket his undershorts showed. But I did not want another neighbor in the house to witness Tucci there.

"I can't walk around like this," Tucci said. "Purdy, you think you could ask her to come in?"

"Sure, Mr. Tucci." Purdy hurried out.

Cocco looked at me. "Now I know where you were going instead of to a ballgame that wasn't played."

"It's not what you think," I said.

"Let him think what he thinks," Tucci said. "He will anyway."

"How can I help it? I see what I see."

"And what do you see, Lou?" Tucci asked. "What?"

"You."

"You see me. So what?"

"I never would have been friends with Vince if I knew he worked for you."

"I don't—" I started to protest.

"Why?" Tucci said, cutting me off. "Because you have some idea about me, about Vince, who we are?"

"I don't want any part of people like you."

"You don't know who I am."

"I know enough."

"You know all you want to know, you mean."

"Maybe so, but that doesn't change anything," Cocco said.

"Did you know your father, Al Bananas, was my best friend, and that we grew up together? You didn't, did you? That I went to one of your birthday parties, gave you a bicycle? I went to the hospital with your father to see you when you had scarlet fever? Did you know that?"

"If that's true, my father died like an animal because of you."

"No, you're wrong there, you're very wrong."

"It may as well have been you who set the match."

"Your father would slap you in the face if he heard you talking to me like this." There was real menace in Tucci's voice now. "You come in here and think because a couple of punks knocked me around, that you can say anything to me? Who the fuck do you think gave your mother the money to live after your father was killed? If it wasn't for me, your mother would've wound up in the cigar factory or picking tomatoes in New Jersey. And you would've been helping her or been out in the street selling fruit or newspapers for a nickel. But did you ever have to work a second before you got out of school? No. Did you ever have to worry about having a good meal, clothes on your back? No. And it was because you had a father who wanted the best for you, never mind where he got the money. And it was because *I* sent your mother money every week for seven years until she remarried. There was no life insurance like maybe she told you. That was me. I gave her money. I put food in your ungrateful mouth. Me! Now you better calm down or I'll forget I knew your father and make you wish you didn't come in here."

Cocco looked at his shoes.

"Now, listen," Tucci said. "I didn't have anything to do with your father's death. In fact, and I told this to Vincent, I took care of the men who did."

"It's true."

After a long pause, Cocco asked, "Why did you do it?"

"Because he would have done the same for me." Tucci walked toward the stairs. "I'm going to the bathroom." He took the steps to the second floor as if the joints in his legs were sticking. Cocco and I watched him make the slow climb, and we did not look at each other until the bathroom door had closed.

"I'm sorry to hear about your father," I said, after Tucci was out of earshot.

"I have the newspaper clipping. He was handcuffed to the steering wheel of his car, gasoline was poured in, and the rest you can imagine, even the 'onlookers standing helpless,' as the papers put it."

"You never mentioned him."

"I was ashamed of him. I was ten but I could read well. When I read about the murder, I couldn't believe they were talking about the same man. I thought my father ran a construction supply business, but here they were saying he was a criminal. I had some trouble sorting things out. By the time I was done, I hated him, and I hated everyone connected to him."

"I feel I should try to explain a few things."

"It's not necessary. Just let me go to the movies and try to forget tonight."

"I'm not in any trouble," I said. He seemed to need assuring on that score, and I think I needed it too.

"I hope you're right."

Cocco started to go out the door when it opened and Purdy came in with Mrs. Falcone. She nodded at me and smiled. I said her name. The last time she was in the house, I realized, was back when Teddy disappeared and she found him on Market Street.

Purdy looked at the sofa and then about the room. "Is he still here?" he asked in a whisper.

I pointed up the stairs.

The bathroom door opened on the second floor, and we watched Tucci walk slowly down the steps, holding his side. When he saw Mrs. Falcone, he smiled, showing the gap in his teeth where his tooth had been.

"Rachel," he said, opening his arms as if to embrace her.

Before Tucci could touch Mrs. Falcone, she said, "Pig," and spit in his face.

Tucci asked me to drive him home a few moments after Mrs. Falcone spit at him. She had spit, then abruptly turned and walked out the door. Tucci blinked once, pulled out a handkerchief from his back pocket and calmly wiped his face as the rest of us watched astonished. Purdy nervously excused himself then and, taking Cocco by the arm, they too left.

"I'm sorry," I told Tucci after the door closed.
"For what?"
"Those guys showing up, Mrs. Falcone."
"It wasn't your fault."
"Why did she do it?"
"I'll tell you later. Take me home."
"I just remembered. My brother Ted has my car."
"Then order me a cab."
"All right." I felt relieved, but before reaching the telephone Ted walked in. "Jesus, it's Grand Central Station," I muttered, returning to the livingroom.

"I was looking for Frank," Tucci said to my brother before I could introduce them. "I'm a friend of his."

"Nice to meet you," Teddy said.

"I came to the wrong house, and Vince was going to take me to the right one. We were just leaving." He started for the door.

"I'll be back later," I said to Ted, then followed Tucci outside into the hot and strangely empty street.

The late afternoon sun, coupled with the humidity, felt as much like pressure as temperature, pressing down as if with the intent to squash. Broken glass glittered on the sidewalk stretching up Jackson Street. Again, that familiar odor of decay hung in the air, the stink of garbage or dead rats in the walls. I heard children squeal, but ghostly, because I could not see them anywhere.

Tucci did not talk much during the drive, and as we crossed the bridge he did not notice my trembling. He said he felt ill and that his ribs ached; he did not think he would be up to talking later. That was fine with me.

Before I completely stopped the car at the house, Mrs. Tucci opened the front door and came down the driveway, reaching us before her husband stepped out.

"What happened to you?" she said to him, seeing his torn pants and the blood on his shirt.

"Nothing."

She took his arm. "Here."

"Let go. I can walk." He jerked his arm from her grasp.

She took his arm again. "What's wrong with you?"

"I don't need help." He jerked his arm from her hand, but he lost his balance and spun into the car. "Goddamn," he said, clutching his ribs.

"You," Mrs. Tucci said to me as I came around to her side of the car, "what happened?"

"Nothing happened," Tucci said, starting toward the house.

His wife grabbed my arm after her husband took several steps and whispered, "You come in." She then sprang after Tucci, walking near enough to catch him if he should fall but not touching him.

She looked behind after a few steps, saw that I still stood at the car, and jerked her head for me to follow.

In the hallway, she pointed behind Tucci's back to the room I had waited in that first night. She wanted me to wait there. Both times I felt as though I were put in cold storage to wait for Mrs. Tucci to return and pluck me from the shelf. I stepped in the room as she guided her husband toward the stairs, his elbow in her fierce grasp. I had been nervous and fretful that first night, cursing myself for being at that house, but now I only cursed, and in the gilt-framed mirror, I saw disgust. I wished Tucci had simply told his wife on the lawn that he had gotten clobbered by petty thieves so I wouldn't have to wait in that room and then tell his scary wife the story.

I was looking at myself in the mirror when Mrs. Tucci appeared behind me in the doorway. I spun around and felt my face go hot, as if she had caught me in an act meant to be done in private.

"He wants to see you upstairs in the bedroom," she said. I could tell from her voice that she was annoyed by that. The bedroom was too intimate a place for a stranger like me.

"I thought he was feeling ill," I said, bothered myself about seeing him up there.

"Go up, he says, so go. First, what happened to him?"

I told her about Tucci coming to my house and repeated what he had told me about the mugging. When through, she stood still for awhile as if breaking down the information I had given her and putting it into mental compartments. I did not mention Mrs. Falcone.

"Come." She led me to the stairs, her feet quiet on the tiles while mine clacked. The stairs were made of walnut and gave up no sound when Mrs. Tucci walked up them. She seemed to float on warm air, whereas I made the steps wince. I was dumbly watching her rump when she suddenly turned and glared at me as if she had felt my gaze on her backside. I nearly apologized, she rattled me so much. She turned abruptly and continued her smooth climb. At the bedroom door, Mrs. Tucci stopped and motioned with her hard chin, then walked away in the direction of the stairs. If she went back down, I did not hear her.

I knocked on the door, heard a voice, and went in. Tucci lay in bed beneath a crucifix that hung on the wall above the headboard. There was a smell in the room of menthol and tomato sauce. The furniture was simple. Only the bedside lamp burned, creating more shadow in the room than light. Tucci's clothes were folded neatly over the arm of a chair, his shoes with the socks in them beneath it. The sheet went up to his chest and he seemed to hold it there with his arms, which were uncovered and straight at his sides; beneath the linen, his legs looked thin and brittle. This is what we become, I thought. Our teeth crack and loosen. Fat chokes our hearts. Flesh becomes tumorous. Our skeletons warp and the mind, if we live too long, uncoils.

Tucci motioned for me to close the door. He looked exhausted, but more spiritually than in body.

"My stomach's bothering me," he said, after I closed the door. "It's like the cancer has teeth, it's an animal chewing at my insides."

"Can't you take your pills?"

"I have to take too many for them to do anything, then I get dopey, like I'm getting now. I don't want to be dopey because, probably not tonight, I want to finish this thing with you. Then I don't care what happens, die of cancer or get shot in the back of the head. Getting shot would be better except for the pictures. Some of my friends, I saw them in the papers lying on the floor of a restaurant and in the street with their mouths wide opened and the blood like a pool of oil they fell in. I don't want to wind up like that. If it happens, I hope somebody at least puts a sheet over me. Not wind up in Life magazine, make some photographer famous." He smoothed the sheet against his chest, then folded his hands on his stomach. "Did you see Marie while my wife had you wait?"

"I didn't see anybody."

"I heard you had a long talk with her, my wife says."

"We talked a bit. I don't know about 'long.'"

Mrs. Tucci must have seen us on the lawn through the window. I wondered if she woke Tony that night and told him Marie and I were out front under the tree, knowing how he would react. I also wondered if Mrs. Tucci or anyone else in that house knew about Tony forcing me from his car on the bridge.

"You're starting to like her?"

"She's pleasant."

"Which means you like her."

"I like her, sure."

After a long pause, Tucci said, "One day, my wife found her diary in the grass out back by the gazebo. Marie must have wrote in it that afternoon and left it there. My wife said I had to read it, she thought it was 'dangerous.' That was the word she used. I know it wasn't right, but I read it. I didn't know she had so much sadness and hatred. I didn't know she felt about me and my wife the way she did in there. I was a monster in that book, Marie's mother not much better. She hates me."

I thought of the night Marie and I had talked under the tree out front before Tony Buttons came out wanting to kill me. She had told me things about her parents to justify her resentment. I had seen her point. She had seemed so tragic there in the dark shadows, talking about Patty, that now I felt little sympathy for Tucci, no matter how tragic he himself looked in that bed.

"That's one of the reasons you're here," he went on. "The more I read about myself, Marie's life, everything, the more I wanted to explain things, my own life. You could tell in the book that I loved her, I only wanted the best for her. Make sure you write that. It's important."

"Why don't you tell her?"

"You think I didn't try?" he said. "When I walk in the same room as her, she walks out. When I touch her, she moves away like I'm a leper. You give up after awhile. But I didn't want to go to my grave knowing that all she knew about me was what was in her diary. So tell it."

"All right."

He fell silent for a while, gazing at the ceiling. I watched the slow rise and fall of his chest, thinking: he will die soon. He had a look in his eyes of a growing interior vacuum, a crumbling of the will, which the body would follow. I felt nothing at the thought. I did not pity him for his troubles with Marie or his failing health. I had no stake in his emotions. There was nothing in my brain then, either, of his memoirs, the stories I would have to harness, his love for Marie that he wanted me to show. The single thought in my head, the image, was of Mrs. Falcone spitting in Tucci's face and his calm reaction. That nagged me.

I said, "About Mrs. Falcone."

"Don't ask me that now, why she spit at me." He pulled the sheet tight against his chin and closed his eyes. "I'm very tired and it's a long story."

"Does it have to do with Patty Leone?" I blurted.

He stiffened. "What do you know about that?"

"Just what Marie told me."

"That he liked her?"

"That he loved her and disappeared, that's all."

Tucci relaxed. "Go," he said, closing his eyes. "It's too much to tell now."

I hovered for a minute beside the bed, hoping he would find a little strength, change his mind and tell me the story. But he did not open his mouth.

"Well, good night," I said.

He seemed to be asleep already; only his chest rose and fell slightly with his breathing. I left the room, softly closing the door behind me.

Turning, I nearly bumped into Mrs. Tucci, who seemed to have dropped from the ceiling. She stood so close, a bowl of plums in her hands not an inch from my stomach, I could see a vein pulsing at her temple.

"Excuse me."

Mrs. Tucci stared into my eyes without saying a word and so flustered me that I looked away.

I cleared my throat. "I'm going now."

She did not budge. I wanted to fold my arms across my chest but there was so little room between Mrs. Tucci and me that I could not bring up my arms without hitting the bowl of plums or her breasts. At the corner of her brutal mouth, I thought I saw a smile.

"Done?" she asked.

"Yes, uh huh."

"For good?"

"I don't think so."

Mrs. Tucci nodded slowly, as if thinking. "You know how to get out." She moved to the side and let me squeeze by.

I went down the stairs, through the hall and out the door, goosebumps on my skin from my encounter with that woman.

The heat and humidity outside Tucci's air-conditioned house flattened the goosebumps on my skin as I headed for my car parked at the end of the driveway. Fireflies winked and drifted in the night air and the crickets chirped loudly. It was a pleasure to be outside in the fresh air after the closeness and smell of age and sickness in Tucci's bedroom.

The thought of returning to the city with its oppressive heat and odors made my heart sink. I could already feel the wall of heat once I came off the bridge and entered the city. With only forty miles between me and the shore, I thought a ride there would do me some good. I could sit on the beach, listen to the waves breaking, and feel anonymous. I could forget about Tucci and everything revolving about him.

"You again?" It was Marie, dangling in the tree swing. She faced away from the house, her shoulders hunched, the ropes of the swing caught in the crooks of her elbows.

"Yes, it's me." I paused on the walkway, remembering Buttoni's rage and my terror on the bridge. But I had not seen or heard Tony all night.

"I saw your car but no one was in the den when I walked by. My mother said you were in her *bedroom?*"

"It wasn't my idea," I said, crossing the lawn to her.

"I wouldn't think so. She had to be outraged by it."

"Your mother doesn't like me very much."

"To her, you're like the camera to certain primitive people who think taking a photograph steals their soul. You're stealing her husband's soul and putting it on tape."

"I'm not stealing it. He's giving it away."

"He's telling you things that he never told her and that he probably never told anyone. Maybe he's even told you stuff about her. It's natural for my mother to dislike you."

"Well, she won't be seeing me too much longer."

"You're almost through here?" She looked up from the ground. I noticed that she had gotten her hair cut and she wore a little make-up. Even in the poor light, Marie looked more attractive now than at the library or the other night I saw her.

"Almost." I was thinking, though, of Tucci in his bed, looking frail and so close to death, not that the taping was nearly complete.

"You must be relieved."

"I am." I turned away to my car.

"Are you going home now?"

"Yes. I mean, no. I thought I might take a ride to the shore."

"What were you going to do there?"

"I didn't have anything particular in mind. I felt like taking a ride, and that's the direction I thought I'd go in."

She put a fingernail at her mouth but immediately took it away. "Want some company?" she asked, barely loud enough for me to hear.

I hesitated a moment, nervous about Buttoni. But Marie had asked me to come along, not the other way around. "Sure."

"All right." But she remained in the swing, as if the habit of hanging there had become stronger than her desire to move.

I said, "So, do you think we should leave now?"

She nodded, then slowly disentangled herself from the swing. I took her elbow for a moment, then let it go. We crossed the lawn to the car. I opened the passenger door for Marie and she slid in. Walking around to the other side of the car, I glanced up at the house and saw a sliver of light in the center of a window between the curtains, then it vanished.

"I think somebody watched us," I said, getting in the car.

Marie looked toward the house. "Is it all right?"

I started the car and pulled away. "I hope so."

TEN

We took the Black Horse Pike instead of the Atlantic City Expressway to the shore. I had suggested the alternative to Marie as we neared the entrance and she chose the slower route. I usually took the Expressway because of the speed, and because the view was more pleasant. Outside of several exit toll booths, casino billboards, and the single service area twenty miles from Atlantic City, with its single gas station and Roy Rogers restaurant, all you saw on the Expressway were trees and the occasional field.

"This is how Patty and I used to go to the shore," Marie said a little past the split.

I said, "Hm," just so Marie knew I had heard her. I tried not to think of them in Patty's car, carefree and happy. When she said his name, I saw Marie as a young girl, the night she was to get married, waiting for Patty to take her away, and her disappointment and worry when he failed to show.

"Looks like you need gas," Marie said.

"What?" I looked at the gauge. "Oh."

We pulled into the next tired-looking gas station we came to. Its neon lights were only half operating, and there was a big greasy dog lying, as if exhausted, by the air pump. A car was perched on a lift in the gloomy bay and a man worked a wrench on the underside. He paused for a moment and glanced at us as we pulled up to the pumps. A teenage boy, his long hair tied back with a rubberband, came from the office toward us, looking disinterested and bored. The man, the boy and even the dog, lying flat out with its chin on its large paws, looked like they knew this was as far as they were going to get in life. I realized they all had the same fatigued and defeated eyes.

Marie sat quietly with her hands pressed between her knees. I could hear the gasoline rushing into the tank and the metallic clicking of the rachet wrench from the man with his hands deep in the car's underbelly.

Marie said, "Tony asked me to marry him yesterday. Again." She did not look at me as she spoke.

"Again?"

"He asks me about three times a year, as if maybe I'll change my mind. I think this time was a coordinated effort between my mother and him, because in the morning she cornered me and tried to convince me, also once again, of Tony's virtues."

"He has virtues? What are they?"

"I don't know. I didn't listen. But my mother thinks he's a teddy bear."

"Maybe she means grizzly bear."

"She says she doesn't want me to become a spinster, which may be true, but mainly she wants to get Tony into the family."

"He told me that. He said he'd be set for life."

"He would be. So would my mother, what's left of her life. Her dream would come true."

"Your marrying Tony Buttons?"

Marie nodded. "I was thirteen when he first showed up at the house, and not long after my mother began to put the idea in my head. Tony was handsome, I didn't know anything, and I probably would have married him in five or six years if it wasn't for Patty. That pretty much destroyed my mother's plans for Tony to become her son-in-law."

"What a terrible shame," I said.

"Oh, yes, a catastrophe."

We left the gas station, kicking gravel into the wheelwells, and continued on the Black Horse Pike.

"Last night, I dreamt that Tony was chasing me," Marie said after a distance. "I kept ahead of him until suddenly the ground became thick mud. I got stuck and couldn't move a step more. I have this dream often, but I always wake up just as Tony grabs my wrist. This time," she said, looking at her hands, her face darkening, "I didn't wake up, not even when he tore my clothes off and pressed me back into the mud." Her voice caught.

"It was just a dream."

"Do you think, by not waking up, my resistance is eroding?"

"What did you say when he asked you to marry him?"

"I laughed in his face."

"Then your resistance is fine."

Some of the roadside motels we passed seemed

nice and well-kept, freshly painted and with swimming pools glowing aqua-green beneath mercury lamps; but the last one had a look of seedy convenience that made me think no families had ever stayed there, only drifters or couples wanting cheap privacy. Shortly after my divorce from Alison, I'd wake up in the morning so numb that I had to fight the impulse, after lifting the teapot from the burner, to put my hand on the red coils and singe concentric circles into my flesh so as to feel something. I stopped at that motel with a woman I had met only a few days before. She was intelligent and beautiful, but the orange vinyl chairs, the odor of pine oil disinfectant, and the pornography we acted out there, left me feeling unclean and fed my self-loathing. I only had to drive by the place to bring that feeling of wretchedness back, which was another reason I did not often take this road to the shore.

"Would you mind going to Ocean City?" I asked Marie.

"That's fine."

I crossed the draw bridge that spanned the bay when we came to it twenty minutes later and then turned right at the monument where the Black Horse Pike ended at Atlantic City. Another five hundred feet straight ahead and we would be in the ocean. Tires screeched from behind us and, looking in the rearview mirror, I saw several cars turn against the light.

"Someone knows if you get stopped at that light, you're there for a while," I said. "It's the longest light in Atlantic City."

"You seem to know this area well," Marie said.

"I worked here five summers while in college,

four of them in a restaurant not far from here. I was a busboy." When we came to Lou's a few minutes later, I pointed to it. "There. It looks exactly as it did when I was in college." In the next breath, I mentioned that I had met my ex-wife Alison there, and that we would soon be passing the street that led to the house she had lived in.

"Ever wonder what happened to her?" Marie asked.

"All the time. Sure."

"You could find out."

"I don't know if that would be a good idea."

But the closer I came to the street that led to Alison's house a few blocks away, the more I thought of her—the spell she cast over me, that strange eloquence that gripped me when we were together our first weeks, the blond hairs on the backs of her thighs—the more powerful was the urge to turn right and at least drive by the house, look at it, and appease for a bit that terrible itch to know. I knew that I would be a fool to turn, that nothing but disappointment and heartache lay that way, along with all the old ghosts, the old madness, the relentless hungers. But I could not help myself.

I turned wordlessly down the tree-lined street and then up a smaller street, following the pattern still in my head from years ago. Another right turn, a few yards, and we were there. I stopped the car under a tree, left the engine running, and stared at the house. A car was parked in the driveway and the downstairs lights were on. As with Lou's restaurant, nothing seemed changed and I had a sense of stepping directly into the past.

"Is that it?" Marie asked.

"That's it."

"Are you going to knock?"

"Would you?"

"It would depend on how badly I wanted to know."

"How badly would you want to know?"

"Very badly," Marie said.

"What would I say?"

"If they still live there, they'll recognize you. They'll know why you're there."

"I don't know. Her parents hated me."

"But wasn't that a while ago?"

"Some people never forgive."

"Maybe you'll be surprised. Maybe they'll be happy to tell you whatever you want to know."

"Will you come with me?"

"I think I should wait in the car."

"Yes, I guess you should."

I did a U-turn in the street, raking the front of the house with my headlights, and pulled up at the curb. Someone's headlights went out up the street, making me feel less conspicuous.

"This is probably not a good idea," I said.

"Don't do it if you'll regret it."

"It's just the curiosity that's pushing me, nothing else, and I don't know if that's enough to risk any ugly scene."

"I understand."

I sat motionless in the dark gazing at the yellow window, listening to the ticking of the engine. If only one of Alison's parents would come to the window and look out, I thought; if I could just see them, that would be enough to make me move. Maybe they didn't live there anymore, had sold the house and moved to Florida for retirement, and I was looking at a stranger's house. Maybe they were dead, from cancer or heart disease or a plane crash. Maybe Alison had been willed the house and received a load of insurance money, like my brother-in-law Cyril. I'd go up to the door, knock, and my ex-wife would answer. We'd gape at each other. We would not be able to speak, there would be a vacuum as if the earth had paused in its rotation. Alison would look older, fuller, soft around the edges, but her eyes would be that same cool blue. I could recognize Alison from those eyes only, because when I looked into them I knew that instantly I would see the world we had dreamed together, the shining moments, her laugh, how we sat that night wrapped naked in a blanket and watched the snow falling into the dismal street until it transformed all the sharp gray edges into soft white. I would see all that in her eyes because I would be looking into myself, too. Maybe I'd feel an electric spasm of emotion in my chest, a giddy rush of love. I would try to hold onto that, try to remember only the good times when happiness seemed eternal and everything possible. But I would not be able to hold onto it long, because in Alison's sapphire eyes there would also be the world we had ruined.

She would not be happy to see me.

"Let's go," I said. "There's nothing for me here." I started the car and sped away, glad that I had not gone to the door.

In Ocean City, we parked a few minutes later alongside the Forum Motel and headed for the Boardwalk, glowing a block and a half away; the lights of some amusement ride twirled above the roof of a beach house and the faint sounds of a merry-go-round reached us.

We soon reached the Boardwalk and slowly strolled on it like old people or vacationers with lots of time to kill. People streamed in both directions. Rock music blared from the arcades and from gigantic radios on the shoulders of teenage boys. Younger boys on skateboards zigzagged through the crowds like slalom skiers. Palmreaders sitting outside their tiny curtained rooms discreetly solicited. Marquees pulsed electric light. The crowds were thick but not as dense as in Atlantic City. It was a different crowd with a different character. There were more children, young people, more families, and nothing in their faces of that particular rage or shock which comes from losing a lot of money. The smells were the same: roasting peanuts, fudge, pizza, sizzling onions, and greasy meat, which we passed through as if through clouds. We shuffled for a long time behind twin girls eating bouffants of pink cotton candy, a parent on either side of them.

"I feel like I'm part of the family," I said.

"Let's just follow them wherever they go."

"And then what?"

"We'll see when we get there."

At an arcade called Funland, its name in bright yellow flashing lights, the girls squealed and jumped up and down and pulled their parents inside. Marie and I followed them into the arcade; they wandered away from us toward the rear as we stood in a cyclone of voices, bells, pounding music, and electronic noises. The arcade smelled of popcorn and damp wood; it was poorly lighted, but intentionally so, like a barroom, so that the pulsing and glowing machines and gadgets stood out against backgrounds of darkness.

"Want to play?" I asked.

"Which one?"

"Any of them. We'll just try a few."

"All right."

I changed bills into quarters and we went among the machines. First, we watched the young people slap at the controls in rapid and hyper movements, as if their lives depended on their score. Then we tried a few machines ourselves, pinball first. These were sophisticated contraptions, not the simple ones that Charlie Shunk had in his bar or the ones of my college summers in Atlantic City. These machines had labyrinthic turns and several levels for the ball to travel; the boards flashed light and noise, and computer voices wisecracked in many of them.

Marie stood rigidly at a machine next to me, moving only her fingers on the flippers as if entranced, hypnotized by the lights and the computer gibberish, while I leaned into my machine or jolted it with stiff arms sometimes violently, trying to put english on the ball or to achieve a greater bounce off the bumpers. I "tilted" often; the machine went dead and the rude "game over" sign came on. We did not win any games of pinball.

I changed more bills into quarters and we next tried whatever video game looked interesting. Kung Fu. Slugger. Top Gun. Starfighter. They were more difficult to play than the pinball machines; it was necessary to manipulate two or three controls with both hands to avoid being destroyed by enemy jets or spacecraft, mutants, monsters, thugs, Indians, animals, or evil geniuses. But the electronic images on the screen were too numerous, too fast or too wily; the situations that our heroes had to maneuver through were too perilous and complex for our dulled reflexes and unsupple brains. Our spaceships or jets or karate men or cowboys were obliterated in bursts of light, or shot, clubbed, or knifed, the violence accompanied by sounds of explosion, grunts, yipes, or death groans. When the mayhem was over, the annoying adenoidal computer voice said, "Try again."

"I can see somebody throwing a chair through one of these things," I said.

"Or hitting it with a golf club."

We dropped quarters in a device with a rifle pointing at a screen where video ducks flew and other animals popped out from behind bushes. With each hit, the animal vanished from the screen. Another game, called Tail Gunner, featured a machine gun for shooting down attacking airplanes. It turned out that I had some skill with the various guns; I won several games and came close to winning a half dozen others.

Next, we sat in dark booths which mimicked the interiors of jet cockpits or racing cars, video screens as windshields, and went on simulated flights or rides that took us through a number of diverse obstacles at a speed and in a direction controlled by a pedal, steering wheel, or joy stick. We did not score many points, but we laughed at our incompetance each time our jet or racing car struck a mountain, a blimp, another jet or disabled cars, road signs, or funny-looking men with exaggerated looks of terror. We sat together in the booths, too small for two adults, touching shoulders and thighs, and when Marie laughed I glimpsed the fillings of her teeth, her delicate tongue and wanted to kiss her.

"Done yet?" It was the twin girls, speaking in unison, that we had followed on the Boardwalk. I did not feel like an overgrown simpleton until then.

"Yes, we are," I said. We pulled ourselves from the booth, and the girls scrambled in, giggling.

"My head is swimming," I said. "Let's get out of here."

We walked through the arcade and the spastic youngsters toward the Boardwalk, and paused at the booth which took four photographs for fifty cents and spit out the prints all together in a vertical line a minute later. The last thing we saw in the arcade were the parents of the twin girls in the booth, making faces at the camera and laughing hysterically as it took their picture.

After leaving the arcade, Marie and I went to a white-tiled stand that sold fresh fruit, either chopped and in cups or pureed to drink. Boxes of oranges and pineapples lined the wall on the floor. One attendant sliced cantaloupe and worked the blenders while the other tended to customers, both their aprons and fingertips stained with the red and blue of the berries. The fruit sat in a row of deep stainless steel trays behind glass, the colors of the melons, strawberries, blueberries, bananas, peaches, and pineapples almost artificially lush under the flourescent lights.

I bought two small cups of fruit, mostly honeydew and banana, and we ate them with plastic forks while sitting on a bench that faced the ocean. We ate slowly, watching the waves break white and slosh toward the shore. When through, Marie and I left the Boardwalk and went down the wooden steps to the beach.

We walked in the sand to the nearest jetty of black rocks; the sounds of the Boardwalk faded but the lights sent enough glow our way to see the gaps between the huge boulders as we walked outward on them. In the daylight, you saw the jumble of broken shells between the rocks, seaweed, and several beer bottles, but now I could only smell the odor of fish and whatever else decayed down there in the crevices. Marie and I stepped carefully over the gaps and made our way to the end of the jetty. We were alone there and I felt a little too exposed, too puny as the waves pounded against the rocks and sent up plumes of water. I thought of sinking ships, and knew that anyone in the water near the rocks would be slammed over and over against them by the waves. Your ribs would get broken and your skull pulverized.

Looking up the coast, we saw the lights of the Atlantic City casinos. They looked closer than fifteen miles, as if walking up the shoreline would bring us to them in no time at all. Looking south, the lights of the shore towns marked the coast. Far down, there was Wildwood, with its droves of teenagers, then Cape May, with its quaint Victorian houses at the very tip of New Jersey. Beyond, there was only the blackness that stretched toward Florida.

Marie and I sat on a boulder, out of the reach of the splashing waves, and gazed out to sea hugging our knees.

"I used to know the longitude and latitude of

Paris," Marie said without turning from the sea. "And Rome."

"Were you a geography buff?"

"A little. But no, I was going there once."

"With Patty?" I asked, already knowing.

"I shouldn't talk about it. It's rude and selfish."

"It's all right."

"It's not fair to you."

"Maybe you have to talk about Patty before we can talk about anything else."

She watched the waves roll toward us and crash against the jetty for a time before speaking.

"I had a world Atlas that we liked to page through," Marie said, her voice resigned. "We could name cities in countries all over the world, and mountains and bodies of water because we looked at it so much. We paged through that Atlas on these rocks once. I have some pictures from the time. Patty standing near the water with his back to the ocean, the big Atlas under his arm; and in another he's doing a handstand. I got sunburned that day and Patty smeared Noxema on me. A few days later, he peeled dead skin from my back like lasagna, rattling off cities and towns in Greece as he did it."

"Did you ever make it to Europe?"

Marie shook her head, no. "I read about it instead. I don't travel much, but when I do I take a train. Trains are wonderful. There's something solid and secure about them. If something goes wrong, they don't have miles to fall or sink." Marie hugged her knees tighter and put her chin on top of them as the breeze picked up. She shivered. "I'm getting cold."

"Do you want to leave?"

"Not yet."

I slid closer to her and put my arm around her shoulders. She leaned into me, tilting her head slightly toward mind but not enough to touch.

"I once took a train to Rhode Island because I saw a brochure of Newport in a shoebox of Patty's letters. The letters were often beautiful. Most of Patty's toughness was exterior; he was much smarter and softer on the inside. He had an inner life that no one knew about." She gazed out into the dark ocean and for a long while neither of us spoke. When she did, it was to say that she had to make a trip to the Boardwalk, implying that she needed to use the public bathroom there. She stood up.

"I'll walk you," I said.

"No, it's all right. Save our spot."

"Ok." I watched her step from rock to rock until she reached the sand, turned, and waved briefly. I smiled and lifted my hand, unsure that Marie could see me in the darkness.

I looked back out to sea. Marie's words, images of her, me, Patty, everything swirled at that point of seamless black where the night sky met the black water. I had pitied Marie most of the night, as I had from the time I met her, because she seemed truly broken by the turns her life had made. Despair seemed to have grown into her flesh. But my pity had worn thin the more time we spent together, and I began to see, without realizing it until she turned and waved from the beach, that I did not just feel sorry for her. I had held her and smelled her hair, felt warm toward her, wanted to kiss her. I wanted to take her home so much that the images of Patty, whom she had loved, and Tony Buttons, who had tossed me onto the Walt Whitman Bridge, were beginning to dissolve.

A wave crashed and the spray hit me in the face. I was wiping off the salt water when I realized, too late, that someone had walked up behind me and that it was not Marie. The waves had been breaking so loudly against the jetty that the sound drowned out not just the music and the random shouts from the Boardwalk, but the footsteps that had come at my back. I heard sand grind beneath a shoe and nearly in the same instant a shock came at the bottom of my neck. My head snapped back and I went sprawling forward, colliding with the rock before I knew it would be there. My ribs seemed to collapse, my lungs froze, and I rolled up in a ball, trying to breathe my own tongue. Tears flooded my eyes. Just before I thought I was going to black out, something let go inside and air rushed in.

I uncurled slightly, gasping on the rock like a fish, and watched shoes come toward my face. Another figure stood beyond the pairs of legs but I could not make out the person through my tears. Then hands grabbed my arms and jerked me up from the rocks. The lights from the Boardwalk streaked crazily. I smelled cigarettes and cologne but could not see the two big men who held me. I expected to be beaten by them but instead the men lifted me completely clear of the rocks and took me to the edge of the jetty.

"How 'bout a swim?" one said. "Do a little Jacques Cousteau number. Whataya say?" He sounded familiar.

My mouth worked but nothing came out.

"Look, we drop you right there in the white stuff

and you tumble for a little bit like in a washing machine. Your head goes ka-klunk, ka-klunk against the rocks." I knew that voice.

"You come outta that, you're lucky if you're only retarded."

I kicked against the air.

"Tony! George!" a voice shouted behind them.

"Hey, you're in luck," Buttoni said.

They let me down and, still holding me between them, brought me away from the edge and back to where I had been sitting. They turned me to face the other person who had yelled for them to stop. My head was still foggy, though clearing by the minute.

"Why do you get carried away?" It was Mrs. Tucci, in her house dress and a cardigan sweater, silhouetted by the Boardwalk glare.

"We were only fooling," George said.

"Don't fool. Bring him to the car."

"What about Marie when she comes back?" Tony asked.

"You, George, you wait for her. When she comes, you tell her stay. Make her stay. We'll come back soon." Mrs. Tucci turned and headed to the beach, stepping nimbly from rock to rock. George let go of me and stayed on the jetty as Tony guided me after Mrs. Tucci, his fingers dug into my arm.

"Why are you doing this?" I asked, finally able to speak.

"It's not me. I just work for people."

"For Mrs. Tucci?"

"For whoever's paying."

My feet caught in the sand when we reached it and Tony had to partly drag me through it and then

BLOOD CONFESSIONS

up the wooden steps. The Boardwalk lights dazzled and made my head ache at the back. Breathing hurt my chest.

"Now smile for the people, and don't try anything funny."

I was too wobbly in the legs to pull away from Tony, even if I thought it would have done some good. Where would I go? Back to the jetty to wrestle George? Or run in some other direction where Tony would certainly follow? Shouting would not help, either. If Buttoni wanted to seriously hurt me, I thought, he would have done it on the rocks. No, better now to stay in his grasp and see what would happen next.

Tony and Mrs. Tucci took me off the Boardwalk.

"You didn't have to hit me like that," I said, as we went down the ramp.

"It wasn't me; it was George. He has a philosophy, which, would you like to hear it? It says that if you have to deal with somebody, deal with them when they're in a position of weakness."

"Like on their back and gasping?"

"Exactly. It's my philosophy, too. Now shut your face."

Their car was parked a block away in a lot paved with small stones, which scattered when we walked on them. There was a small booth in the center of the lot and the cars were arranged around it in a horseshoe pattern. An attendant sat in the doorway of the booth smoking a cigarette; he barely looked at us when we walked by, the flick of his eyes cold and emotionless. Mrs. Tucci slid into the back seat of the car. Tony shoved me in after her, closed the door and stood against it. Mrs. Tucci kept the windows closed, for privacy, I guessed, or because she preferred the suffocating heat that soon built up, which seemed to suit her. I sat as far away from her as possible, sweating and on the verge of gasping.

Mrs. Tucci did not speak for awhile, and instead looked through the windshield at the attendant sitting in the doorway of his booth. She had a ruthless profile, just this side of sadistic. If I had wanted to escape, I would have to go through Tony on the other side of the door or through that woman. I did not know which would be worse.

"You are surprised to see me?" she asked.

"At first, but now it seems perfect."

"I wanted to know where you were going."

"Did your husband send you?"

"My husband is sleeping."

"Does he know you're here?"

"Never mind that. Where were you taking Marie?"

"We just took a ride. Nothing serious." I rubbed the ache at the back of my head; my brain still seemed to move independent of my skull.

"You took her to that house. Who lives there? Who were you there to meet?"

"Meet? What house? Oh, the house in Margate," I said, remembering the stop. "My ex-wife used to live there."

Mrs. Tucci looked at me steadily. "Don't lie."

"I'm not lying. Marie suggested we go there."

"To do what?"

"It was personal and not very important."

Mrs. Tucci suddenly grabbed my throat. "To do what?"

Her grip was so tight, I could barely breathe let alone speak. Even without Tony there to protect her,

I wasn't sure I'd wrestle with her or try to slug her so she'd let go.

She released my throat. "The truth. Why did you stop at that house?"

"I told you," I said, swallowing. "I was going to see if my ex-wife still lived there, that's all."

She stared at me with contempt. "Idiot."

Mrs. Tucci looked away and toward the attendant in the booth; he was burning the hairs off his forearms with his cigarette. Above the booth and a rooftop beyond, the top of a ferris wheel arced in yellow and white light.

"Falling in love with my daughter is not a good idea."

"I'm not falling in love with your daughter."

"Tony wouldn't like it. He wants to marry her."

"But Marie doesn't want to marry him. She hates him."

"So? One man is as good as another, hate or like."

"Marie doesn't think so."

"Forget about Marie."

"What are you going to tell her happened to me?"

"She'll know what happened to you."

"I don't want her to think that I abandoned her."

"Enough about that," Mrs. Tucci snapped, turning to me. "I'm not here to chase you away from my daughter. Tony will do that. I'm here to talk to you. My husband made it necessary. In his old age he has gotten foolish. He's been a fool before. But even a fool, he is still my husband, he has provided, and I do not want to see him on the ground with bullet holes. He should have retired years ago, but he stayed. No, worse. He wants to say things to strangers. He wants to tell things, secrets, what happened years ago and put it on tapes. I heard some of the things he said to you. Never mind how."

Staring at the side of Mrs. Tucci's head, I imagined her crouched down in the hallway with her ear pressed against the door of the den or with a stethoscope held against the wall.

She looked out the window again toward the attendant. He was throwing a basketball into a bottomless milk crate attached to the side of his booth. Every time the ball hit the crate, it made a racket; the booth vibrated and the light inside wobbled.

"Yo!" Tony shouted at the attendant.

The attendant paused and looked at Buttons.

"You're making a lot of friggin' noise, pal."

The attendant looked back to the milk crate and continued shooting the basketball.

Mrs. Tucci turned back to me. "I want the tapes," she said. "Where are they? Your house?"

"*You* want the tapes?"

"I want the tapes. Are you hard of hearing?"

"I don't understand. Are you asking me without your husband's knowledge?"

"He's not right in the head. He takes pills that make his brain funny. The tapes are dangerous and he doesn't know."

"They're his; I can't give them to you. And if I did, what would I tell him?"

"If you give them to me, I won't let Tony get mad at you for taking Marie here. Nothing will happen to you."

"I'd only give them to you if your husband told me." I wiped sweat from my forehead with the back of my wrist.

Mrs. Tucci reached into her sweater and pulled out a wad of money. She tossed it at me and it hit my thigh. "Five thousand for not telling him."

"I can't do that." I put the money between us on the seat.

"What, you like him?"

"That wouldn't have anything to do with it."

Mrs. Tucci took the money from the seat. "Roll down the window," she said, pointing with her chin toward the handle.

I did as she said. Before the glass completely slid into the door, she called Tony. He ducked his head into the opening and looked at her. "Yeah, Mrs. Tucci?"

"Tony, tell him," she said.

He jerked his head toward me, his face six inches from my own. "We want those tapes, fucker," he said. "Or you're going to be in real trouble."

"Ok, Tony, thank you." She dismissed him with a flick of her wrist and told me to roll the window back up. "Now, how much do you want for the tapes and for not coming back to the house?"

"I'm sorry. I made a deal with your husband. They're his tapes, and I can't do anything with them without his permission."

"Is Maglio paying more?"

That made me pause. "Maglio?"

"I know Frank had dinner with him."

"That doesn't mean Maglio was offered the tapes," I said, but thinking it was possible and maybe likely. "Anyway, he'd have to get them from me."

"Ha! You think I'm stupid?" Mrs. Tucci replaced the money in her cardigan. "Frank met Joe Maglio.

You're Frank's brother. You have the tapes. It's clear. And my husband would not like to hear it."

"What are you saying?"

"You figure."

Tony shouted at the attendant again to quit throwing the basketball.

The attendant said, "Screw you, man, this ain't a library out here," and continued to shoot. Tony abruptly left the side of the car and rushed toward the attendant. Mrs. Tucci quickly rolled down her window.

"Tony!"

Buttoni went straight to the attendant, grabbed the ball as it came off the milk crate, and hurled it far into the street. The attendant watched the ball sail and stared as it bounced and rolled toward the beach. Tony, not much taller than the attendant, stood facing him, as if waiting for an answer to something he had asked. The attendant looked slowly back at Buttoni and smiled.

"Tony!" Mrs. Tucci called, maybe seeing something in that smile that she did not.

Buttoni turned slightly and held up his finger, as if to say, "One minute." That's when the attendant punched him.

Tony was a big man, used to his largeness and solidity, and he fell as big men do, more surprised than hurt that he could be knocked off his feet by someone smaller. He fell hard, grunting once and scattering stones. Tony scrambled up quickly, as if embarrassed to stay on the ground long, but the attendant, in a boxer's stance now, hit him quickly under the chin with an uppercut and then hit him again in the cheek. Tony pitched backward and fell spinning onto the hood of the car.

"Tony!" Mrs. Tucci said, jumping in her seat, though this time it was more a shout of concern and worry than a call to bring him back.

Tony blinked at us through the windshield, looking puzzled, still unable to grasp what was happening to him. He frowned, shook his head as if to clear it, pushed himself away from the car and turned. But the attendant was waiting for him and he hit Tony with a hook that sent him stumbling to the left and into another car. Buttoni rammed the fender with his head and fell out of sight. The attendant moved toward him, his fists still up.

This time, Tony started up with a gun. But as soon as it appeared, the man kicked it out of Tony's hand, then kicked him in the side. Buttoni went, "Oof," and dropped again.

"You want more, get up," the man said, picking up the gun.

"Stay, Tony," Mrs. Tucci pleaded.

But Tony spit blood, cursed, crawled up the side of the car and staggered toward the attendant. When Tony awkwardly swung, the man stepped neatly aside, paused as if for the drama of it, stretched back his fist and hit Tony with a punch in the jaw that sounded like a cantaloupe hitting a sidewalk. Buttoni spun a complete turn before falling. As he collapsed, I pushed open the car door and ran for the sea.

My side ached with each step and deep breath, as did the back of my head where I had been hit, but I did not slow up. I ran down the street at full speed toward the garish lights, the food smells, and the jaunty music. Then I charged up the wooden ramp and weaved through the streaming mothers and fathers, the children, the slow-walking elderly, the clots of young people, the band of nuns together like a school of fish, running as I hadn't done since playing football in high school. I ran along the railing, trying to avoid collisions while at the same time looking at the shoreline.

I saw them.

Marie sat in the middle of the jetty, hugging her legs, forehead on her knees, as if waiting resigned for the tide to rise high enough to drown her. She faced the ocean, her back to the big man. George stood behind her, but nearer the water, his back to the Boardwalk, watching the waves break against the rocks. They were both motionless, sculpture-like, though Marie seemed like motion stopped, George motion about to erupt.

I took the wooden steps that dropped to the beach in threes and slogged across the sand in a straight line, my eyes focused on a spot in George's back, everything else streaking by as if on the outside of a moving car. The sand thinned as the rocks began below it, and then it was just rock with the spaces between them filled in with concrete, and then rocks only with the gaps I did not watch or think about, seeing only that spot on the big man's back, aiming for it as I began to pick up speed, then to fly.

I lowered my shoulder and rammed into George's kidney. I dropped to the rocks as George, flailing at the air, fell over the side of the jetty and out of sight.

"Marie!" I shouted.

She turned and saw me, something first of incomprehension in her eyes and then relief.

"Hurry!" I waved her toward me, then scrambled on my hands and knees to the edge of the jetty to look for George.

Marie stepped quickly over the rocks. "Where is he?"

I pointed to the side of the jetty. George burst coughing through the surface, facing out to sea. I stood up as he turned and grabbed hold of the nearest rock, but a wave crashed on his head and he vanished in frothy white.

George's head popped out of the water. He chopped briefly toward the rocks before another wave came and battered him. He disappeared in the suds again, but a few moments later he was hammering at the water, trying to get to the rocks before another wave came. He reached the rocks in time, and when the next wave smashed against his back he held on.

"Come on," I said, taking Marie's hand, and starting toward the beach.

We wheeled and hurried over the rocks. As we ran across the sand, the sound of the waves faded, but before we reached the steps to the Boardwalk I thought I heard a voice yell for help.

ELEVEN

By the time we reached the Atlantic City Expressway, I had told Marie nearly everything: how I had been struck in the back on the jetty, the two men holding me over the water, the talk with her mother in the car, Tony's run-in with the parking lot attendant. I did not mention that I was a little frightened that George and Tony would come after me.

"Are you still in pain?" Marie asked, noticing my hand against my side.

"A little, but I don't think anything's broken."

"It's my fault you got hurt. I should have known what would happen if I went with you tonight. Those goons! My mother!"

"You're not to blame."

"I can't live in that house anymore, not after this. I'm going to move out, get an apartment, maybe in another state, maybe another country. I'm going to leave. Yes." She seemed to be trying to convince herself.

Thirty minutes later, Marie had me turn off the road that led to her house and onto another. A short distance later, she told me to turn right. It was a country road with a few houses spaced far apart and without lights burning in them. In the daylight, the houses would look ramshackled, I thought, with collapsing porches and cockeyed windows. We rode a distance through darkness, then Marie told me to slow down and to turn again.

"It's an apple orchard," Marie said, as I turned onto a dirt road. "Probably the only one left in New Jersey that hasn't been turned into a housing development or a shopping mall. It's close enough to the house that in the daylight you can see it from my bedroom window. Turn off the headlights so they don't see us from there," Marie said, just before the trees ended.

I flicked off the headlights and drove by feel in the sudden darkness for a few moments before stopping.

Marie turned to me. "I want to thank you for the night. It would have been completely wonderful if not for the thugs."

"You don't have to thank me."

"But I'd still be in the tree-swing if it weren't for you."

"We'll do it again sometime."

She looked down at her hands.

I put my hand under her chin, turned her head toward me and kissed her. I felt her fingers lightly on the back of my neck, briefly, then she broke away.

"Keep on this road to get out," Marie said hurriedly. "It loops around the orchard and ends where we came in. Bye."

She stepped quickly from the car and into the crickets and the fireflies. Marie left as if afraid to be caught at something. A half moon had come out, and I watched her fade in the pale silver light, the winking fireflies closing in behind her.

I started the car and turned on the headlights, just glimpsing Marie's back before she left the reach of the beams. I imagined her crossing the field, entering the house from the rear and going quietly up to her room to plan her departure.

I put the car in gear and rumbled around the perimeter of the orchard. The beams of my headlights bounced as I drove over the ruts. After a few minutes, I came to the paved road and the black shapes of the houses. I found my way back to route 42, which led to the city. It was after midnight and few cars were on the highway.

The trip went fast.

Instead of going straight home after reaching the city, I drove to Frank's apartment on Dickenson Street, not caring that it was one o'clock in the morning, not really thinking about it. I parked a half block away in front of a corner butcher shop; getting out of the car, I noticed the eyeless head of a pig on a rack in the wide window. The sight gave me a jolt. Even without eyes, the pig seemed to stare at me. I hurried away from the head up the sidewalk. Air conditioners blew hot air into the street and fans hummed in the windows of nearly every row home I passed. Cockroaches scurried across my path with the same bad luck omen as black cats. Again, the warm moist air smelled faintly of rot, and a film of oil seemed to cover every inch of my skin. Thunder rumbled in the distance.

I rang Frank's buzzer in the unlighted vestibule of his building, having to read his name beneath the pushbutton from the pale light of the streetlamp coming through the transom.

"Yeah?" a voice said over the speaker after a few minutes.

"Frank?" I said into the same black box. "It's Vincent. I have to talk to you."

"Now? I got somebody here."

"It's important, Frank."

I soon heard a door open and close from within the building and then footsteps coming down the wooden stairs. The inside door opened and Frank came into the vestibule. He wore a tee-shirt, loafers without socks, and his hair was slightly out of order.

"What is it?"

"I'm sorry I bothered you," I said. "I just want to ask you a question that I need a straight answer to."

"Whoa, this sounds serious."

"What were you doing with Joe Maglio in the restaurant?"

"Oh. So you recognized him."

"Not until later, and that was after I ran into Tommy Green; he told me a friend of his had seen you and Maglio there. It looks like Tommy told Buttoni and he told—get this—Mrs. Tucci."

"*Mrs.* Tucci?"

I told Frank about the trip to the shore with Marie, what happened on the jetty after she had gone to the Boardwalk, and my conversation with Tucci's wife.

"*She* wants the tapes?"

"I don't get it either," I said. "What is she doing following me to the shore and how is it that guys like Tony and George go with her?"

"I don't know. That's very weird." He seemed puzzled. "I want to hear what Mr. Tucci has to say about that."

"Is it true what she thinks, that you meant to give the tapes to Maglio?"

Frank took the handle of the outside door and pulled the door open. "You can't breathe in here," he said, stepping out. "Let's take a walk."

"For Christ sake, Frank, just tell me."

"You're getting excited. And when you get excited, your voice gets louder and people look at you. Calm down." He stepped onto the sidewalk.

"I want to know, Frank," I said at his heels.

"Where's your car. We'll go there."

"You going to tell me?"

"I'll tell you."

"Ok. This way."

I walked with him up the street toward my car. The air was so hot and still, it seemed as though a toxic cloud had settled over the area and chased all but the foolhardy indoors.

"Get in," Frank said at the car.

I felt the pig head's eyeless stare at my back as I opened the door and slid behind the steering wheel. Lightning flashed at the end of the street as I leaned over to unlock the door for my brother.

"So?" I asked after he settled in the seat. "Is it true?"

"Yeah, Maglio wants the tapes. Like everybody else, he's afraid he's on them."

"And you intended to sell them to him, counting on me to just hand them over to you?"

"Is that what you think? Just like Tony and Mrs. Tucci?"

"That's what she told me."

"They tried to muscle you. Christ, you can't believe everything people tell you."

"I don't know what to believe. I got a maniac who wants to kick the shit out of me and this old woman who, Christ, I think she has acid in her veins. She hinted that if her husband knew you were dealing the tapes to Maglio, Tucci would do something drastic. I don't give her the tapes, you get in trouble. That was her message. But they're Tucci's tapes. I'm responsible for them, goddamn it!"

"Settle down, will you?"

"Tell me what you were doing with Maglio, then I'll settle down."

Frank gazed through the windshield at the lightning and seemed to wait until its thunder reached us before speaking. "I didn't call Maglio; he called me. Somebody told him about the tapes."

"Who?"

"Maglio didn't say, and he wouldn't say if I was ignorant enough to ask him. But it had to be somebody in the house, one of the few people who knew what Mr. Tucci was doing with you."

"Why would they want Maglio to know?"

"To help stop you and Tucci."

"*Me* and Tucci?"

"You're the one going to the house to make the tapes."

"That's why Maglio called you instead of somebody else?"

"You're my brother," Frank said. "Maglio expects me to have some influence over you."

"But the tapes aren't for sale."

"Who said Maglio wanted to buy them? All he has to say is to get the tapes from you or you're dead."

Heat burst in my stomach. "Did he say that? He threatened to kill me?"

"He didn't have to say exactly, but that's what he meant. I get the tapes from you or he takes matters into his own hands. Why do you think I said you were a friend of mine and hustled you out of the restaurant that night you came in?"

I remembered that now, the man with the black hair combed straight back looking at me with annoyance and Frank, apologetic, taking me by the arm and ushering me to the door.

"Frank, I'm not dying because of some tapes," I blurted. "Can't we explain things to Mr. Tucci? He seems reasonable."

"We already talked. You think I would meet Maglio without telling Mr. Tucci? He told me to go, see what Maglio wanted. Afterwards, I told Mr. Tucci. He wasn't happy; he knows somebody in the house had to fink. But he doesn't want to give up the tapes to Maglio, if only to spite him for threatening us. If we did, it would be the same as spitting in Mr. Tucci's face. Anyway, like you told his wife, they're not yours to hand over, they're his."

"Then what the fuck are we going to do, Frank?" My voice cracked, but I didn't think Frank heard it over the increasing thunder.

"Copies," Frank said, as the rain started to dot the windshield.

"Copies?"

"We tell Maglio we have copies."

"But I don't have copies."

"Then make them. Next time I see Maglio, I'll tell him we have the originals locked in a safe deposit box with notes in our wills that say if anything messy happens to me or you, the tapes go to the D.A."

"Will he buy that?"

"It doesn't matter, because just them thinking there might be copies is enough. It's already working."

"How do you mean?"

"Why you didn't get dropped in the ocean is because whoever has the tapes is safe as long as the people wanting them don't know where they are or if there are copies. Understand? Same thing why Maglio's going through the trouble with me. They have to know for sure about the tapes, where they are, are there copies, before they do anything serious."

I nodded slowly, seeing my brother's logic.

"In one way, you're lucky Tony's a hothead. If he didn't go after that parking lot attendant, who knows what he and the old lady would've done to find out where you have the tapes, and to get them." He watched the rain slash through the lamplight.

"You think you could get Tony off my back?"

"I'll talk to him."

"Thanks."

Frank slapped his thighs. "Now, I have some business to finish. See you." He jumped out of the car and ran toward his apartment through the rain.

I sat for a time in the steamy car, glancing at the pig head as the rain came down hard and thick and hammered against the roof.

Ted woke me at seven Monday morning to go running. Without considering how badly out of shape I was, I crawled out of bed, dug some old running shoes from the closet, threw on shorts and a shirt and went sleepily after him out the door. We loosened up a little on the sidewalk in the bright sunlight, and then shoved off toward Eleventh Street.

I kept up with Ted for a few blocks before my lungs and legs began to give out and I slipped behind. He slowed for me but I told him to stay at his own pace. He nodded and stretched out his stride and pulled farther and farther ahead of me. Watching Ted, I realized we had taken the same path as my parents when they went looking for him that night he ran away from home. It was a late fall night, and my parents sat in the front seat of the big Buick with our dog between them and Frank and I in the back seat. Jamie had been left home on the chance that Ted returned. My father drove up Eleventh Street to Snyder Avenue and turned toward Broad. The green light of the dashboard shown on my parents' worried faces like fine dust, and the streetlamps expanded and contracted the light inside the car as we drove, peering along the sidewalks and into doorways and alleys, and any dark spot that could hide a boy. We checked the schoolyards and the playgrounds and the subway stops all the way to City Hall. My father parked the car on the curb and all of us went looking in the urine-smelling stairwells that led to the subway tunnels. My mother questioned the bums. Ted had not been seen by anyone. We piled back in the car and headed toward South Philly. At Wharton Street, my father made a left and drove to Ninth, where we rode between the piles of rotting fruit and the empty display stands and the darkened stores and the rusted steel drums, some ablaze with trash fires. No luck there, my father turned the car south again and we drove to the Lakes and looked about the ponds and the bushes and the boat houses and the Swedish Museum. We searched the darkness under the section of I-95 that ran there, shining our headlights among the graffitied pillars; we checked the tennis courts and the closed refreshment stand and the police horse stables, and before leaving the park my mother rapped on the steamy windows of parked cars, disturbing startled lovers to ask them if they had seen her son. Some cursed her. We left the Lakes and drove slowly home, a funereal silence in the dark car.

Unable to run any farther, I stopped and watched Ted grow smaller as he continued up Broad Street, imagining that he was heading for the spot where Mrs. Falcone had found him years ago on Market after three days of being missing.

I turned around, slightly nauseous, my throat raw, and wobbled toward home. At the PSFS bank, I thought of the copies I still had to make of the Tucci tapes that I meant to put in one of the bank's safety deposit boxes, as Frank suggested, later that morning. I bought blank cassettes at the Oregon Mall the day before, meaning to make copies by the end of the night, but Ted hung around the house all day and, not wanting him to know anything about my association with Tucci, I did not copy the tapes with him in the house. That evening, Ted wanted to see a movie. We went in town and had ice cream after the show, again killing any chance that I could copy the tapes without inviting his curiosity. I would try to make the copies while he was out running.

Just as I reached the house, two men stepped out of a gray car and came up to me. They had neat haircuts and wore lightweight suits with white shirts and pin-dotted ties.

"Recognize us?" one asked. I glimpsed gold in his mouth.

"No," I said.

"We're Guildenstern and Rosencrantz," the other said.

"Be professional, Carl."

"We're Rocky and Bullwinkle."

"Come on, Carl, cut it out."

"We're the guys who plucked you off the bridge the other night."

I looked from one to the other, thinking back to the hysteria of the bridge and the men in the car who had saved me. I made a vague connection.

"You're wondering why we're here, right?" Carl asked. "You're saying to yourself that this is an incredible coincidence."

"Something like that," I said. I was.

"All right, show it, Carl."

The two men briefly opened their jackets where, pinned to the inside, were identification cards with their pictures and official-looking stamps.

"I'm Rick Russo. This is Carl Silver. Will you let us come in with you for a couple of minutes?"

"What do you want?" I asked, blood coming into my face.

"Talk, mostly," Russo said.

"Did you know a man named John Nunzio, a Johnny Plum?" Carl asked abruptly.

"No," I said, immediately.

"Carl, I don't think we should do this on the sidewalk."

"You did hear that he was murdered?" Silver went on.

"I caught something on the news, yes."

"Aren't you Frank Vespers's brother?"

"Inside, Carl?"

"He doesn't want us to go inside," Carl said. He turned back to me. "Did you know that your brother was friends with John Nunzio?"

"I didn't know that."

"Did you know that he's friends with a man named Tony Buttoni and that they're both associates of Carmine Tucci?"

I did not say anything to that.

"Tell me you never heard of Tucci."

"Carl, calm down." Russo looked at me. "We just want to talk about a few things involving your brother."

"I don't have anything to do with my brother's affairs."

"You don't know Tony Buttons?" Carl said.

"I may have heard the name."

"Rick, just show him the fucking pictures."

Russo tightened his lips, obviously displeased with his partner. He took a manila envelope from a folder under his arm, undid the flap and pulled out several large photographs, handing them to me.

"Read 'em and weep," Carl said.

The photographs showed Tony Buttons, Tommy Green and me talking on the sidewalk at the corner of Eleventh and Jackson. The pictures were clear and unmistakable. Tony wore a suit, and I immediately remembered the Maglio wedding and the photographer taking pictures of the arriving guests. I felt like Russo had kicked me in the stomach.

"You don't know the other twerp either, I guess," Carl said.

"Tommy Green," I said.

"Hey, your memory's coming back."

"Once we got his name," Russo said, "we tapped it into the computer and out pops his record. He did a year and a half for rape a little while ago."

"He jazzed a sixteen-year-old girl but he had a good lawyer," Carl said. "Your brother Frank's lawyer, as a matter of fact."

"Can we maybe talk inside now?" Russo asked.

Without speaking, I climbed the steps and opened the door, leaving it ajar so they would follow.

TWELVE

Cyril and Jamie breezed in several hours later, overloaded with shopping bags. They had bought clothing, books, and "things for the house," theirs not mine. They had gone to Macy's, Gucci for the fun of it, Barnes and Noble, and the Metropolitan Museum. They saw an off-Broadway play. They took the ferry to Staten Island.

After they settled in, I made bacon and eggs for all of us, and at noon we started for the Home to see our mother.

We drove down Eleventh Street to Passyunk Avenue, passing Jamie's first apartment and Pat's Steaks, the odors of onions and meat in the air, then turned right onto Washington, driving past the high-rise housing project, laundry hanging to dry on the balconies, and then the Mummer's Museum, painted in garish colors, and then to Delaware Avenue that ran along the river. Ted sat beside me in the front; Cyril and Jamie sat in the rear. None of us spoke much.

We turned left onto Delaware Avenue. The dark river looked solid; a few cargo ships anchored in the middle of it appeared to be mired in tar. Camden, on the other side, seemed deserted.

A few minutes later, we took the Aramingo entrance onto I-95. I quickly pushed the car up to sixty. It felt good to be driving fast after going so slowly through the city. I heard safety belts click behind me. We soon entered the chemical stink of Bridesburg. It was on this section of the highway, in the shadows of the mauve clouds billowing from the tall smokestacks not far beyond the guard rail, that Alison and I had had our accident. The car had slowed because of a clogged fuel line, an oil truck smashed into our rear, glass exploded, the front seats collapsed. We came to rest on the shoulder of the highway. I looked at the spot now. Alison's arm had been broken and she suffered a concussion. I had bruised ribs and a banged up nose. The car was mangled; staggering out of it, I couldn't believe we were conscious. At the hospital, we went to X-ray together. In the bathroom, I spit up a blood clot the size of a walnut. We spent the next three days in bed, our bodies aching. We treated each other tenderly. For awhile, it seemed that the accident had saved our marriage. But as we mended, the recriminations returned, and we jumped back on the road to our dissolution.

We passed the heaps of rusted metal in the junk yards, and eventually rushed by Holmesburg prison, a structure that looked, with its turrets and thick windowless walls, like nothing else but a prison.

Tony Buttons and Tucci had done some time there. Twenty minutes later, we exited at the Newtown ramp. We made a few turns and then were soon in the country, driving along tree-lined roads, passing joggers, bike-riders, and expensive houses, a few with turquoise pools shimmering in the sun. Lawns were being cut with noisy power mowers and we could smell the grass. Behind one stretch of picket fence, we saw a few horses.

After another turn, we could see the maroon brick of the Home through the trees that lined the road. The main building sat far back from the road and was connected to it by a meandering driveway that discouraged high speeds. Despite the curves, there were times when I drove so fast away from that place that my tires screeched.

"It's such a beautiful day," Jamie said. "Let's take mom for a walk."

Good idea, I thought, turning into the driveway. Anything would be better than sitting in that place with its odd smells and strange noises.

"Why are you so distant, Vincent?" Jamie asked.

"I'm not distant."

"You've been preoccupied all day."

"I'm sorry. I get like this whenever I come here."

"Yes," Jamie said. "I know what you mean."

But more than the minor horrors of the Home, the men who had met me on the sidewalk that morning were on my mind. They had followed me into the house and wasted no time in telling me that they were part of a special task force conducting an ongoing investigation.

The situation, Russo told me, was this: for the last two years, the task force had been trying to build a case against Carmine Tucci and a number of his associates, Buttoni and Frank included, and were getting close to an indictment. They had less on Frank than the others, Russo admitted, but it was enough to put him away for a few years, if only for tax evasion, which the lawyers were certain they could prove. The big interests, however, were Tucci and Buttoni; there was evidence to bring charges against them but it was not as much or as strong as they would like. The Plum murder was a break, but they didn't have any solid evidence connecting them to it, even though they believed Buttoni had done the killing after Tucci's order. Why Plum was killed, they could only guess.

It was because of a wire tap on Tucci's line, Russo said, that they were alerted to me. Mine was a new number, and it was routine to check out new numbers immediately. Russo pulled a sheet of paper from his folder and showed it to me; it was a transcript of the first telephone conversation I had had with Tucci. I read it. Tucci had asked me if I got the money that Buttoni had put through my mailbox. I had said that I just counted it. So I would come out to the house Monday, Tucci had asked. I hadn't answered. Tucci then said that Frank had told him I agreed. To which I said that I guessed I did. Tucci said, Good, and told me that someone would pick me up.

"Familiar?" Silver asked. I ignored him.

They found the call very interesting, Russo said. They knew that I periodically met Frank and suspected that I may have had something to do with his business, but they did not know, or say at least, what. They had not examined any of my bank records—"Not yet," Silver threatened—and so could not tell if the numbers were out of line with my teacher's salary. They knew about my safety deposit boxes at the Fidelity Bank, which contained Frank's cash, gold, and certificates, but there was no way they could get a search warrant from a judge to look in them because I was just a school teacher. Even with that, I was an "unknown, a new element," Russo said, and here I was talking to the "big shot" who had obviously given me money for something that I was supposed to do. From the surveillance, they saw Tony Buttoni pick me up and take me to the Tucci house in New Jersey, and that I continued to go there for a full week straight. They also did not miss that I met Tucci's daughter at the library and that Tucci had visited my house alone, which they thought was extremely peculiar.

The phone call from Tucci was enough for them to watch me. That's how they spotted me on the Walt Whitman Bridge. Did I want to share with them why Buttoni had dumped me on the bridge? Silver asked. I shook my head no. Did I want to tell them why I was going to the Tucci house nearly every night for over a week? I told them it was personal.

"Or maybe you have some insight into why your brother met with the other heavyweight scumball of the city at the Villa restaurant the other day," Silver went on. "That's gotta look a little strange to you, right Shakespeare?"

"Ease up, Carl," Russo said.

"This guy, saying he don't know Tony Buttoni, which he does, comes out of left field and the next thing you know Tucci's calling him on the phone and going to his house. He gets himself tossed out of a car onto a bridge. Then his brother, Tucci's right arm, has a sit down with Maglio. Something screwy's going on and it's bugging the shit out of me."

"Well, maybe Mr. Vespers will help us."

What they wanted mainly, Russo said, was to ask me to consider a few things. They didn't know if what I was doing with Tucci was illegal or not, whether I was paid for it or not, but if there was anything I learned while at the house that could help in their efforts to build a solid indictment against Tucci and Buttoni, would I let them know? For the information, they would be very considerate if charges were brought against me for tax evasion or for something I may be doing with Tucci. They would also see to it that Frank be shown leniency when he was indicted.

"You can help him," Russo said. "Think about it." He gave me a card with his phone number on it and started out.

Silver began to follow but paused at the coffee table where I had dumped the stack of cassettes I bought.

"What's with the tapes?" he asked. "You a music freak or are you interviewing all the wise guys at the big house and seeing what makes them tick?" He laughed harshly and followed Russo out the door and into the dense summer heat.

If only they knew.

The Home smelled like a discount drugstore, though it was not as cool. The walls and floors were white or beige. The pictures on the walls were of landscapes or waves crashing against beaches. It was quiet, though now and then I heard odd sounds I could not identify.

At the front desk, we were told that my mother was not in her room but in the "sun room" down the hall. In the Sun Room, marked by a sign above the doorway, old people sat about, most of them looking bored or tired, or angry. One woman cried softly in the corner. There was a table covered with tattered magazines. An attendant, with a splotch of ketchup on his white shirt, sat behind a desk sullenly eating his lunch and listening to the radio. Two old men sat on either side of a checker board, but they stopped playing to look at us.

Our mother was sitting in a rocking chair and looking out the bank of windows. The windows faced the parking lot, and it was possible that my mother, who did not say, had watched us park and come up the steps to the tall white doors. She seemed smaller than the last time I saw her, and smaller still than the time before that, as though, instead of dying, she was shrinking out of existence. Sadness pulled at me.

We went to her. Cyril, part of the family but not by blood, stood slightly back. My mother looked at us as at strangers, then as we said hello and touched her, she tentatively smiled. It was always difficult for me to see that struggle to grasp our faces and then, on a good day, mumble our names, as if my mother wasn't quite sure what they were. I gritted my teeth as her mind worked through the clutter to find our faces and then to put a name on them. She did not always succeed.

Jamie hugged and kissed my mother and smoothed

her tangled hair away from her cheeks. My mother did not open her mouth, but by the way her lips leaned inward, I knew her dentures were not in.

"Mom," Jamie said, "we're going to take you for a walk."

My mother's expression remained unchanged.

"But first, let's fix you up a bit." Jamie turned to us. "I'll meet you in the lobby."

I nodded and we followed them out of the room, then watched them walk slowly down the white hall, Jamie's arm about my mother's stooped shoulders. I started away first, and Teddy and Cyril followed me.

Later, we all sat at a picnic table beneath an oak tree. There was very little to say to my mother; her mind was so fogged or jumbled that whatever you said to her became lost or distorted beyond meaning.

It was always the same. You went there, you didn't quite recognize the woman as your mother, you tried to establish some common ground, tried to talk about something, anything, and you always wound up frustrated, sad, bitter, ultimately silent.

I turned to looking at ants in the grass, swishing away gnats, gazing about the grounds in intentional efforts at distraction. It was hard not to think how much simpler and easier it would have been if my mother'd had a coronary or some brief fatal illness, instead of her mind going and the slow decay of her body that followed.

"Mom, guess what?" Jamie said with false enthusiasm. "You're going to be a grandmother."

My mother received the news with knitted brows,

saying nothing. Maybe she did not know anymore what a grandmother was, I thought.

"Yes, Cyril and I are going to become a family!"

She did not say it, but my mother's eyes said, *Who's Cyril?*

Jamie kept up a stream of talk, telling my mother about her trip back from Ohio, the lunch at Frank's place, the day in New York City. It was better for her than to sit in silence as I did most of the time.

I looked away and across the grounds, to the trees lining the road, the sky, the other residents in the Home walking about or sitting at other picnic tables. Glints of sunlight to my left made me turn, and I saw that they had come from the spokes of a wheelchair before it, its rider, and the person pushing the chair went behind a stretch of shrubs at the side of the walkway. I looked back to the trees lining the road, and then the glints of sunlight shot from my left again, and I saw the chair and the figures. You saw wheelchairs every time you went there, but something about this pair was familiar, even if they were a hundred feet or so away. They were coming toward us down a path, and I kept watching for them to emerge after they disappeared behind more shrubs.

"Hey, look who it is," I said, after they had come closer.

The others turned.

"It's Frank," Jamie said. "I thought he never came here."

"Why is he pushing that man?" I stood up and waved to him, but Frank was already heading toward our table.

When Frank was twenty feet away, Ted gasped

and stood up; and when the wheelchair drew close enough to hear the squeak of its wheels, Ted dropped back a step.

"What is it, Teddy?" Cyril asked.

Ted, his face going white, stared wide-eyed and speechless at the two men coming our way.

"Teddy," Jamie said. "What's wrong?"

Frank stopped before us; he stepped on a brake and locked the wheels. In the chair, the man's head was bent slightly down and he stared vacantly somewhere past his feet. He had black hair, with gray at the temples. The left side of his face had collapsed; the eye, the cheek, the side of the mouth had melted downward.

Frank took out a handkerchief from his pocket and wiped spittle from the man's mouth, then he pulled the man's collar away from his moist neck.

My ears popped, and I heard the trees rustling, the sound of bees, the giggle of a child in the momentary vacuum that came with the man in the chair. I stared at his lowered head, empty eyes, mouth wet with spit. The face not just older but altered. The leanness now of the invalid and not of youth, the poorly shaven beard of the idiot. No more wit or charm. No more laughter. No more good looks. For a moment, I thought he could have been someone else. I wanted him to be. Get this wreck away, the flaccid muscle, the dull vegetable face, the blank brain. But it was him. To think that he had come to this.

"Patty," my mother mumbled.

Jamie gasped. "Is it really, Frank?"

Frank nodded, but kept his eyes on Ted, still white and rigid.

"I thought he was dead."

"So did a lot of people."

"I don't understand any of this," Cyril said.

"I told you about him, honey," Jamie said. "Mrs. Falcone's nephew who disappeared about fifteen years ago."

"And this is the first you've seen of him?"

"Yes. Frank, does Mrs. Falcone know?"

"Nobody knows but us."

"But how did *you* know he was here?" I asked.

Frank took out a comb and ran it through Patty's thin hair; the face did not alter at the touch. "I was visiting a few weeks ago and I saw Patty under a tree. It took me a while to recognize him, even if he was my best friend." Frank brushed dandruff from Patty's round shoulders and put away the comb. "Pretty sight, huh?"

"What happened to him?" Jamie asked.

"His brain got damaged. I don't know how, though." Frank turned to Ted. His lips were parted slightly and his eyes were still wide and fixed on Patty in an expression of astonishment. "Ted, you ok?"

He did not speak or move.

"Ted, do you know something we don't?" I asked.

His brows came together in an effort, it seemed, at sorting out a puzzle. Ted's lips began to tremble, but instead of answering, he bolted. He ran across the wide green field toward the road on the other side of the trees. Frank and I started after him, but it did not take us long to realize that Teddy, who daily ran at least five miles, was not going to slow down and that we did not have a chance of catching him. I didn't know what we would do if we had. We stopped in the middle of the grassy field and gazed after him.

"Where's he going?"

"I don't know, Vince."

"*Why's* he going?"

"I don't know that either, but I want to find out."

We watched Ted slip through the trees, cross the road and vanish. But Frank and I remained in the field, catching our breath and gazing at the trees with our backs to Cyril and Jamie as though waiting for Ted to reappear.

Frank said, "It was Mr. Tucci who told me about Patty."

"Tucci?"

"I wasn't visiting; he sent me here to ask for somebody with a name that wasn't Patty's. But it was Patty they wheeled out."

"What's that mean? He knew all this time?"

"I don't know what it means. I don't know how Patty got hurt, how he got here, why Mr. Tucci told me, nothing. But he knows something about it and, going by Teddy's reaction, so does he."

"What could Ted know?"

"He ran away the same night Patty disappeared. Maybe there's a connection."

"He saw something?"

"I'd bet on it."

Thinking of Ted's look of shock and astonishment at the sight of Patty, I would bet on it, too.

"Can I ask you why you didn't tell me about Patty when you found out?" I asked. "It being big news."

"Tucci told me not to say anything about it to anybody. Course, he didn't say why. But you figure he knew you were going to meet Marie and also spend time around Tony. If you knew, it might get out about Patty and there would be trouble."

"What kind of trouble?"

"Well, suppose you told Marie. She was so crazy about Patty, she might want to come here, get him, and bring him to live with her at the house. Can you see that? Somebody like Tony or George rolling Patty across the lawn, Mrs. Tucci feeding him canned peaches?"

"I see what you mean."

Frank turned around and started back to the picnic table where Jamie stood behind my mother and Cyril flanked Patty.

"Wait," I said, touching his arm and halting him, "I have something to tell you. I tried to call you before leaving to come here but you were apparently on your way, too."

"What is it?"

"A couple of agents met me outside the house this morning"

"Agents?"

"They showed me badges."

"They say they were agents?"

"They weren't plain cops."

"What did they want?"

I repeated everything Russo and Silver had shown and told me, including the deal they wanted to make for providing them with information.

"They're not agents, they're saints."

"They said I could help you."

"What help? You don't have anything to give them. And don't say the tapes, if you were thinking it. You give them the tapes, you also have to testify against people. Which means if you didn't want to change your name and move to an Indian reservation in North Dakota, you'd get killed by anybody who even *thinks* they're on the fucking tapes."

"But you're under investigation."

"There's always some kind of investigation going on," Frank said. "But I'm ninety-five percent legitimate and they can't have much on me. It's you they're squeezing, figuring you're soft. But you're all right. There's no law about visiting somebody."

"What about the money that Tucci mentioned on the phone?"

"Could be four dollars for a collection you're handling for starving kids in Africa," Frank said, looking toward the picnic area. "All you have to worry about is keeping it in cash and not to make a trail for the tax people, which you already know."

"I can't go to jail, Frank."

"Listen to me. You give Russo and the other prick the tapes and your life's over. All we can do now is put the tapes in a vault to protect you from Maglio and the other bastards who want them, and then take your chances with the courts, if you even get there."

"I could always run."

"I guess you could. But right now we better get back before Jamie starts thinking we're planning a heist."

We walked back to her and the others.

"What were you guys talking about over there?" Jamie asked.

"Where Ted might be," I said.

"I'm sure he's on his way back home," Jamie said.

"Unless he's running back to his cabin," Frank

said, wiping spittle again from Patty's mouth and combing his hair.

It had been an odd sight, that show of tenderness by my brother, who had displayed so little of it all the years I knew him. What had Tommy said about Frank? That he wasn't "right" these days, that even Tony said Frank was acting strange. I could only think that finding out Patty Leone was alive had something, if not everything, to do with it.

We looked for Teddy later along the roads we had travelled getting to the Home and, even though we backtracked and circled, we saw nothing of him.

THIRTEEN

After returning my mother to her room, Jamie met us at the car and announced that she wanted to cook a big meal for everyone. "Any objections?" It sounded like a threat.

"No. None," I said, looking at Cyril.

"It's therapy," he whispered. "She does it when she's upset. And I think she's upset about Ted."

Jamie had me stop at Ninth Street on the drive home, and Cyril and I ran from shop to shop and stand to stand behind her as she bought mushrooms, onions, romaine lettuce, red peppers, imported parmesan in a chunk, and other things to eat. She bought two kinds of olives, a loaf of bread with sesame seeds clinging to its hard brown surface, red potatoes, and asparagus. For the main course, she dragged Cyril and me into a poultry shop for five cornish hens, one for each of us, including Ted, if he showed up.

Frank was already in the house when we arrived, the air-conditioner vibrating in the window.

"Teddy's not with you?" Frank asked as we came in.

"He'll be here," Jamie said, almost cheerfully.

"How do you know?" I asked.

"I know."

"I believe you," Frank said, and went upstairs. A few minutes later, he called me up.

The second floor of the house was stuffy and hot; midway up the stairs, you abruptly entered jungle heat. Frank had taken off his shirt and I saw close up what he had done to his body with the weight-training. Looking at his muscles, I imagined him shattering things, including bones. He walked ahead of me into the bathroom and turned on the shower. I stood at the door as steam began to billow.

Frank sat on the closed toilet and untied his shoes and removed his socks.

"Can't we talk later? I'm suffocating already," I said.

"The heat'll do you good, sweat out the poisons."

"Which I have a lot of."

"Why don't you come to the gym with me. We'll work out together, get you in shape."

"I'll keep it in mind."

Frank bent over the tub and adjusted the water. "There's one thing I didn't tell you about that visit when I saw Patty." He straightened up and turned to look at his face in the mirror. "I wasn't alone."

"No? Who were you with?"

Frank turned each cheek to the mirror and examined them. Staring into his own eyes, he said, "Johnny Plum."

Hearing that was the same as being punched, because Plum had been found strangled in a sewer on Mifflin Street, and the image of his body, stuffed upside down in the filthy hole, flashed in my mind.

"How was that?" I asked. "Tucci send him, too?"

"No. On my way, I ran into him on the street. He was looking to kill some time, so he asked to come along. I didn't know what I was going to see at the Home, so I said sure."

"He saw Patty, too?"

"Yeah, but he swore he didn't recognize him." Frank turned from the mirror and began to remove his pants.

"Did he, do you think?"

"I don't know. But he was dead three days later, and nobody knows why, or can even guess because Plum was a simple guy who didn't seem to want more than he had." Frank took off his pants and stood in his briefs, looking in the mirror again. "It's a shame. He had a family, a girl getting married in a coupla weeks. The invitation's on my table."

"And no one knows anything?"

"No. That's all I'm going to say about it." He turned away from the mirror. "All right, get out and let me shower. Tell Jamie to hurry up. I'm starving."

He closed the door. I stood on the landing, my clothes damp and stuck to my skin, thinking about Plum, his garroted neck, and the wedding of his daughter he would miss.

The diningroom table was set as if for Thanksgiving dinner. Cyril had put out the dishes, silverware, wine glasses and cloth napkins Jamie must have dug out of a drawer somewhere. The cheeses and the olives Jamie had bought on Ninth Street sat in the middle of the table as appetizers, along with the length of bread and fingers of carrots and celery on small white plates. I walked into the hot kitchen. Butter sizzled in a skillet. Gravy bubbled.

Despite Ted running away, Jamie seemed cheerful, her eyes bright and her cheeks rosy from the heat of the oven she opened as I walked in. I glimpsed the cornish hens, their skin brown and crisp, and surrounded by potatoes flecked with parsley.

"Hand me the wooden spoon," she told Cyril. "Cut the melon and arrange it nicely on a plate with the prosciutto. Where's the pepper?" He handed her the shaker. "The thyme."

"Five o'clock."

"The spice."

"Oh."

Cyril went into cabinets, drawers, the refrigerator, flashed a knife like a sword, jumped back and forth across the kitchen, spun, streaked into the diningroom, and came back. In the middle of all the motion, he stepped over to Jamie and they kissed over the steaming pots and pans.

"When do we eat?" I asked.

"It won't be long." In her face I saw my mother, who was always happiest when at the center of a maelstrom of cooking. She touched her finger to the brown liquid and tasted, then added salt, stirring the gravy slowly, watching the swirls of oil on the surface. Jamie put a lid on the gravy and started to break off the bottoms of the asparagus.

"Maybe I should go look for Teddy," I said.

"I think it'll just be a waste of time. He'll be here."

But Ted did not show by the time Jamie finished cooking. She had us wait a little longer while the cornish hens cooled, but then she began to worry that they would cool too much and become unappetizing, so she allowed us to eat.

We did not talk about anything that had happened that afternoon, not a word about Patty, the Home, or Ted bolting. We stayed topical, commenting on the food, the heat, politics, and for the most part managed to avoid sounding false.

After an hour, we still sat at the table with the brittle carcasses of our hens stark on our plates and the food left in the serving bowls now cold. All the aromas except for the wine were gone. Cyril, the last one of us chewing, munched on grapes. I worked tidbits from between my teeth and sipped wine.

Finally, with the oil in the gravy beginning to congeal, Jamie sighed and began to clear away the dishes and the leftovers. Cyril helped her. Frank and I offered to pitch in too, but they told us to stay put. We did not insist.

After Jamie and Cyril had gone into the kitchen, I asked Frank if he wanted to tell Mrs. Falcone about Patty.

"If you think she should know, you tell her," he said. "It'll break her heart, though."

"But she should know; she'd want to. Also Marie."

"You want to see somebody go completely nuts, you tell Marie that Patty's like he is. She'll kill somebody, then herself. Let her father tell her."

Cyril returned and took more plates from the

table. After he left the room, Frank asked if I wanted to take a ride.

"I'm going to sell the pizza shops and I got a meeting with somebody who's interested. I could use you there for advice."

"You didn't tell me you were going to sell."

"It's something I've been thinking about. I wanted you to liquidate everything because I need a change. I might even leave the country. Know anything about Venezuela?"

"Are you serious?"

"Yeah. I'm getting out. Too much stress."

I looked him fully in the face; there was no joking in his eyes. "It's in South America."

He laughed slightly. "I got a genius for a brother."

"I'd go with you but I'm supposed to see Mr. Tucci tonight."

"That's more important, yeah. Go, I can handle the meeting myself."

Jamie returned, smiled tightly at us, and took more dishes to the kitchen. Just as she walked out, the front door opened and Ted walked in, his clothes dark with sweat.

"It's like a dream that doesn't seem to be mine," Ted began. He did not look at us; instead, he kept his eyes on the floor, talking into the carpet. "A lot of it I don't remember at all, or didn't allow myself to remember until this afternoon." He paused, seeming to be making an effort to talk. "I remember that it started with the telescope falling out the window."

"When I dropped it out," Frank said.

"All right," Teddy said. "I remember the sound

of the crash most of all, coming from the sidewalk below the open window. There were nights afterwards where I would hear the sound, and in my mind I would see the telescope striking the pavement and obliterating, just coming apart in a thousand pieces, as if bursting. I heard that noise and I instantly went outside of myself. A sense of unreality came about my head like fog. Frank and Jamie, you were fighting on the floor, but it was as though on a screen and not at my feet. Then I drifted out the door and, on my hands and knees on the sidewalk, I collected bits of glass, put them in my pocket, picked up the tube of the telescope, walked away—but numb, blind, automatic, watching myself from a height." He stopped, stood up, glanced out the window and sat down again.

"I walked up Jackson toward Broad Street, but at Twelfth the trolley was sitting at the red light between the brush factory and the rectory with no one on board but the driver, a black man, and I walked into the street just as the light changed and the trolley began to move. The trolley driver had to hit the brakes. There was that screech of metal on metal, the trolley lurching, shuddering. And the single headlight at the nose of the trolley three feet from my chest, that powerful light, humming I thought, but it was the dynamos, the spinning coils of the trolley's electric engine. The driver clanged his bell. I looked up at him, that mock angry black face backlit by the soft yellow light of the car's inside, that furrowed brow, the pursed lips, the face as high as a judge's. I was so close to the headlight that I could feel heat from it. The telescope tucked under my arm. The driver glaring down at me. I was standing between his two tracks." He fell silent for a few moments, then began again.

"I looked up as the glaring driver clanged his bell, but stood there, fog in my head, the headlight bright in my eyes, heat coming from it. He motioned for me to get out of the way, and then I heard the doors rattle open and the driver came out and said, 'What are you doing, boy? Can't stay in the middle of the street. You got to move.' I went around him and stepped onto the trolley. The driver came on after me. I sat in the front seat, the telescope on my lap. I didn't have any money. I didn't think to pay. The driver asked me once, but after I didn't say a word, he shrugged, sat at his controls, pressed the pedal, and the trolley rolled down Twelfth Street. No one else got on the trolley the rest of the run. The lights blinked off and on. At Moyamensing, the light was red and we stopped. I could hear the trolley humming, feel the vibrations of the mechanisms under my feet. The driver said, 'You running away, boy?' I don't think I answered him. He asked me again if anything was wrong. I just looked at him. 'You deaf and dumb?' I heard him, but his voice was just noise. The driver shook his head at me, and then the light changed and he eased the gears in and we were rolling again. In the window, I could see my reflection; on the other side, there were the row homes, and at every corner, a shop or store or bar with a sign hanging above the door. I rode to the end of the line, Bigler Street, then I sat there until the driver told me I had to get off. He was heading back uptown, he said, and if I wanted to ride I would have to pay this time. If he hadn't spoken to me, I would have continued uptown with him. But he swung the doors open with that lever, and said, 'Go home, boy, if you're all right. You all right?' I got off the trolley, he said, 'Goddamn,' the doors closed behind me, and the trolley swung slowly onto Bigler, the wheels screeching, and went away." Ted stood up, parted the drapes, looked out the window.

"Are you ok?" Jamie asked.

Teddy sat down, nodded, took a deep breath. He picked up his turned bowl from the radiator cover and held it in his hands.

"I walked up Bigler Street to Broad. South on Broad to Pattison. I made that right. The old boxy Naval homes are there behind the cyclone fence. I left the sidewalk and walked onto the grass, then through some trees, crossing the road that loops around the Lakes, then over the open grass fields where once we flew kites with dad." Ted pressed the bowl against his forehead.

"There were some parked cars by the road or under the trees or in the parking areas. In one, I saw the flicker of a match and the outline of two heads, but briefly. I stopped under a clump of trees, and I tore out clumps of grass sod and then dug a furrow in the ground with a tin can and a stick. I put the telescope in the hole and put the bits of lens in a candy box I found and put those in the hole. It seems silly now, but there it is. I was a kid. When I finished, I sat with my back against a tree. I started to feel cold for the first time. The Swedish Museum was a hundred yards away, and I went there to look for a spot to huddle up that didn't smell like urine. There was a big flattened cardboard box and a sheet of thick packing paper in one of the doorways, and that's where I sat down. I covered myself with the paper and fell asleep."

"You slept there?"

"I didn't mean to."

"A pervert could've gotten you."

"It didn't happen, but I was woken up by a man going through my pockets, looking for money. He said I was sleeping in his bed. He called it a bed. I can still smell his terrible breath. It was a clear enough night to see that he had on a ski cap and a couple of shirts. He had some kind of sore on his cheek, which was wet. He wasn't deranged. He was just a bum. He told me to get lost, but it wasn't with anger. I ran down the steps of the museum and kept running until I was out of the park and walking on Pattison Avenue again. I was thinking about home now, because of the cold, and about all of you, what happened, how you, mom and dad might be worried about me, when a taxi passed, then stopped suddenly. Somebody called out the window. I didn't know the voice and kept walking. The man called me again as I was nearing the cab, about to pass it. He said, 'Hey, aren't you one of the Vespers kids?' I stopped at that and looked. His face was sticking out the window, and the streetlamp above cast a shadow on it, so I had trouble seeing who he was. He asked me what I was doing out at that hour. He had a kind voice, nothing threatening in it. I told him I was walking. He sort of laughed softly. 'Whatever you say, boss,' he said."

"It was Patty," Frank said.

"Yes. He told me that as I was standing there trying to make out who he was. 'I know your father,' he said. I recognized him, then. I saw him on the street a few times or going into Mrs. Falcone's. He asked me if I wanted a lift home. I hesitated a little but because I knew him and I was tired, I got in the taxi. Patty told the driver to go, and we headed toward Broad Street. Veteran's Stadium was under construction then, and you could see the outline of the cranes and the trucks in the darkness as we crossed Broad. We should have gone left but we didn't. Patty said he had to stop somewhere first for a few minutes, if I didn't mind, then he would take me home. If I would have said to take me home, he would have. I knew that. But I didn't mind, and I told him. Strange to say, I wanted to stay with Patty." Ted paused for a breath, then continued.

"After I got in the taxi, Patty lit a cigarette. There was that flash of light from the match. In that instant of light, he did not seem tough or cocky; he seemed inward and thoughtful. The car filled with smoke. After the construction site, there was nothing much to see on either side of the road. Open lots, an Acme sign, the silhouettes of low buildings. Pattison became Delaware Avenue near the river a few minutes later. There were a couple of tugboats at a dock and strange buildings I had never seen, acute angles and weird proportions. Not a soul around. That scary desolation. A place where serial killers would dump their dead victims. Soon we were passing under the bridge, the stretch before it went over the river. You could see the steel gridwork of the underbelly of the bridge. I saw a sign on a building on the riverside right after passing the bridge. Publicker Industries, it said. And then there were a bunch of large cylindrical tanks. When the tanks ended, I could see the river off and on between unmarked buildings, dock lights, lights from the Camden side reflected in the water, ships anchored out there. I saw the noses of a couple of ships on our side, wedged between the piers, tied up. I thought of the ships crawling down the river to the ocean and sailing across the sea to other countries, and I wanted to be on them." Teddy paused, as if seeing himself at the rail of a great ship, the green ocean moving beneath him.

"Patty didn't talk much until we turned onto Oregon Avenue a few minutes later. He had the driver stop a little before Front Street, paid him, and we got out. There were no homes on the street, only dark warehouses, a tire distributor, and more open lots. Leone said he would have taken me home right away but that he was late for his meeting already. He told me that he would only be a few minutes, that he just had to say no to somebody. I had no idea what that meant, but I didn't question it, didn't think to question it, being a kid. I was simply *there*. I didn't know who Patty would be meeting. I didn't care. He said that we would catch another taxi or a ride when he was done. Then he said that, no, he should have sent me home in the taxi, and in fact he wanted to flag down another one and put me in it. I realize now that he was nervous. It was late, and Oregon Avenue near Front had few taxi cabs on it. The minutes we waited there, none passed. I said it was all right, that I could get home easily from there. It was only a matter of taking the bus to Broad Street, then the subway—or I could just walk. He wouldn't let me do that. I was his respon-

sibility now, he said. He would see me home safely. But there was his meeting. Ok, he said, I could come with him but I had to stay out of his sight. Whatever I did, he said, I wasn't to let anyone he met see me."
Teddy fell silent. He relaxed his grip on the wooden bowl, let it dangle a moment between his knees, then dropped it to the floor. He had fixed his eyes on the wall across the room; but he did not stir when the bowl thunked against the carpet.

"Teddy," Jamie said.

He did not move or speak.

"You can't stop now," Frank said.

"Let him rest, if he wants," Jamie said.

"He's not resting, he's fading away."

"Shhh, Frank." Jamie turned back to Ted.

"I lingered on the sidewalk near a splintery telephone pole, watching Patty walk away. When headlights flared, I saw him well, sharply outlined. He turned once to look back at me, his shoulders hunched against the cold. The headlights turned and Leone vanished for a moment until my eyes adjusted. He was getting too far away. I followed him up the street. I heard car doors slam, and three figures met Leone on the sidewalk. They stood there only briefly, then all of them seemed to rush off the sidewalk and out of sight. He didn't want me to lose sight of him, and because he was gone, I ran. The cold made my eyes tear. I began to feel afraid, sensed something wrong. Something in the way the men waited in the dark car for Leone, the way they hurried out of sight. No friendly greetings. I reached the spot where all of them left the sidewalk. A used car lot was there, and set back from the street a garage and, connected to it, a smaller structure, an office. The office was dark, but there was light in the single tiny window of the garage door. I hesitated, thought to keep to myself, but I was drawn to the window. I crossed the driveway, looked through the glass, but a pick-up truck was there and I couldn't see anyone. I thought maybe they weren't in there, that the men went somewhere else, when I heard something fall, a crash of metal things against concrete. I went to the side of the garage, saw white light in several windows in the wall, but they were high up, and I couldn't look in without climbing on top of the covered barrels there. I looked around for a step onto the barrel, found a milk crate, moved it into position. I climbed up in seconds. The glass was sooty but I saw well enough. Too well." Ted's hands began to tremble. True terror had come into his eyes. He tried to continue but the words got hung up in his throat.

Jamie said, "Teddy?"

Teddy shook his head as if to clear it. "There were bars on the garage windows and I clutched them to keep from falling. The men were to my right and below, standing in the center of the car bay, cars on either side of them. I didn't look at their faces because when I looked through the window I saw Patty in his tee-shirt on his hands and knees, holding his stomach and coughing. Tools were scattered on the ground behind him. He jumped up suddenly, a wrench in his hand, and moved toward the big man of the group, but the man was faster and hit Patty in the face. Patty fell to the concrete, his mouth bloody. He got up again, but again the big man hit him, again Patty fell. The big man grabbed Patty by the back of the neck, picked him up, said something to him, rattled Patty for an answer, but Patty spit at him. The big man hit Patty in the stomach and shoved him across the garage where he collided with the wall and dropped. He stayed on the floor. The big man turned around to the other men. One of the men was hidden by a girder and outside the ring of light; the other was visible. He had a birthmark on his face."

"Johnny Plum," Frank said.

"I watched them, my eyes burning, and it was as if Patty rushed in from the side of a stage. He was a red blur, his arms flailing, some object in his hand I couldn't make out until, taken off guard, it connected with the cheek of the big man and stayed there."

"That's where the dent in his face came from," Frank said.

"Whose?" I asked.

"Buttoni's."

"It was a bailing hook," Teddy went on, his eyes still on the wall, but an intensity coming into them, and a feverishness in his voice, as if he were rushing to finish. "A hook attached to a handle at right angles, yes, there in the big man's cheek. Patty tugged him across the garage floor while the man howled, his mouth as red with blood as Leone's, his eyes wild. Good for him, I thought, I hope Patty pulls clean through. But Leone was staggering from the beating he had already taken, he had no strength. The big man reached for Patty's wrist, grabbed it, kicked him in the groin. Patty crumpled to the oily floor. The big man fell back against a car, holding his jaw, the thing still in his cheek, yelling but through clenched teeth. He took the hook and, screaming, pulled it from his cheek, dropped it on the concrete floor, slapped one hand against the blood, the other grabbing hair as he howled and kicked first the body of the car and then Patty—over and over until he missed, lost his balance and fell into the scattered tools. He wasn't finished. He grabbed a pipe from the floor and hit Patty in the head a number of times before the man with the birthmark lunged into him and made him stop. He calmed him down. Before guiding him away, he tossed something onto Patty's motionless body; it looked like money. Then he spoke to the third man. The man came out from behind the girder and into the light. I saw him but the image didn't want to make sense; it was a trick, an absurdity. I squeezed my eyes shut but he was still there when I opened them. Something happened to my legs then and I fell between the barrels to the ground." Teddy picked up the bowl he had turned years ago from between his feet and held it as if waiting for someone to fill it with fruit. His throat quivered, the adam's apple moving up and down, as if something were lodged there.

"It was Dad," Ted got out.

An absolute silence filled the room.

I said, "What?"

"Dad?" Jamie said. "Are you sure?"

Ted's voice broke. "I saw him. It was the man with the birthmark, the big man, and our father."

"You're sure, Ted?" I could not imagine my father at that scene.

He nodded slowly.

"Positive?" Jamie asked. "Absolutely positive?"

Ted continued to nod sadly.

"Crazy," Frank said.

So it wasn't just the telescope crashing against the sidewalk that had marked my brother, I thought, not his innocence and trust shattering with it that turned him inward. He could have accepted and lived with that. As he could have accepted seeing Patty getting battered by Tony. It would not have been easy but he could have tucked it away into some corner of his brain. But our father had stepped out of the shadows in the garage. He had walked into the light and stood with Patty Leone, bloody and unconscious, at his feet, and Ted had seen him through the milky window. We saw the effects of the sight on Ted's face when Mrs. Falcone handed him over to my mother. Years later on television, I saw that same look on a child who, during a flood in Mississippi, had watched his parents get swept away. It was a look beyond physical shock and disbelief, rather a look from experiencing a force that had abruptly and completely altered the world.

"It must have been terrible for you," Jamie said, putting her hand on Teddy's shoulder. He did not act like he felt it.

"What was dad doing there?" I said. "Do you know, Frank?"

"No idea."

"It happened so long ago, can't you two let it rest?"

"No, Jamie," Frank said.

"But why? It's just old pain that we don't need."

"We have to know," Frank said. "People might have to pay."

"Pay? For God's sake, Frank, what's a vendetta going to do for you but get you in trouble?"

"It's not for me. It's for Patty." Frank looked back to Ted. "So what happened after that, Teddy?"

Teddy frowned, as if it were an effort to pick up where he had left off. "I was curled up there between the barrels. My head was spinning. I heard the garage door open, then the car doors open and close, a gunned engine, the car speeding away."

"Did they leave Patty there?" Frank asked.

Teddy shook his head no. "I'm sorry. I don't know. The next thing I remember is meeting Mrs. Falcone on Market Street."

"But you were gone for three days."

"When I was told that, I couldn't believe it; yet, as time went on things came back to me. They still do. Scenes and people, but they're as if from somebody else's life. Or from a bad dream." He put the wooden bowl on the radiator beside him. "I could never look at dad without seeing the other two men and what they did to Patty. I avoided him. I did not look at him. He would try, in his pathetic way, to talk to me, to draw me out, but I would turn away. I had to. There were those images in the garage between us. He was a kind man, wasn't he? All right, he sold stolen merchandise a few times, he stole copper pipe and plumbing fixtures from his jobs, he gambled, but this—" Teddy stopped. "If only he had helped Patty, or at least stopped the others from hurting him." Teddy choked.

"But Patty lived," Jamie said.

"He's an invalid." Teddy stood up, opened the drapes wide and stood facing the window, looking into the graying street.

No one moved or spoke for a while.

Then, one by one we joined Ted at the window. Jamie first, then me, then Frank. Cyril hung back. We stood watching a small girl drawing figures with chalk on the sidewalk, which Mrs. Falcone would promptly hose off when she discovered them.

FOURTEEN

We stood at the window for a long time, Ted between Jamie and me, Frank on my other side. My shoulders touched both Ted's and Frank's. I had the sense that Jamie and Ted leaned together on the other side, too, so that we were all connected while we watched the girl. No one spoke. Jamie did not want to know more than she heard, and Frank had gotten everything he could from Ted. We knew now what had happened to Patty. How he left the garage and wound up at the Home was anyone's guess. What our father was doing at the scene Ted described was a further mystery. More than anything, I was bothered that our father could hold a secret like Leone's beating to his grave. What other secrets did he retain during those silences at the kitchen table when he played solitaire for hours?

Ted left the window first and walked slowly up the stairs. Jamie turned away next, took Cyril by the hand and led him back to the kitchen. Frank and I continued to watch the street.

"There are a few things I'm not clear about in Ted's story," I said. "Why would Patty go to that garage, for one?"

"That's probably where he was going to get paid not to run away with Marie and marry her."

"But he didn't take the money," I said.

"No. Somewhere along the line he changed his mind, said no to the buy-off. Maybe he even told Tony that he'd never see Marie again. But that maniac, he had his eye on Marie himself, waiting for her to get three or four years older, he probably got pissed off. You can almost see it. There's some words, Tony can't hold his temper, then things get out of hand."

"Or it was intentional. They planned to beat up Patty or kill him from the beginning."

"That's more like Tony Buttons, sure."

"All right," I said. "But what was Dad doing there?"

"I don't know."

"I'm going to go see Tucci in a little bit and ask him."

We stood at the window a little longer without speaking, watching the girl draw her fantastic shapes.

Buttoni's car was not in the driveway; I felt relieved not to see it. Leo's BMW was there and, by the house, Tucci's Buick.

Mrs. Tucci answered the door and gave me a look first of surprise, then hatred. I stepped past her into the house before she could curse me or move.

Mrs. Tucci fixed a gaze on me that had the quality of a drill. "Why did you come back?"

"I'm not finished."

"You're finished."

"I have some questions I want answered."

"What questions?"

"They're for your husband."

"No. That's over."

"I'm sorry, I have to talk to him." I started down the marble hall.

"You! Stop!"

I kept walking until Leo stepped from the livingroom.

"I have an appointment," I said to him.

"I don't care what you have," Leo said. "She says to wait, you wait."

Mrs. Tucci came up. "I don't like you doing that."

"Should I throw him out?"

"No, Leo, you go back." She gently pushed against his thick arm, encouraging him into the livingroom. Turning to me she said, "Go," and pointed with her chin down the hall. She waited until I moved, then followed me closely to the room off the front entrance. "Sit."

"I'd rather stand."

She looked at me with that old hatred, her hands balled into fists at her sides; I expected her to throw a punch at me.

"Where's my daughter?"

"I don't know." Marie said the night before that she could no longer stand to live in that house. Good for her if she decided to leave immediately.

"She didn't tell you where she was going?"

"Why should she?"

"She at your house?"

"I said I didn't know where she is. Now please tell your husband I'm here."

Mrs. Tucci narrowed her eyes. I stared back, mimicking her. "More tapes, bastard?"

"More tapes."

I waited for her to swing her balled fists but she spun and left the room.

In five minutes I sat across from her husband in the den, the tape recorder quietly whirring between us. The single lamp on the table burned and cast thick shadows, and the twin clocks ticked on the mantle. Tucci wore slippers and a bathrobe, his bald legs sticking out from the bottom and looking brittle. He still had the gap in his teeth from the mugging and the faded purple of a bruise on his cheek. He did not look well, and when he told me to close the door his voice itself sounded cancerous.

"I want to ask you some questions," I began.

"Ask."

"What was my father doing at the garage where Patty Leone was beaten up?"

Tucci stiffened slightly. "How do you know about that?"

I told him about Ted running away, meeting Patty, and what my brother saw through the garage window. He listened closely, nodding at points, frowning at others. When Tucci went to speak after I finished, he coughed deeply, his lungs sounding wet and spongy.

"Excuse me," he said, bringing up sputum and spitting into a handkerchief. He returned the handkerchief to the pocket of his bathrobe. "Your father ran money for me once in a while. He was just filling in for somebody that night. He was told to take the money to the garage and give it to Tony."

"The money he brought was for Patty to leave the city?"

"Yeah. I didn't want Patty running away with my daughter. She was just a kid, sixteen, but she was crazy about him. Tony couldn't scare him away, so I thought I could offer Patty money, get him out of Marie's sight long enough for her to forget about him. She had a crush, I figured. It happens. But maybe it was true love. That happens, too. It was something deep, because look at her, she never got over it. If I knew how deep it was, I would've told her to wait a few years and she could marry him with my blessing. But I didn't get the chance to do that. Tony came to me that night with a bandage on his face and told me what happened. He said Patty refused the money and attacked him. Tony had to rough him up in self defense. He didn't tell me how bad he hurt the kid. But I told Tony to make sure Patty didn't show up at the house all banged-up for Marie to see. That would be the end of her; she'd follow Patty to the moon. But they said they didn't know where Patty was. Johnny Plum had gone back to the garage after taking Tony to the hospital but Patty wasn't there. I had people watching out in front of the house to grab him if he came around but he never did. Nobody knew what happened to him. He disappeared."

"But he didn't."

"No." Mr. Tucci said, winded, "but Tony and Plum thought he did. They thought Patty came to and decided it was better that he get out of the city. I thought that myself. I mean, where was he? It was messy the way things turned out, but they turned out. Patty was gone." He coughed again and spit what he brought up into the handkerchief.

"Where did Patty go? Do you know?"

Tucci slowly nodded. "It was none of his business but your father went back to the garage."

"My father?"

"About a week after the thing in the garage, I got your father over here to do some plumbing work. When I went to pay him after, he wouldn't take any money. Not just that, he pulls out a wad of dough and says it's mine. Then he tries to leave. I made him tell me what he was doing. He didn't want to talk about it, you could see, but he did. He said he went back to the garage after Plum and Tony went to the hospital. Patty was still knocked out. Your father took him to a hospital uptown so he wouldn't run into anybody in South Philly. They had to operate on Leone's head to save his life. He had a fractured skull and a couple of blood clots. They saved him but his brain was screwed up. I asked your father if anybody knew what he did, and he said no. He took Patty's wallet from him and told the people at the hospital that he was a cousin. Your father had a good head. A good heart, too. He could take pity but he was smart enough not to make tracks."

"Tracks to you."

"Tracks to me, tracks to anybody." He paused and breathed deeply, the air passing loudly and wet through his lungs. "Leone was still in the hospital when I talked to your father the day he did the plumbing. We went to see Patty in the hospital the next day. Turned out your father was seeing Patty every day. One of those days, Patty was awake but he was like he is now, an empty bucket. You stood in front of him, talked to him, and it was like you weren't there. The thing about his legs, why he couldn't walk, was from his bad brain, too. This kid wasn't anything to me, but I started to think if Marie somehow saw him like that, she would lose her head. I mean, he wasn't even a person anymore; he was a turnip. So I thought about getting him out of there." Tucci paused, looking fatigued, and I thought he was going to leave the story at that. "Your father just wheeled Patty out."

"Why not Tony Buttons or Plum?"

"There was no reason for them to know. But it was something else. Your father. A guy like Tony might think your father had slighted him by coming to me. Accidents could happen. I decided to keep it a secret. Let everybody think Patty took off for another city. Slim the chance of Marie finding out. Your father I could trust not to say anything. I was waiting outside with a car when he wheeled Patty out and we drove away. I put him in that place where your mother wound up. Patty up there, without any sense, a new name, it's no wonder it looked like he disappeared. Only thing was, Marie didn't forget him. His aunt either."

"Mrs. Falcone."

"Yeah. She called me up a few days after that night in the garage. She introduced herself. She said Marie had been around to see her, looking for Patty, so she knew who I was. She wanted to know if I knew what happened to her nephew. What could I tell her? I said I didn't know anything. She said she knew I was lying, just like that, and I knew that she knew. She called me again. Again I said I didn't know anything. Again she said I was a liar. She called about once a week for a month, then every month for a year, then every year for six, seven years. It was always the same. 'You are lying.' She believed that I was responsible for Patty disappearing. That's why she spit at me." Tucci coughed again, and when the handkerchief came away from his mouth I saw blood. He didn't seem surprised or concerned.

"You said you wanted to keep it quiet, but you sent Frank to the Home."

"Yes," he said, nodding slowly, as if deep in thought. "When I looked at my daughter, how gloomy she was, I thought of how happy she'd been when she was seeing Patty. It worked on me. Then I found out about the cancer. I started to worry that I would die with Patty being in that place and nobody knowing. It's a nice place, the best for him, but if they didn't get paid, what could they do but kick him out? You read in the newspapers about those places run by the state for people like Patty and it's always bad. The patients getting beaten, raped, having to sleep in their own shit. It wasn't just thinking about Marie that got to me, how hurt she would be if any of those things happened to Patty when I could've done something about it, and especially if she knew I didn't. I started to feel responsible for what happened, too. You understand? So, I had to tell somebody about Patty, somebody who would make sure he got the best care. That was Frank. Because he had liked Patty so much and because I could trust him to do it."

"Does he know that yet?"

"We talked."

"Does Marie know?"

"I'm afraid what it will do to her to see Patty like that," Tucci said. "I decided to tell her anyway. Let her scream, curse me. But she left the house early in the morning and hasn't come back. If she doesn't come back, you'll tell her what she has to know when you see her. Ok, Vincent? Promise me?"

I nodded.

"And you'll give her the memoirs. Let her decide what she wants to do with them."

"All right."

He coughed again. After his lungs settled, he asked weakly, "All your questions answered now?"

I hesitated before speaking. "Johnny Plum went to the Home with Frank, and a few days later he was killed. Who killed him?"

"I know he went with Frank; your brother told me. But I don't know why he was killed or who did it. Could be Tony. Maybe Plum *did* recognize Patty when he saw him, went back to the city, told Tony, and then, I don't know, said something that made Buttons nervous. Tony whacked him maybe and made it look like a hit. But I could be wrong."

"He wants your tapes."

"I know." Tucci sighed; I heard liquids in his chest. "Everybody wants the tapes. Somebody in the house even told Maglio about the tapes. You got any ideas who?"

I had barely drawn a breath to speak when the door burst open and Mrs. Tucci charged in.

"I did! I called him!" She seized the tape recorder and, lifting it over her head, threw it against the wall, where it shattered, pieces of it flying outward and the cassette dropping to the floor. "I did! I did! I did!" Mrs. Tucci shrieked, bringing the heel of her black shoe down upon the cassette over and over.

"What are you doing?" Tucci worked himself out of the seat and tried to stop her, but she shoved him away with one arm as easily as a child. He stumbled back down on the sofa as his wife continued to stomp the cassette.

"Stop that," he said, working himself up again.

"Shut up, you fool!" Again, when he reached her, Mrs. Tucci shoved against his thin chest, knocking him over the coffee table and to the floor.

I went to help him. Taking Tucci under the shoulders, I lifted him to the sofa and eased him back into the cushions. That close to him, I *could* smell something of his decay.

His wife spun toward us, her eyes wild, fists balled, mouth open as if she meant to bite as well as punch. "You idiot!" she yelled. "Telling him everything, telling the tape. My God, so stupid you are, so weak. Leo! George!"

Leo already stood behind her, filling the doorway; beyond him, George stood in the hallway, looking anxious to rush in.

"Yes, Tony killed Plum," Mrs. Tucci screamed, "just like he should've killed that half-Irish shit Leone. That dumb man Johnny got sentimental and wanted to tell Marie that he was alive. Then she would never marry Tony. No, he had to go." She turned her glare to me. "And you! I want the tapes."

"No," Tucci said.

"Shut up, dead man. I talked to your doctor. I know what's wrong with you. Why did you have to be so weak, so stupid? Why those goddamn tapes?

Now you can't die in peace." She looked over her shoulder. "Leo. George."

The men started into the room.

Mr. Tucci said their names, his voice frail.

"Don't listen to him," Mrs. Tucci said to them. "He has cancer. He'll be dead in a week."

The men took me each by an arm and pulled me roughly out of the room and down the hall. Behind me, Mrs. Tucci continued to shout and curse at her husband, while he coughed so powerfully it sounded like bloody chunks of lung were being worked loose.

Passing the dark alcove, I said, "People know I'm here."

"Shut up," Leo said.

"You can't—"

"Shut—"

I heard the thunk and felt the shock transferred from George's neck to my arm where he held me before I saw anything, and even then it was a blur. George stiffened for a moment and began to fall even before the second thunk made me wince as if it was my head getting cracked. Leo made a noise then, a kind of strangled yipe, somebody's name half-formed in a terrified throat, before the blur struck him, too. I heard the thunk, winced, heard it again, and felt Leo let go of me and pitch against the wall, then slump to the floor, the back of his head trailing blood down the wallpaper.

I turned around and saw Frank, holding one of the baseball bats from our cellar.

"Stay here." He pulled out a gun and started down the hall.

When Mrs. Tucci stuck her head into the hall to see what the commotion was, he pointed the gun at her. She froze, and Frank brushed past her into the den. He came out a few moments later, carrying Tucci in his arms. Tucci held the gun.

"Vince, open the door," Frank called.

I stepped over the bodies of Leo and George to get to the front door. I opened it and stepped outside into the warm country darkness.

"My car's down the road," Frank said when he came into the doorway. "Take us to it." He did not stop but continued walking past me over the lawn and toward the car as he talked.

"How did you know?" I asked beside him.

"Don't ask questions. Just get us out of here."

At the urgency in his voice, I hurried and reached the car before he did, opening the back door. He put Tucci down and took the gun from him. Tucci went slowly into the back seat as I got behind the wheel and started the car. Frank closed the back door and came around to the passenger side.

"Let's go," he said, getting in. "Make a left at the entrance."

I backed down the driveway and onto the unlighted road, stopped, and sped in the direction of Frank's car. No one else was on the road, the sides of it deep black except for the scattered buildings.

"Frank?" Tucci said from the back seat, his voice raspy.

"Yes, Mr. Tucci?"

"Frank, what time is the flight?"

"Seven in the morning."

"You have clothes for me?"

"Everything you need."

"And Patty?"

"They're moving him to the other place before noon."

"Good."

I glanced in the rearview mirror at Tucci, then at Frank. "What's going on?"

"There's not time. I'll call you later."

"Frank, tell him," Tucci said weakly from behind us.

"Vince, don't tell this to anybody. We're leaving the country tomorrow."

"Is that why you wanted to know how much cash you could get in a short notice? You *are* leaving."

"Only temporarily."

"How long is that?"

"Until I die," Tucci said from the darkness.

Frank pointed to the side of the road. "There's the car."

I saw it in my headlights and began to lean toward the shoulder of the road. "Was this planned?"

"Look, Vince, we don't have time to go into that."

"It's ok, Frank," Tucci said, making an effort, it seemed, to speak, "tell Vincent, tell him everything."

Gravel pocked in the wheelwells as I went onto the shoulder and pulled up to Frank's car.

"Mr. Tucci has always intended to do this, but a few things made it necessary to do it now," Frank said quickly, "like people trying to kill him, for one. Mr. Tucci, we should hurry."

"Because of the tapes?" I said.

"Tell him."

"The tapes were made to keep them from killing him in the first place," Frank said, impatiently. "Look, a month ago I was approached by a coupla big guys about knocking Mr. Tucci out of the way.

I said I'd think about it, then went to Mr. Tucci and told him. He told me to stall them, then a little later he wanted to meet you. You know the rest, except that was the first I heard about the memoirs and the tapes." Frank turned around in his seat. "Mr. Tucci, you ready?"

"Tell him the rest," Tucci said.

"Ok, look, he didn't try to hide the taping because he knew what the scum would think when they caught on. They would worry they were on the tapes, and they would think they couldn't do anything to Mr. Tucci unless they had them, were sure the tapes weren't sitting somewhere to be found or sent to somebody. Like for how we handled Maglio."

"But why did you bring me into this?" I asked.

"I needed an outsider," Tucci said, weaker still, "somebody who would throw them off. Plus, you're Frank's brother."

"Mr. Tucci, we have to get going. Something could've gone wrong and Tony's on his way back from the poker game Petie Bird took him to."

"Yes, ok." Tucci leaned forward and put his hand on my shoulder as Frank left the car. "You'll find the rest of your money in the mail. Thank you."

I turned. I could barely see his face in the darkness. "You're welcome," I said, feeling bewildered.

Frank opened his door and helped Tucci out, holding onto his elbow as he walked Tucci to his car, then ran back to me.

"One other thing," he said, "send Jamie and Cyril back to Ohio first thing in the morning, if you can't get them to go tonight. Send Teddy back to the woods. You get out of the city, too, at least for a while. And thank Lou Cocco for me. He'll tell you why." He put his hand behind my neck, briefly squeezed, then ran back to his car.

"Frank!"

Within seconds, he did a sharp U-turn and tore up the road.

It was in the brief flare of his headlights close to my windshield that I saw the note on the dashboard. I turned on the inside light and read it. "Meet me in the orchard. Marie," it said, and under her name she had drawn a small map. I started the car and did my best to follow the map in the dark.

I drove down those quiet lonely roads made vaguely familiar the night Marie had me take her to the orchard after our trip to the shore, passed the few simple houses and the open fields and did not get lost. The back of the car scraped against the macadam when I turned and bounced into the dirt road that ringed the orchard. I continued to bounce as I rumbled beside the apple trees, looking for a sign of Marie. I drove a few minutes, the headlights scattering darkness, made a left turn and stopped when I came to a barrel blocking my way. In a few seconds, she appeared from the black trees and tentatively walked toward the car. I rolled down the window.

"It's me," I said.

Her steps quickened as she crossed through the headlight beams and went around to the passenger side of the car.

"I'm so glad you came," she said, excitedly and almost breathless, as she slid in beside me. "I didn't know if you would. Maybe you didn't want anything more to do with me after George and Leo. But you came. I'm happy."

"Marie—"

"Wait, let me finish. I know I'm going a mile a minute but if I don't say this now I won't say it at all. I didn't want you to think that I didn't like you. I do. It's just been hard for me to act normal. You kissed me when I saw you last and I panicked. It's because I haven't been kissed since—well, for a long time. I didn't know how to act. I'm not peculiar, just out of practice. Well, maybe a little peculiar, but I'm not nuts. You can see that, can't you? Say that I'm not nuts."

"You're not nuts."

"Thank you. It's just been that for years I don't know what I've been doing with my life. It's as though I had locked myself in a cellar and lived like a nun. But I've swept that all away. I'm starting over."

"Marie—"

"Wait, let me tell you about my day. I woke up early, which I never do, and went out for a walk, which I also never do—you see, I wanted to break all my old habits. I walked across the field in the back of the house to here. There was dew on the grass, some gossamer. The orchard was empty and very quiet. I knew I was there for the last time, saying goodbye. I walked through the orchard, then went home. An hour later, I drove to Philadelphia to the train station and took one of every brochure they had, describing trips all over the country. Then I went around to travel agencies and collected brochures from them. Then I went into a bookstore and picked a half dozen travel books, looking for a place I might want to go to and live in. After that, it was to the library to research cities and jobs, to figure out how I wanted to make a living, because I was going to have to do that now. No more living like a dependent child at home. I ate lunch at—"

"Marie," I said, trying again to stop her. But she hardly paused, and went on in that breathless manner as if a train already waited for her and she had only a few minutes to tell me everything she wanted: how she had gone around the city and in the afternoon the suburban malls buying new clothes because she wanted to throw out, if possible, everything she had worn before yesterday, anything that would remind her of the life she was ending. She bought running shoes for jogging and a tennis racket because she wanted to get into shape. Along with the travel books, Marie bought cook books because she had never learned to cook much more than eggs while living at home all those years. She allowed a salesgirl in a department store to make-up her face with expensive cosmetics. She bought newspapers and scanned the want ads, called about apartments for rent, and looked at several in town, not because she decided to move into the city but because she wanted to familiarize herself with the process.

I went to say her name again, stop her, but she rushed on, that imaginary train about to creep away from the platform without her, her "new life" on it, the old one escapable only by telling me how she had done it, as if speaking her reversals of habits and the changes underway would validate and make them permanent.

"I ate supper at a place called Marabella's, then went to a movie. I didn't want to go home, back to that house with all its reminders there like a quicksand just waiting to drag me down and drown me. I also had some difficult things to do there, the final things that would cut me loose completely. I meant to build a fire and burn anything I owned that was attached to a memory, especially the sentimental ones: a few books, some clothes, journals, letters. These things were like radiation that kept me weak. I—"

"Marie, wait," I said, determined to say what I had been trying to since she came into the car. "Patty's alive."

She stopped in the middle of a word, her mouth frozen open, her eyes, in the pale moonlight, suddenly frightened.

I touched her arm. "I'm sorry."

"How? Where?" she uttered, her voice quivering.

I said, "There are a lot of things to explain, and some to Mrs. Falcone as well. Let me take you there."

"What things? Are they bad?"

"Marie, this is hard for me. Let me take you to Mrs. Falcone's and do it once." I started the car.

Marie leaned back into the seat and wrapped her arms around herself as if cold. "Hurry."

That was the last word between us until we reached Philadelphia. I maneuvered the car around the barrel in the middle of the dirt road, the weeds brushing against the floor, the beams from the headlights knocking against the trees, and I rumbled around the perimeter of the orchard. I tried to stay in the ruts but they were uneven and the car jostled and bounced. On the third bend, a lone parked car sat nestled between two trees; as the headlights passed over the back window, I saw a head pop up, watch us pass, then duck back down out of view. I looked in the rearview mirror as we drove on, and in moments the darkness swallowed all of the parked car except a glint of silver moonlight reflecting off the chrome bumper. That dime of light, too, vanished when I turned into the last leg surrounding the orchard. I picked up speed and the car bounced harder. The moon streaked crazily into and out of the black windshield. I rushed so quickly through the final bend that the tail of the car briefly skidded sideways in the dirt. The main road came quickly, but I barely slowed down for the gully or for anyone driving without headlights. The rear scraped in the dirt and we lurched onto the macadam. In a few minutes we were speeding on Route 42, heading back to Philadelphia.

A half hour later, after fighting the panic on the bridge, we were in my neighborhood. I parked in front of the Church of the Epiphany just as the carillon went off and dropped its somber bongs on our heads. Mrs. Falcone came to her door before we reached it, as if the bells had announced our arrival.

I introduced the two women.

"We remember each other," Mrs. Falcone said.

"Yes," Marie said.

"I have something to tell you, Mrs. Falcone."

Mrs. Falcone nodded, held the door open for us, and we walked into the anise-smelling house. She led us to the diningroom and offered us tea. We both declined.

The women sat down at the table and I told them everything I knew, but avoided their reactions by looking at the viney thing that ran in green and maroon sinuations through Mrs. Falcone's carpet.

I told my story and answered their choking questions inside an hour, and then I walked out of Mrs. Falcone's house, leaving the two women in the diningroom holding each other and crying. I had passed on my secrets to them as Tucci had to me, and they knew as much as I did now. I held nothing from them. There was no more mystery, except Patty's appearance, the way he looked, and they would satisfy that in the morning. They would go to the Home, they would see him, there would be more grief.

I stepped out of the house and into the warm night, feeling light and unburdened until those few intense minutes between Mrs. Tucci bursting into the den and Frank running back to his car came rushing in on me. He had saved me from Leo and George, but now I had to get Jamie and the others out of the city, and I was to follow. Tucci had led me to believe that his desire to have his memoirs written was to explain himself to his daughter and to others, and thereby gain their understanding. I still believed that to be partially true, but in the car by the road I learned that the tapes had mainly been created to protect Tucci from those forces he had spent a lifetime nurturing. Nothing but money had been gained from my experience with Tucci. But had I expected anything more?

I thought of sitting in the orchard with Marie, poised to fall in love with her, but I could not keep from her what I knew about Patty. Instantly, I lost her to him.

When I walked in the house, it was quiet. No one was in the livingroom, and the kitchen, when I walked back there, was empty too. I peeked into the cellar but it was dark.

"Hello," I called, "anybody home?"

I heard a thud from upstairs.

"Jamie? Ted?"

There was another thud.

"What are you guys doing up there?" I started up the steps. "Cyril torturing you?" It was dark in the hall because I had not changed the dead bulb in the light fixture, but I could see from the light coming up from the livingroom that all the doors were closed.

Another thud came from my parents old bedroom.

"Jamie?" If the light were on in there, it would have shone at the bottom of the door, but it was dark at the floor too. I halted. "Hey, are you guys in there?" The thudding answered me and, with it, a muffled yell. I hurried then, threw open the door and switched on the light.

My breath caught. I saw Cyril first, lying on the floor with his hands tied behind his back, the rope going to his feet, then to the radiator. Duct tape covered his mouth. One eye was swollen nearly shut and a split at his cheekbone had made a small pool of blood on the floor. Ted lay near him, tied and gagged in the same way and tethered to the same radiator. His face too was bruised and beneath each nostril a stream of blood had run.

"Jamie?" I asked, going to them.

Cyril banged his head on the floor, making noises in his throat.

"Is she here?" I peeled the tape from Cyril's mouth.

He gulped air. "Other room."

I peeled the tape from Ted's mouth and hurried

out and down the hall. I threw open the door to the middle room; it had been ransacked, but Jamie was not in it. I dashed to the last room at the back of the house, pushed open the door and flicked on the light. My breath caught again, but for long moments it would not start.

My sister lay naked on the bed, an arm and a leg tied to each one of the four posts, her mouth taped closed, hair dishevelled, her upturned watery broken eyes looking at me in both fright and sorrow.

I took the sheet from the floor and covered her. Then I put my thumbnail under the edge of the tape and lifted it slowly so as not to hurt her. But once I had the tape in my fingers, Jamie jerked her head and pulled the tape away from her lips. Immediately, she turned her head to the side and spit several objects from her mouth. I looked at them, first in puzzlement, then I understood.

They were buttons.

FIFTEEN

I slapped the buttons off the sheet and untied Jamie's arms and legs.

She sat up, holding the sheet to her chest, looking dazed. "Cyril?" she asked.

"I'll get him." I gathered her scattered clothes from the floor and put them on her knees, my eyes burning.

I hurried back to the front room, untied first Cyril, who staggered out as soon as he was free, then Ted. His nose looked broken.

"You all right?" I asked, my hand on his shoulder.

He nodded slowly, staring at his purple wrists where the ropes had been.

"Come on," I said, helping him to his feet. "We have to get you washed up."

He looked at himself in the mirror. His hand came up slowly and he scraped dried blood from his face, then gently touched his nose and the broad welt from the tape around his mouth. He moved his jaw from side to side, loosening it.

"Jamie?" he asked.

"Let's go see."

Jamie was sitting in the same spot in the bed, Cyril holding her, slightly rocking, their cheeks together. Jamie faced us, Cyril faced away. She opened her eyes when we came in, then closed them. Ted and I stared speechless until I took my brother by the arm and drew him out of the room.

"It was the big man from the garage and a smaller man," Ted told me downstairs.

I described Tommy Green.

"Yes, that was the other one. How do you know him?"

"He worked for Frank until about a week ago. Tell me what happened."

Ted had gone out for a walk and came in the house to find Tommy pointing a gun at him and Buttoni pointing one at Cyril and Jamie. Ted was punched when he told the men to take what they wanted and leave, and Buttoni pistol-whipped Cyril for not answering a question.

"Something about tapes," my brother said.

Buttoni and Green took them upstairs. They tied up the men and left the room with Jamie.

Ted heard the crashing sounds from my room as the men looked for the Tucci tapes. He heard their voices and then their steps going toward the back of the house, then the door closing, a sound of scuffling, a short half-yell from Jamie, then footsteps coming toward him and Cyril. It was Green. He grabbed the tape and the rope from the bed. Cyril yelled behind his gag and flopped about on the floor trying to lunge at Green. Tommy kicked him and turned out the light as he left the room. The footsteps receded, the back door closed again, there was another brief yell from Jamie, then more sounds of struggle that went on for a time. All the while, Cyril flopped on his chest from shoulder to shoulder, inching toward the closed door, pulling against his ropes, making noises in his throat. He would stop to listen for the struggling sounds, hear them, squirm again. Only when the back bedroom door opened again and the steps of the two men went down the stairs and out the door did Cyril stop moving. I came in the house from Mrs. Falcone's almost two hours later.

Ted and I heard someone coming down the stairs, looked up and saw Cyril.

"How long before the police get here?" he asked.

"We didn't call them."

"What the hell are you waiting for?"

"A few things have to be considered."

"Consider your sister, consider us. You saw Jamie. You know what happened to her. Look at Ted and me. We got our heads clobbered because of Frank and you. They told us that. I don't know what you've been doing that people like that would want to hurt us. But I'll be goddamned if I'm not going to tell the police what they did." He started for the telephone.

"Cyril, wait."

"I'm not waiting. I'm calling them and then we're going to the hospital." He picked up the receiver.

"Cyril, they could've killed you if they wanted. There's a reason they didn't. Ted?"

Ted looked at the floor. "It's true, Cyril."

"I don't believe this." Cyril said. "Never mind what happened to Ted and me. My wife, your sister, has been raped by two men. Not smacked around, not puched in the stomach. Raped. You want me to spell it out for you, give you the specifics?"

"You have to understand something—"

"I don't want to understand! I've been taught that the reason we have police is to protect us from the kinds of creeps that attacked us. That's what I understand. I don't care about these mob formalities. There's a crime committed, you call the police." He began to dial.

"Hold on, Cyril." I took his hand away from the digits.

"Goddamn it, Vincent! It's your fault what they did and you care only about yourself. You're one of them."

"That's not true."

"Then what are you going to do about it?"

"Call Frank." I thought I might catch him at his apartment and, if not, at the Hilton Hotel near the airport.

"All right, call Frank. After you do, I'm still calling the police, even if I have to go outside to do it."

I dialed Frank's number with Cyril standing beside me. After several rings, the phone was answered but no voice came at the other end.

"Frank?"

Still nothing.

"Frank, it's Vincent."

"Turn on the TV, you sorry bastard," a familiar voice said, "see what else could happen to your fam-

BLOOD CONFESSIONS

ily if I don't get any copies of those tapes." The line went dead.

Blood drained from my face.

"What's wrong?" Cyril asked.

"I don't know." I crossed the room and turned on the television.

"What are you doing?"

I didn't answer Cyril as the picture came into focus. The late news had just begun and the lead, "late-breaking story" was a shooting at the airport Hilton, "possibly mob-related," that left two men dead. The anchorman disappeared as the news station switched to a live camera at the scene of the murders. A woman reporter, facing the camera with a microphone to her lips, stood in a hallway of the hotel. Behind her, police and plainclothes detectives swarmed. Apparently, the reporter told us, the men were gunned down as they were about to enter their room; the key was still in the door. There were no eyewitnesses but several hotel guests in nearby rooms heard the gunshots, looked into the hall, and saw one of the men stagger about ten feet before collapsing.

The camera left her face and focused on a body beneath a sheet some distance down the hall beyond the police barrier.

Asked by the anchorman if she had the names of the victims yet, the reporter said she did not. All she was told, she said, was that one man was in his thirties and the other in his sixties or seventies.

"It could be somebody else," my brother said, behind me.

"Yes." But I knew otherwise.

"What is it?" Cyril asked.

Neither Ted nor I answered him.

The reporter went on. "I'm trying to get one of the many policemen here to talk to me but it looks like they've been told to keep their lips tight on this one. Officer? Sir?" She grabbed a cop by his sleeve. "Can you tell us what happened here tonight."

"Ask the suits," he said, brushing past her.

The phone rang.

"Don't answer it," I said, turning off the television.

"Maybe it's Frank."

"Cyril, it's not Frank!" I shouted. "Now get out of here. Take Jamie to the hospital."

"Vince."

"Go!"

Ted said my name.

"You, too," I said more gently. "See about those cuts and your nose."

Cyril lingered in front of me, then went up the stairs as the phone continued to ring.

Shortly after they had gone, two detectives, along with the special agents, Russo and Silver, showed up at the house and asked to come in. I left the door open and walked back into the livingroom. The detectives were cordial and polite; the agents hung back without speaking, letting the detectives take charge.

"I have some bad news for you," one detective began.

"I know what it is," I said.

"You saw it on the TV?"

I nodded.

"Did you see where another man was shot with him?"

"They got Tucci," Silver blurted.

"For Christ sake, Carl," Russo said.

"What? Tucci's nothing to him. Is he?" He looked to me for an answer. I looked away.

Russo took the detective's arm. "You think we can have a few minutes with him?"

"Sure."

The detectives moved a few feet away and the agents came closer.

"What can you tell us?" Russo asked.

"Only what I saw on the news."

"Which isn't much."

"I thought you had surveillance."

"We're on a limited budget like everybody else, plus it's August and people are on vacation. We can't watch everybody all the time."

"It's a shame because you missed a lot."

"I guess we did. Can you help us out by telling us about your time in New Jersey?"

"Tucci's dead. What do you want, something to make sure he goes to hell instead of purgatory?"

"Another wiseass."

"Carl, take it easy," Russo said. "Vincent, we were hoping you could give us something on Buttoni and anyone else. Leo Leonardo? George Capaldi?"

As Russo said their names, I saw those two on the marble floor of the hall at Tucci's house, their heads haloed by blood. I heard Buttoni's voice on the phone, warning me about further hurting the family if I did not give him the copies of the tapes he thought existed.

"I can't help you."

"That's final?"

"Yes."

Russo turned to the detectives. "He's yours."

Did I know who might want to kill my brother? the detective asked. I said I didn't. Who was the last person I saw with Frank? Myself. Were there any names Frank had mentioned in connection with any kind of disagreement? No.

"Ok. We just need you to come down to the morgue to identify the body."

The men preceded me out the door. Several of the neighbors stood in front of their houses and watched the detectives and me as we came out into the humidity. They had known my parents, they had watched us grow from children into adults, they had seen my father being carried out on an ambulance stretcher for the last time, they had seen my mother's mind crumble. Here was more of my life for them to share. They watched me serious and grave as I walked down the steps, turned and started up the sidewalk. None of them were talking. I saw Lou Cocco, looking grim, and wondered what he would tell me about Frank when I spoke to him. Mrs. Falcone, her house dark, was not among the neighbors. I thought briefly about Marie. Was she still in there?

Walking up the block toward the detectives' car, I saw Purdy Gant standing at the corner in a circle of lamplight and facing me, his hands twisted together in front of his stomach. Like the others, he watched us without moving and kept his distance. When I got in the car and was driven past Purdy, he moved only his head to watch me. I smiled at him, and when he saw it his sad face contracted as if he might howl.

We arrived at the morgue in fifteen minutes. The detectives led us past a guard—"Hiya, Andy"—and down a cool hall that smelled of disinfectant, then into a colder room where a man sat at a steel desk reading the newspaper. One detective stayed talking to the man at the desk and the other led me into another colder room where the bodies were. My brother was on the nearest table. The detective led me there and pulled down the green sheet.

"That him?"

The face was unmarked, the eyes slightly open, the mouth parted enough to show a little of his teeth. The face did not look surprised, irritated, in pain or peaceful. It looked nothing but dead, and I hardly recognized that face as Frank's. Without life, without that tension in his face, the bitterness in his eyes even while laughing, he was not Frank but only flesh that happened to be in a shape similar to that of my brother. I did not look at him long. I did not touch him. A dull throb in my stomach that would last for days began then.

I nodded. "Yes."

"Good." He wrote something on a form. "They'll scoop the body tomorrow."

"What?"

"Autopsy. We'll need the bullets for evidence." He told me where they were, where Frank had been shot. "Then you can have a funeral home pick it up."

"It?" I said, angry. "That's my brother there."

"The *body* of your brother."

"You shouldn't refer to him in that way. You don't know anything about him."

"I know what I see."

I glared at him.

"Sign the form," he said.

I signed and started from that chilly room with the shadowless light and odd smell.

The detective followed me closely and we walked down the hall together.

"Phillies win, Andy?" he asked the guard without stopping.

"Lost in the eleventh."

At the door, I told the detective that I didn't need a ride.

"You don't want to walk that far through some of those neighborhoods," he said.

"I'll take a cab."

"Suit yourself." He opened the exit door for us. "I'll be in touch."

I didn't take a cab but walked home without trouble.

I entered the house around one o'clock. Jamie and Cyril had not returned from the hospital. Ted had come home and sat, stitched and bandaged, in the wing chair.

"Doing ok?" I asked.

"Fine."

"I guess you won't be coming back here any time soon."

"I don't know about that."

"Need anything?"

"Just to rest."

I went upstairs, looked into my ransacked bedroom, felt the throb in my stomach turn into a stab

BLOOD CONFESSIONS

and backed out. I closed the door, not ready to face that scene yet. Then I went into the back bedroom where I had found Jamie. As I gathered the pieces of rope and duct tape, I kept my eyes away from the bed because I would start thinking about what happened there and begin to shake. Even when I stripped the sheets from the bed, I did it with my head turned to the side. Carrying the sheets under my arm, I walked into the front room where Cyril and Ted had been tied and picked up the rope and the bits of tape from there. I threw the rope and the tape in a trashcan and returned to the middle room. I looked in again, stared for several moments and closed the door.

I went downstairs and took several plastic trash bags from the kitchen cabinet and went back upstairs with them. Ted watched me go by but remained quiet. I emptied the trashcan with the ropes and tape into a bag, followed that with the sheets, and tied the bag closed. Then I went into my bedroom. I began there by returning the drawers, where the tapes had been, to the dresser. I gathered the clothing and papers and everything else that had been dumped on the floor and filled the trashbags with it. Anything Green and Buttons may have touched, I threw out. Like the sheet, I didn't want to have anything around that would remind me of that night. It was just as well that they took the cash in my drawer; I would have gotten rid of that too.

I put the trashbags in the hall and checked the rooms a final time. After satisfying myself that, short of setting the rooms on fire, I had removed or straightened everything the men had touched, I took the bags downstairs and went out into the back yard.

The dog across the alley barked at the sound of my door. I put the bags against the green wooden fence nearest the alley, wanting to put the bags as far from the house as possible. I lingered out there in the darkness and the dead humid air, gritting my teeth against the hurt in my stomach and the urge to shake. The dog stopped barking, whimpered for a short time, then quieted entirely. I heard the fans and the air conditioners humming in the windows and nothing else. All the windows were dark. I smelled garbage. Looking up at the sky at the sound of a jet, I saw blinking lights moving across deep purple. Beyond it, the light of the stars did not pierce the haze.

Frank was dead.

I went back into the house and sat on the sofa across from Ted. He was asleep in the wing chair. He was still there four hours later when Jamie and Cyril came in as the windows began to lighten with the morning. I was still on the sofa, wide awake. If I had slept, I dreamed that I stayed awake all night sitting in my livingroom, watching Ted and fighting off images.

After Jamie came in, I went to embrace her but she went straight up the stairs without a word. Her face was pale, her eyes dull. Ted had woken at the sound of the door and looked after Jamie as she climbed. We heard her turn in the hall and walk into the front bedroom.

"How is she?" I asked Cyril.

"Numb. She just wants to go home."

"I'm sorry about all this."

"So am I." He shook his head. "A TV was on in the emergency room and I saw the news about Frank while Jamie was being treated. I didn't realize what we were watching earlier."

"They shot him four times," I said, "twice in the chest, once in the stomach, once in the upper arm. I was at the morgue." My voice cracked.

"You had to identify the body?"

"Detectives came after you left and took me there. His face was unmarked."

"I didn't know Frank well. I knew that he was the black sheep, the troublemaker, but no one deserves to be shot down like that."

"Does Jamie know?"

Cyril shook his head. "She didn't need another shock so I didn't say anything."

I said, "She has to be told."

"Yes, I know."

"I'll tell her," Teddy said, and went up the stairs.

Cyril sat down at the other end of the sofa. "You read about it but you never think it's going to happen to you," he said. "Or you hear about it. Somebody breaks into somebody's house and assaults or kills the innocent people there. You feel momentarily bad for them, knock on wood that it wasn't you. But you can't know what it's like unless yours is the house the misfits have broken into, yours is the head they strike. The physical pain is nothing next to the other, the anguish, what happened to Jamie. And now Frank." He touched his bandage, seemed to listen for a sound above our heads. "You should be up there, too."

"Yes. I'm going." I stood up, my legs wobbly from having sat all night, and climbed the stairs to the front bedroom. I could see the open suitcase on the bed from the hall, but not Jamie or Ted until I entered the room. They were standing by the open dresser, their arms about each other. I crossed the room and joined them.

SIXTEEN

At the wake, a steady stream of relatives, Frank's friends and strangers passed by his casket. Many of them kneeled briefly at its side and gazed at Frank, even more handsome in death than in life, and many of them, the strangers too, shook my hand or embraced me as they made their way past the front row of mourners: Jamie, Cyril, Ted, me, and our grandparents. I tired quickly of the condolences, all the touching, squeezing hands, and the hushed, awkward words of sympathy. I left the building a number of times and walked slowly around the block in the sticky summer heat. I returned to find that nothing had changed. I could see Frank's unnatural profile from the entryway, empty of everything, even peace, and people continued to approach and look down on him in attitudes between dread and grief.

It was a long exhausting night. I was relieved to see it end.

A day later, the hot morning sun warmed the mahogany casket as Ted, Cyril, several uncles and I carried Frank's body up the Church of the Epiphany's granite steps and into the cooler interior of stone. The casket gave off heat and a smell of lacquer. The priest waited between banks of flowers directly in line with the vertical axis of a ten foot crucifix on the wall behind him; it seemed to float above his head. From up front, as if calling us, came the sound of weeping. It was my mother, understanding quite clearly at the moment that her son was dead. A girlfriend of Frank's had cried openly at the wake and sniffled loudly now. Purdy Gant, standing beside Lou Cocco, cried, as did grandmom Vespers. I never thought my brother could stir such emotion.

As we carried the casket past the pews to the alter, I tried not to think of Frank inside the box. I tried not to think of his wounds or the medical examiner groping inside his body for bullets. I tried not to think at all as we placed the casket on the catafalque and sat in the first pew for the mass. But the thoughts came and came.

The priest began as soon as we settled in the pew and delivered his words in such perfect tones of solemnity that he seemed to be acting. I listened closely to his every word, staring at the priest's face for the twenty minutes it took him to finish. When he did, we carried the casket back out of the church and put it into the hearse, the friends and relatives coming after us and then everyone following the long black car through the city in a long line of cars with our headlights on to Holy Cross Cemetery in Yeadon. The same priest said a few words there with the coffin poised above the sharply rectangular hole and the relatives and friends gathered around it, their faces beginning to look impatient and weary, some distracted entirely, other things on their minds now as daily life began to take over.

The priest finished and Frank was lowered into the hole beside my father, beginning our family of bones. I turned and started away before Frank touched the ground.

Lou Cocco, having parked near me, was leaning against his car smoking a cigarette.

"I didn't know you smoked," I said as I came up.

"I don't, except at funerals."

"That's peculiar."

"There are stranger things."

"I suppose you're right."

I leaned against Lou's car beside him, feeling the sun reflected against my back, and we both gazed toward the knot of people still gathered about my brother's raw grave and the acres of white stone and grass beyond.

"I didn't like Frank that much," Cocco said, "but I felt bad when I heard what happened."

"Frank could be hard to like," I said, thinking about him, and not offended by Cocco's remark. Frank was too direct, too demanding, rarely sympathetic. He liked few things himself, and people even less. He did like money and the power it gave him, but that was because he hated and feared poverty so much. He liked physical conditioning, going to the gym and working out, but that stemmed from his hatred of any kind of weakness. If he loved any woman, he never told me. With us, his family, he seemed always ready to continue some endless argument, until recently. "He had a lot of hatreds. But he liked Patty Leone very much. And he liked Mr. Tucci. He died because of his loyalty to them, to the friendships."

"The code," Lou said.

"Yes, the code."

"Something I never had, and maybe never want. It can get you in trouble."

"Or get you killed."

"When Tucci asked me to go to that restaurant and get Frank, I didn't want to go. It wasn't any of my business."

"Frank said to ask you about that."

"He didn't tell you?"

"He didn't have time when I saw him last. Then he was killed an hour later."

Cocco dropped his cigarette and crushed it in the dirt. "I was sitting in front of the TV watching I don't know what when the phone rang; the wife answered it and said it was for me. She didn't know who it was. I got on and the voice said, 'It's Carmine Tucci. I need a favor.' I hung up on him. It was bad enough what happened at your house when he told me my father was his best friend. I wanted to forget that day, but here he was calling me, making it all fresh again. He called back. My wife answered again, and she talked to him a minute while I'm waving at her from the livingroom to say I'm out, I'm in the shower, I killed myself, anything. But she put the phone down, comes over and tells me when I'm about to holler at her that you're in danger. You, Vince. I got back on the phone and Tucci said that all he wanted me to do was to go to Oscar's and, without attracting attention, tell Frank to go to his house in Jersey, and to 'come quietly.' He said to make sure I used those words: come quietly, like it was a code. Tucci told me to do it for you, not him."

"I'm glad you did."

Cocco lit another cigarette. "I went in the place and sat at the bar, looking around for your brother. I saw him at a table with another man and a woman. After the waiter put food on their table, he came to the bar for drinks and I flagged him. I gave the guy ten bucks and told him I wanted to play a practical joke on my buddy sitting at his table and told him not to let on. I told him to tell Frank that his car was being towed, then I went outside, hoping that Frank rode to the place. But he came out seconds later, looking mad, and I grabbed his arm and told him what Tucci said: 'Come quietly.' Frank didn't go back into the restaurant, but shook my hand and ran to his car, which *was* parked at a fire hydrant. The next thing I know, him and Tucci are dead." He threw his barely smoked cigarette into the grass. "I'm sorry. I'm sorry I said I didn't like him."

"You probably saved my life, Cocco."

"So I'm a hero. Forget it."

Tucci must have known or suspected something, I thought. He must have overheard a conversation or something of my encounter in the hall with his wife and Leo. Or, living in that house with her and the men for so long, he sensed a shift in mood that he read as threatening. Whatever the cause, he must have called Lou shortly after learning that I arrived at the house.

Cocco and I watched the crowd break up from around Frank's grave and begin to filter toward us.

Heads down, watching their feet, they were careful not to step on the dead.

My sister and her husband left the city for Ohio immediately after the funeral. They stayed at the house only long enough to load their bags into the trunk of the car and, when done, guided my mother into the back seat to return her to the Home before they headed across the state. They did not linger on the sidewalk, and our good-byes, moments later, were hurried and embarrassed, as though too much knowledge were between us now. I wanted to speak my anguish at their hurt, but I could not gather the words.

"Come visit," Jamie said, forcing a smile.

"Try," Cyril added.

"I will."

Cyril slid behind the wheel and Jamie into the passenger side. My mother craned her neck to look at me and the house as they pulled away—Would she remember the funeral or would Frank still be alive in her ramshackled mind?—but Jamie and Cyril kept their faces rigidly to the front, as if not wanting to see more than they had to. Watching them drive up the street under the hazy sun, I thought it would be a long time before I saw them again.

I walked into the house and found Teddy preparing to leave.

"So you're going," I said.

"Yes." He told me about a crafts show in Boulder, Colorado that would be held in a few weeks. "I don't have much time to spare if I want to be there for the beginning."

"I'll give you a ride to the train or bus station."

"I think I want to hitchhike."

"All the way to the cabin?"

"It'll do me good." He told me that he would start trying to get a ride on Broad Street, heading north to the Pennsylvania Turnpike.

"Can I walk with you to Broad?"

"I'd like that." He took his backpack from the floor and we left the house.

"Why don't you come to the cabin with me?" Ted asked at Eleventh Street.

"I wouldn't know what to do there."

"Well, feel free to come up any time you want."

"I'll keep it in mind."

We walked the length of the Church of the Epiphany. I tried again not to think of us in there that morning, Teddy and me holding onto opposite brass handles of the casket between us. When I thought of Frank, I imagined his last moments, the four bullets slamming into him, his stumble down the hall, the blood leaking out, and I felt sick. I felt sicker when my thoughts turned to Jamie in the bedroom with Tony Buttons and Tommy Green. So I tried not to think of Jamie either. I kept my eyes straight ahead as Ted and I walked past the church toward Twelfth, understanding Jamie's and Cyril's rigid heads as they drove away.

Ted and I walked straight up Jackson Street to Broad; he had a long steady stride, forcing me to walk faster to keep abreast of him. Now that Ted had a direction in which to travel, he moved with a resoluteness he never otherwise showed, and I felt as though I slowed him down by tagging along. Looking at him, Ted seemed the least affected of all of us by what had happened in the last few days.

"You look better now than when you came," I said.

"In what way?"

"You had a look of dread when we drove into the city; now, you look almost happy, even after what happened."

"What happened can't be undone," he said. "It's over and we have to go forward. Also, I'm going home to carve wood. Work. It's a soothing thought."

"And then hitchhike to Colorado?"

"Probably."

"You won't let me give you any money?"

He shook his head no. I had tried earlier to give Ted some of the money Tucci gave me but Ted didn't want it, not because it had come from Tucci, he had said, but because it was not money he had earned. I did not try to persuade him, but when he left the house to run in the morning I put five thousand dollars in his backpack. I had done the same with Jamie, secretly sticking the cash into an inner sleeve of her suitcase where she had packed the few books she bought in New York. If they wanted to send the money back or give it away, they could.

We reached Broad Street. The cars, buses, and trucks pushed warm drafts over us as we stood facing but not looking at each other.

"Well," my brother said, turning to me.

"Sure you don't want a ride?"

"I'm sure."

The subway train rumbled beneath the sidewalk into the Snyder Avenue stop. "Why don't you at least take the subway to the end of the line?"

"It's not as interesting. Besides, I'd rather be out in the light and air."

BLOOD CONFESSIONS

"So you'll just put out your thumb here?"

"It's not a good idea to stand in one spot waiting for a ride. You should walk with your thumb out because that gives the impression to drivers that you're willing to walk where you want to go and makes them feel like they're doing a good deed when they pick you up."

"Can I walk with you awhile?"

"Well, they'll think we're both hitchhiking, and it's much harder for two people to get a ride than one."

"Yes, I guess that figures," I said. "How about if, while you're in the street, I just walk over here on the sidewalk. Would you mind?" I did not want to go home yet and be alone in the house.

"No, not at all."

I put out my hand. "I guess we should say so long now then."

Teddy nodded and took my hand, looking in my eyes with his deep browns, which still seemed to hold things he would probably never tell, even to lovers.

"Take care, Vincent." He turned and walked across the sidewalk into the street, gave me a look over his shoulder, then turned in the direction of the traffic and began to walk, his thumb pointing to City Hall. He walked between the parked cars and the nearest lane of traffic, a space of four or five feet, and I walked parallel to him on the sidewalk—first, along the wrought iron fence of Southern High School where my parents had been educated, then across Snyder Avenue and past the Burger King, Woolworth's, the Electric Company, and the PSFS bank on the corner of McKean Street. A red light stopped us, but Ted stayed in the street and did not walk over, only smiled at me, a friendly stranger already.

The light changed and we continued up Broad Street, St. Agnes Hospital across from us. Someone shouted at Ted from a pick-up truck and several other cars tooted their horns at him, but no one slowed to pick him up that block. Ted had no luck for the next several blocks either, and at Tasker Street, when he looked at me, I pointed to the subway entrance. But he only gave me a smile, shook his head no, adjusted his backpack with the five thousand dollars he did not know was in it and continued those long patient strides of his. He looked like he could walk the two hundred and fifty miles to his cabin without tiring. I had no doubt that if no one stopped to give him a ride he would walk all the way home.

Ted and I walked nearly to Washington Avenue before a car slowed as it passed my brother, then stopped. He hurried to the car and, reaching it, looked back to me on the sidewalk. I stopped when he did and waved. Ted lifted his hand and stretched out his arm, not waving to me, it seemed, but blessing me. He ducked into the car; as it pulled away, I saw that he had been picked up by three nuns.

I turned around and slowly walked home.

From a block away, I saw two figures on the sidewalk in front of my house. For several steps, I thought Russo and Silver had stopped by to badger me again; but, drawing closer, I made out Mrs. Falcone and Marie. I had not seen them except briefly, since that night I brought them together to tell them about Patty. They seemed now to be waiting for me.

BLOOD CONFESSIONS

Reaching them, I saw that they had the same grief-stricken faces I had left them with that night. Mrs. Falcone wrung her hands and her lips shook. Marie, whose father's funeral was being conducted then, appeared ill.

"What is it?" I asked. "What's wrong?"

It came out as a wail: "Somebody killed Patty."

SEVENTEEN

My family was gone. I thought of the departures as I sat at night in my car on Passyunk Avenue near Shunk's Tavern, waiting for Tommy Green to come out. In my feverish mind, I saw Jamie and Cyril driving away with my mother in the back seat. I saw Ted ducking into the car full of nuns. I saw Frank on the morgue's stainless steel table. I also thought about Tucci, violently killed when so close to death by disease. And about poor Patty Leone.

Mrs. Falcone and Marie had gone to see him at the Home but were told that he had been taken out and moved to another facility several miles away. The women drove there immediately. When she finally saw Patty, Marie barely recognized him; her shock, she said, was lessened because of it. Patty was more familiar to Mrs. Falcone. The older woman and Marie sat with him all afternoon in the shade of a tree. They both spoke to Patty, recalled instances of his life to him, and hoped that in doing so his eyes would focus and he'd respond. He continued to stare. Marie said she realized then that Patty would always be that way. There was nothing left of the young man she had known. But at least she knew now what had become of him; that was a consolation.

The women visited again the next day and were told that Patty had been found dead in his wheelchair, apparently strangled.

"Strangled?"

"Who could do such a thing?" Mrs. Falcone moaned.

I knew. With Marie and Mrs. Falcone softly crying in the livingroom, I searched for Rick Russo's telephone number and called him.

"I'm glad to hear from you," he said.

"I'm ready to talk now."

"When can you come to the office?"

"Immediately."

"Good." He gave me the address.

I left Marie and Mrs. Falcone in the house and went out into the staggering heat. Twenty minutes later, I sat across from Rick Russo, his cluttered desk between us. Carl Silver stood leaning against a steel filing cabinet, biting the edges of his fingernails and peeling them off.

I told them what my dealings with Carmine Tucci had been about.

"Tapes?" Russo said. He sat in front of a window, a building of glass and steel behind him across the street, reflecting the brutal sunlight and causing me to squint. "To protect him from a hit?"

"That, and because he wanted to tell his story."

"Oh, that's rich, that's lovely," Silver remarked.

"But they hit him anyway, *and* your brother," Russo said.

"Buttoni had broken into my house and stolen the tapes by then. They weren't a threat anymore."

"But he still thinks you have copies."

"He threatened to hurt my family and me if I didn't give them to him."

"Those tapes would've been beautiful to have, eh, Rick?"

Russo and I ignored Silver.

"You said you wanted me to help you. What can I do?"

"Did you tell us everything?" Russo asked.

I told him about the last meeting with Tucci when his wife burst into the room, smashed the tape recorder and screamed that Tony had killed Johnny Plum.

"Would you be willing to testify to that?"

"Yes, I think so."

"Good. Anything else?"

"I think Buttoni killed Patty Leone."

"Who's that?" Silver asked.

"Maybe you'll see something about it on the news." I told them about Patty, Marie's attachment to him, and how, because of Buttoni, he wound up in the wheelchair. "He and Plum were strangled. Maybe you can make a connection."

"Damn, those tapes would've been beautiful."

"Forget the goddamn tapes, Carl! They're gone. Let's just work with what we have, ok?"

"Which ain't a shitload of a lot." Silver chewed off a fingernail and spit it toward the trashcan. "We need some solid stuff, Rick. What we have now might put that creep away for a few years, but that's all, if it even sticks. We need something like the tapes."

"Don't you think I know that?" Russo turned to me. "You said that Buttoni thinks there are copies of the tapes, right?"

"Yes."

"So if you told him to meet you somewhere to hand them over to him, you think he would?"

"But there aren't any copies," I said.

"But he thinks there are. So he'll meet you."

"I don't know. I guess he would."

"Rick, tell him already, would you? Can't you just say something without all this bullshit?" Silver took a few steps toward me. "Look, would you wear a wire for us?"

"A wire?"

"A transmitter. Don't you watch TV or go to the movies?"

"Vincent," Russo said, "if you want to get back at Buttoni for what he did to your family, you can do it by helping us get some hard evidence on him so we can put him in jail for a long time. If you meet him and get him to talk about the murders, we'll tape it. He'll incriminate himself. What do you say?"

I did not think long. "Say when."

"As soon as possible."

Late the next evening, I took a new clothesline and cut it into six-foot lengths with a butcher knife. I put the rope and a roll of wide adhesive tape in a paper bag. At the desk, I dug beneath the old papers and brought out Frank's .38. Earlier, I had blown dust from the chambers and the hammer and worked the trigger several times, then I loaded the gun. I wrapped the gun in a towel and put it in the bag with the tape and the rope, even though Russo had told me not to bring any weapons. Before leaving the house, I taped the tiny microphone to my chest and attached the transmitter to my waist with a belt of velcro, as Russo had shown me. I called Russo and told him that I would be near Passyunk and Moore in fifteen minutes.

"I thought you told me you were meeting Buttoni on Broad Street at eleven o'clock," Russo said.

"I am."

"Then why are you going to Passyunk Avenue?"

"Something I have to do."

"Vincent—"

I hung up on him.

The streetlamps had just begun to sputter on as I stepped from the house, a final rim of orange-purple at the end of Jackson Street all that was left of the day. I hurried to the car, drove to Passyunk Avenue, got lucky, and parked close enough to the bar to see the faces of the patrons coming out. It was another hot and humid night and I sweated as I waited.

An hour passed. Men came out of Charlie Shunk's but none of them were Green. I recognized several of Frank's friends. To pass the time, I counted the seconds between light changes at the corner: twenty-six. I put my fingers against my throat and took my pulse: seventy-eight. I thought I should have been more nervous, my heart pounding wildly, but I felt relatively calm.

Another hour passed. I was beginning to think that I had missed Green when the door opened and he stepped out with another man. I sat up. They talked and laughed for a few minutes in front of the bar before splitting up and walking away in opposite directions. The man came toward me, weaving slightly from side to side. I sunk lower in my seat as he passed. Green walked the short distance to Moore Street, crossed it at the corner, and disappeared around the convenience store. I started the car and went after him.

The traffic light had changed to red and I stopped, but I could see up the street and Tommy on the left side walking toward Broad. I watched him cross Thirteenth before the light changed. I turned and drove past Green without looking at him, not chancing that he would recognize me. I sped to Juniper Street, which ran between Broad and Thirteenth, turned and parked on the corner where I could see Green pass in my rearview mirror. I took the towel from the bag and unwrapped the gun. Tommy came into the mirror a few moments later. I let him walk out of it before putting the gun in my pocket and leaving the car with my bag.

Green turned sharply into an alley with his hand to his zipper. I crossed the street and took out the gun when I reached the sidewalk. I rushed the thirty feet to the alley and stood at the mouth of it, listening to splashing and whistled bits of a song. When the splashing stopped, I pressed myself against the wall. Footsteps came toward the mouth of the alley. Green, his head down, was zipping up when he appeared.

"Tommy."

He looked up, smiling, ready to be friendly. Then he recognized me and his smile vanished. I hit him in the face with the gun before he could speak and knocked him back into the alley. His hands went to his nose. I stepped after him and kicked him. Tommy grunted and collapsed, clutching his groin. I stooped over him and jammed the barrel of the gun in his ear, forcing his head to the concrete and into the puddle he had just made. He winced.

"I want you to take me to your apartment. If you try to run, shout, say anything to anybody, I'll shoot you. Understand?"

"Uh huh," he said, bleeding from the nose.

"All right, get up." I took him by the arm and dragged him to his feet. "The gun will be two inches from your back."

I put the gun in my jacket pocket and held on to it with the muzzle pointing at Green. "Move."

Tommy led me from the alley and turned toward Broad Street. I walked slightly behind him, keeping an eye on his hands. At Broad, he wiped blood from beneath his nose and turned left into the brighter light of the streetlamps. Traffic was slight at that hour, few cars travelling north or south. The subway rumbled past beneath our feet, the uprush of air through the grates sending bits of paper into eddies. We passed a woman surrounded by bundles lying in the doorway of a medical supplies store; one of the bundles, I realized, was a child.

"Spare some change for food," the woman said to us.

We didn't stop. An old man walking his dog passed us a little later but he did not look at our faces.

"Where is it?" I asked.

"Next block."

We walked the rest of the way to Mifflin and crossed the street. Green pinched his nostrils.

"I think you broke my nose. I can't even breathe through it. Not a drop."

We continued down the street and walked halfway before Tommy stopped at a brownstone triplex across from St. Agnes Hospital.

"This is about what happened at your place, right?" Green asked. "Tony made me do all that, Vin. He's the guy you want."

I put the gun against his spine. "Open the door."

"Vin, I got a wife and kid in there."

"All right, I'll shoot you in the back right now."

"No, wait. Ok, I lied. Here, I got my keys. I'll unlock the door, we'll have a drink." He hurried up the steps and I followed him through the outer door. In the vestibule, Green fumbled for another key. He opened the inner door and I followed him into a hallway smelling of pine oil and cigarettes. He paused there.

"Look, Vin, I got close to twenty-eight hunnert dollars I collected for Tony tonight. You want it?"

"Keep going."

"I got some coke, weed, a bunch of pills I'll give you too. You can get some good money for the shit, or use it yourself, whatever."

I pulled out the gun and put it against his chest.

"Ok, ok." He led me down the short hall, opened the door there and turned on the light. We stepped into a kitchen of white steel cabinets, yellow linoleum, a cheap dinette set, dishes piled high in the sink. A skillet with congealed grease in it sat on top of the filthy gas range and gave off the odor of bacon. The open doorways to the left and right were dark, the apartment quiet. Somewhere in the building a television was playing.

"Sit down."

He pulled a chair from the dinette and sat. "What're you going to do?" His nose had stopped bleeding; dried blood ringed his nostrils.

I dropped the bag on the table. "Take the stuff out."

Green pulled the lengths of rope and the tape from the bag. "I think I know what this is for."

I grabbed a handful of his hair and yanked his head back against the chair. "You raped my sister."

"Vin, I didn't touch her, I swear. That was Tony."

"I should shoot you in the knees and work my way up." His hair smelled of urine and I let it go, but I kept the gun a few inches from his head.

"Vin, listen to me for a minute. Will you listen to me? You don't want to hurt me. Let's work something out. Take the twenty-eight hunnert I collected for Tony tonight. Whataya say?"

"Don't you get it, Tommy?"

"Vin, I told you, Tony made me do everything."

"Did you think that by killing Frank you wouldn't have anything to worry about?"

"I didn't kill Frank. That I definitely didn't do. I liked Frank. I was going to quit Tony and ask Frank for my old job back. Really, Vin."

"Who killed Frank then?"

"I don't know. I swear to my mother."

I paused, trying to decide if Green was telling the truth, wondering if hitting him with the gun again would give him second thoughts about lying.

"Do you want to live?" I asked.

"What? Sure, I want to live."

"Then do what I say."

"Sure, ok, sure."

I said, "Take one of those ropes and make a slip knot, then put the loop around your right wrist." I pointed the gun at his forehead to encourage him.

"Yeah, that's it," Green said, eagerly taking a piece of rope and starting a knot, "just tie me up, maybe hit me again but not too hard and take the money I collected for Tony, take my dope, make it look like a robbery." He made the knot and put his hand through the loop it made, then he put both hands behind his back. "And I won't say anything, who did it or what."

I stooped behind him and tied his hands together, wrapping the rope around his wrists until I used up the entire length. Taking another piece of rope, I tied his hands to the back of the chair.

"Hey, you're pretty good at this, but not so tight. You'll cut off the circulation."

I ignored him, took two more lengths of the rope from the table and tied each of his ankles to a chair leg.

"Where's your stash?" I asked Green, standing up.

"You gonna take it? Good. Look in that right cabinet, you'll see a coffee can. It's in there."

I went to the cabinet, opened the door and took down a Maxwell House can from the middle shelf. I took the can to the table and dumped the contents in front of Tommy. Plastic sandwich bags of pills, white powder and pot fell out. I opened the bag of pills, poured them on the table and separated them by color and size.

"What are they?"

"You got your xanex and your valiums, there, those tiny ones. You got the benzedrine babies, the darvons for pain, any kind, and the hammerhead qualudes, my personal favorite."

"These the qualudes?" I asked, lifting a pill.

"Yeah, the beautiful barbits. Coupla those and you're walking under water."

I put all the qualudes and darvons in my palm and turned to Green. "Open your mouth," I said, holding the pills under his chin.

"What, and take them? Vin, I can't take that much shit. I'll o.d."

I took the .38 from the table and put it to Green's temple. "If you don't swallow them, I'll shoot you right now."

"Vin, listen—"

"No. Take the pills."

"Look, Vin, I'll give you the hunnert—"

"Shut up."

"—the dope, my stereo system. Hey, there's this girl I know you can do anything you want to."

"Keep going and I'll pull the trigger."

"Wait, Vin. Wait! Vin, you don't want to kill me. You woulda shot me in the alley if you did. Listen, it's not even fair. I didn't kill nobody, so I don't deserve it."

I went to the sink, filled a glass with water and dumped the pills into it. I went back to Green and put the gun to his bony chest. "Drink it."

"I'll go coma, man!"

"Not if you can make it to the range after I leave and burn the ropes from your wrists."

"Yeah, I'll make it to the stove. I'll fly over there."

BLOOD CONFESSIONS

"Ok, pick a knee for me to start with. This one?" I pressed the gun against his left knee.

"They'll hear the shots, somebody in the apartment will see you leave. You'll get caught, Vin. You'll go to jail."

"I'm going to start counting to three. Either drink it or I shoot you."

"Come on, Vin. Vin, listen. Ok, you want to get even for your sister. I can understand that. But what you're doing ain't even. You're goin' overboard. It's cruel, Vin."

I moved the gun to his groin.

"Vin! All right, all right. I'll drink the shit. Give it to me. But you have to make me a promise. If I go into a coma, you have to kill me. You have to come in the hospital and pull out the tubes and shit. That ain't no life. Promise me, Vin."

"Why should I after what you did?"

"Because you're Vin."

I looked down at him, his nose cut and swollen, his hair wet with urine.

"You're pathetic." I took the glass and the rest of Green's dope to the bathroom and flushed it down the toilet.

"Thanks, Vin," Green said when I returned. "I knew you wouldn't hurt me real bad. You're a good guy. But you flushed the stuff? That was, like, nine hunnert worth."

"Where's that money you collected for Buttoni?"

"The drawer to the left of the sink, there's an envelope," he said. "G'head, take it, buy yourself some nice suits, do some high rollin' at the casino."

Before going to the sink, I peeled a length of adhesive tape from the roll and put it quickly over Tommy's mouth before he could protest. I was tired of hearing him. He shook his head, tried to speak, but I got the tape in place and covered it with another piece. Then I went to the drawer and removed the envelope. Behind me, Green rattled the chair legs against the floor as I put the money in one pocket of the jacket and the gun in the other.

"Stop that shaking," I said, going back to him.

He looked at me in wide-eyed panic, his face a deep red. Green's nostrils must have swollen shut as he said earlier and he couldn't breathe because of the tape over his mouth. I reached out to lift the tape but stopped. Tommy's eyes went wider, looking worried and more frightened. Strangle noises came from his convulsing throat. He rocked in the chair, pulled against the knots that held him, and violently shook his head. I watched his face turn from red to deep purple. His eyes bulged and began to tear. True terror showed in them before they rolled upward and his eyelids fluttered. His head fell back on the seat but his body continued to shudder.

After three or four minutes of watching him, I peeled the tape from his mouth and smacked him several times. As Green began to suck air, I left the apartment, turning out the lights before closing the door.

The woman with the bundles and her child were still lying in the doorway of the medical supplies store when I walked toward Mifflin Street.

"Spare some change for food," she said.

I stopped. "Here," and I gave her the envelope of cash.

* * *

BLOOD CONFESSIONS

I stood nervous and sweaty on the corner of Broad and Wharton, watching traffic and waiting for Buttoni. I had the gun in my jacket pocket and the bag of blank tapes in my hand. Somewhere close by, Russo, Silver and their men were supposed to be sitting in cars, waiting to follow Buttoni and me, and to keep me unharmed.

I had called Buttoni late that afternoon, saying I didn't want any more trouble with him and that I wanted to give him the copies of the tapes. That was smart, he said, and told me when and where to meet him.

I waited close to a half hour, watching cars pass, before the Lincoln appeared and slowed. Buttoni briefly hit his horn as the car stopped. I walked into the street, my heart pounding in my head now, and got into the frigid air-conditioned car. Buttoni sped up the street as soon as I closed the door.

I noticed stitches in the corner of Buttoni's eye and a purple ear from his run-in with the parking lot attendant. His jaw was also swollen and bruised.

"Pretty, huh?" Buttoni said.

"What?"

"My face. I have to give it to him, that parking lot guy was a tough bastard. Course, he wound up very sorry we had that misunderstanding. Now he's—what do they call it?—a statistic. Least me and you don't have to fight like that, huh?"

"No." I briefly imagined Buttoni returning to the Ocean City parking lot, armed and not alone, and brutally taking revenge upon the man who had so neatly beaten him.

"Yeah, I'm glad we can do business," Buttoni

said. "After maybe we can be friends. We sort of got off on the wrong foot."

"That happens," I said, barely conscious of my words.

We drove a few blocks without speaking. While wondering how I would get Buttoni to say something about the murders of Frank and Tucci, I also saw myself shooting him, and not just once.

At Christian Street, Buttoni pointed across my nose at the old central public library. "Look at that place. You'd think the city could do something with it."

I looked at the old classical building with its massive columns, resembling a Greek ruin now except for the plywood covering the windows and doors; plans to turn it into something useful came up periodically but the building squatted there year after year and never changed.

When I looked forward, Buttoni had a gun against my neck.

"Your piece, Mr. Assassin," he said. "Drop it over your right shoulder into the back. Do it slow."

I reached into the pocket of my jacket.

"You get brave and I put a bullet through your jugular."

I withdrew the gun from my pocket and, lifting it slowly, let it fall over my shoulder into the back where it thumped on the floor.

"Very nice." Buttoni took the gun from my neck and rested it on the seat, pointing upward at my ribs. "You shoulda made sure Tommy couldn't get outta that chair for a while. His landlady heard him yelling, let herself in with her key, and untied him. He calls me when I'm about to leave and tells me what happened. I didn't think you had it in you. And now you meet me with the same piece you broke Tommy's nose with. You think I'm some dope-eating punk like Tommy Green you can bang up? You sick?"

"You hurt my family, killed Frank."

"Your family coulda been hurt a lot worse. But I didn't touch Frank. What, you think I'm Superman? I can fly to the airport, whack Frank and Tucci, and fly back to take your call? Don't be stupid."

"Who did it, then?"

"You don't have to know that. What good would it do you?" He turned sharply onto Lombard Street, cutting through a long line of traffic going in the opposite direction; a pick-up truck barely missed us, the driver angrily blasting his horn.

"You were in Frank's apartment. You set it up."

"I didn't set up shit. That's Mrs. Tucci's department. Picture that scene: there's George and Leo laying in her hallway with their heads split open compliments of Frank, and she's on the phone sending everybody in motion. Even got somebody over the house to get rid of the bodies and put them in a landfill."

"She sent you to Frank's?"

"It wasn't the first time." He raced the yellow light at Fifteenth Street and we sailed toward Sixteenth, catching another yellow, which Buttoni raced through as well. "Mrs. Tucci knew Frank was up to something, and she said the best way to find out what was to check out his place, look through his mail and stuff. That's a smart lady. Because Frank's phone bill had some interesting calls, like to Italy around where Tucci used to live as a kid, and there was something from the hotel at the airport. Things clicked after that. Two days later, Frank clobbers George and Leo. When you called Frank's, I was tape-hunting. Which reminds me. See the tape deck." He pointed with the gun at the dashboard. "Stick a tape in there, so I can see what we got."

"What do you mean?"

"I mean, I want to see if you're giving me the tapes of Tucci and not something else. Get one."

I reached into the bag as we passed Nineteenth Street and slowly withdrew one of the blank cassettes. I took the cassette slowly from its plastic case and intentionally tried to stick it backwards into the loader.

"The other way," Buttoni said.

I turned the cassette around and let it drop.

"What do you have, palsy? Get another one."

Again, I reached into the bag and withdrew another cassette, removed it from its case and stretched toward the tape player. Trying to buy time, I dropped that one, too.

"Something wrong with you? Give me one, I'll do it."

We whipped by Twenty-first Street and would soon pass the spot where, racing around the corner in the stolen car, I had killed that woman. I shivered, seeing her face just before the thump.

"Throw it over here. And do me a favor, don't grab for the gun. I'd have to shoot you or bust your face."

I took another cassette from the bag and tossed it across the seat, hitting Buttoni in the thigh. He switched the gun to his other hand and, with it still pointing at me, he fingered the cassette from its case and jammed it deftly into the player. Buttoni hit a button and waited. No sound came out of the speaker so he adjusted the volume.

"What the fuck?"

"Maybe you're at the end of the tape. I didn't rewind it."

Buttoni worked the controls of the tape player. The cassette whirled in reverse for less than two seconds, then stopped spinning.

"Maybe that tape got mixed up," I said, hoping for some heavy traffic to suddenly materialize or for a red light so that the car would slow and I could jump out and run. But the street remained empty and the lights green. Where the hell was Russo?

Buttoni grabbed the bag of cassettes and dumped them onto the seat. He took one and jammed it into the player. Again, no sound.

"I must have brought the wrong ones."

"Yeah, you musta." He removed the cassette from the player and dropped it on the seat. Then he backhanded me across the mouth. "The fuck is wrong with you? You think you can play with me?"

"I made a mistake," I said, wiping blood from my lips.

"You made a mistake, all right. There ain't no copies, are there? No notes in nobody's will about tapes?"

"They're in the bank." There were no copies in any bank.

"Don't give me that shit. You met me tonight to whack me, get even about your sister and Frank. Are you mental or what? You actually thought you could do something to me? You? Christ, Patty Leone and Johnny Plum together were easier to kill than you're gonna be." He swung the car sharply around the deserted end of Lombard Street where it turned toward South and the bridge entrance, and where I had run down the woman.

I immediately noticed the orange sign and the barricades, and realized then why the traffic had been so thin on Lombard Street. The bridge was closed for repairs; drivers had to take another bridge to get to West Philadelphia.

"Pretty convenient, huh? Nobody around but us." Buttoni stopped the car at the foot of the bridge and pointed the gun at my head. "Yeah, I knew the bridge was closed. Now, get out."

I stepped out of the Lincoln, anxious to see someone, a lone jogger, a dogwalker, hoping that Russo and Silver would roar around the corner, their portable bubble lights flashing. But the area was deserted. Even if I shouted, no one concerned enough would look out their window before Buttoni shot me.

"All right, killer, walk on the bridge," Buttoni said, coming around to my side of the car.

"Wait. They're repairing it; it's unsafe."

Buttoni laughed. "So live dangerously, at least for another few minutes." He shoved me.

I stumbled past sawhorses with blinking yellow hazard lights attached to them and began walking along the pale green railing of the bridge. Buttoni remained slightly behind and to the left of me. The bridge surface rose in a slight arch and, over the railing, the tops of the few trucks in the ATT lot below receded with each step. Several trucks were parked against the brick wall that separated the lot from the railroad tracks. Just beyond, in the dim light, the water began. My legs weakened and my head began to spin.

"Let's pick it up. I don't have all night." He nudged me with the gun.

I barely heard him, his voice as distant as the rushing cars on the expressway across the river.

We walked past several air compressors, piles of wood and steel rod. I noticed patches in the road surface of deeper black; they were holes where concrete had fallen away, and the deeper blackness was the river below.

I dragged my feet. "I—" It came out as a croak.

"I, what, you chickenshit? I'm scared? I'm sorry for fucking with you, Tony? That's too late. Game's over."

Where were Russo and that bastard Silver?

We passed the first concrete support and neared the spot where, years ago, I had clung to the railing as the police raced from both directions of the bridge to catch Frank, then fallen into the river.

I glanced over the railing, close enough to touch, and saw the water shimmer. Only sixty feet.

"You're forgetting about something," I said, trying to keep the quaver out of my voice.

"Yeah, what am I forgetting?"

"Frank's money."

"Yeah, what about it?"

"It's mine now." I glanced at the river. Only sixty feet. "I'll give it to you and leave the city if you let me go."

"How much are you talking?"

"About two hundred thousand."

"Two hunnert?"

"In cash and gold. And—"

I planted my foot, threw back my elbow against Buttoni's forearm, and spun, swinging. The gun went off in front of me as my fist connected with Buttoni's stitched eye. He staggered, the gun firing aimlessly again as he tripped backwards over a plank, cursing me, and as I, continuing to spin, took one step to the rail and vaulted over it.

The collision with the water came suddenly, before I expected or was ready for it, as though the black river had come up to meet me. I shot straight through the tepid water to the bottom, my limbs and face stinging from the impact, pressure in my ears, the river as inky as the first time. The ooze on the bottom grasped my feet and held them. I kicked in panic, managed to free myself, and flailed toward the surface. I burst into the air, gagging on the water I had drunk, and heard Buttoni's enraged voice from above and the sound of gunshots and what I did not realize until moments later were bullets *thwapping* into the water near me. I knew it was too dark for Buttoni to see but, afraid he'd get lucky, I dove and swam breaststroke under water toward the nearest bank. I did not reach it before my lungs gave out and I had to surface. I drew air quickly and dove again to claw through the water, then once more before finally reaching the bank.

I crouched with my cheek against the cool fetid mud of the bank and paused to listen for Buttoni and his gun. I heard nothing but the rushing traffic of the expressway on the other side. Grabbing ahold of saplings, I pulled myself from the water and scrambled up the bank, pausing by the railroad tracks to look around. I was about to start for the brick wall when I saw a figure appear at the top of it and drop down to my side. I flattened myself against the ground, watching the man hurry directly for the river. He reached it and turned on a flashlight at the same time lights from the bridge appeared, shining down toward the water.

"Vespers!" the man by the river called. "Vespers!"

I stood up from the ground and walked up behind him. "It's about time, Russo."

He wheeled, the flashlight coming around to shine on me. "Damn! You scared me."

"Did you get what you wanted?"

"Yes, we got it, excellent stuff, the murders, plus the attempted murder of you. Also the business with Green. I have to tell you, you had us crazy on that one." He turned off the flashlight.

"Did you get him?"

"He's already locked up."

"Buttoni, I mean."

"He's cuffed and in the car, whining for his lawyer."

"Good." I started away.

"Hey, you all right?"

I thought I was until I reached the railroad tracks. My brain seemed to flip-flop and my stomach contracted. I stopped, doubled over and, as Russo came up behind me, vomited the river into the gravel.

EIGHTEEN

Marie and I sat quietly on the lake in Ted's wooden boat, our fishing lines slanting into the glassy water. In the still surface, I watched clouds drift across the impossibly blue sky. The dense woods had quieted and the sun had dropped behind the trees, casting our dark shadows over the side of the boat.

"Looks like the weather's changing," Marie said.

"Yes."

I felt a slight evening chill on the back of my neck and wondered what it would be like there in the winter. Would the lake freeze over? How would it feel, to a city person like me, to trudge from the cabin to the outhouse in a foot of snow? What if we ran out of food or one of us came down with appendicitis?

"Are you worried about winter?" I asked Marie.

She hesitated only slightly. "No. You?"

I looked at the sky, the trees, the calm water. "Not at all." And I wasn't.

About the Author

Albert DiBartolomeo lives and teaches in Philadelphia. The holder of a master's degree, he is a recent graduate of Temple University's Creative Writing program, where he studied with David Bradley, Toby Olson, Ryszard Kapuscinski, William Van Wert, and Joan Mellon. Before that he spent some time as a cabinetmaker. *Blood Confessions* is his first novel. He is currently at work on a second.

(0451

ON THE EDGE OF YOUR SEAT!

- ☐ **SOUL/MATE by Rosamond Smith.** A psychopathic serial killer with lover's face ... "Headlong suspense ... What if a well-meanin intelligent woman should encounter a demonic twin?"—*The Atlan Journal and Constitution.* "Taut, relentless, chilling!"—*Chicago Tribun* (401905—$4.9

- ☐ **NEMESIS by Rosamond Smith.** "A terror-invoking psychothriller brimmin with atmosphere."—*Cleveland Plain Dealer.* "Extraordinary ... a mu der mystery with a literary twist ... rich in social observation an psychological insight ... well-written ... the dialogue has rhythn pitch, melody and mood"—*Boston Globe* (402952—$5.5

- ☐ **PRESSURE DROP by Peter Abrahams.** Nina Kitchener has no idea wh lay behind the disappearance of her baby from a New York hospital. An nothing will stop her terror-filled quest for the donor who fathered h child ... nothing—not even murder. (402359—$4.9

- ☐ **OVER THE EDGE by Jonathan Kellerman.** The death of a former patie leads Alex Delaware through a labyrinth of sick sex and savage gree penetrating to the inner sanctums of the rich and powerful and t lowest depths of the down and out. Alex's discovery of the secret life one of California's leading families sets off an explosion of shatteri revelations. "Mesmerizing!"—*Booklist* (152190—$5.9

- ☐ **BLOOD TEST by Jonathan Kellerman.** A child psychologist and a hon cide detective hunt through a human jungle of health cults, sex-for-sa haunts and dreams-turned-into-nightmares to find a kidnapped child (159292—$5.9

Prices slightly higher in Canada.

Buy them at your local bookstore or use this convenient coupon for ordering.

NEW AMERICAN LIBRARY
P.O. Box 999, Bergenfield, New Jersey 07621

Please send me the books I have checked above.
I am enclosing $_____ (please add $2.00 to cover postage and handlin Send check or money order (no cash or C.O.D.'s) or charge by Mastercard VISA (with a $15.00 minimum). Prices and numbers are subject to change with notice.

Card #_____ Exp. Date _____
Signature_____
Name_____
Address_____
City _____ State _____ Zip Code _____

For faster service when ordering by credit card call **1-800-253-6476**
Allow a minimum of 4-6 weeks for delivery. This offer is subject to change without noti

ⓓ SIGNET

PAGE-TURNERS!

(0451)

- **EDEN CLOSE by Anita Shreve.** This novel of love, terror and mystery weaves a tale of obsessive passions, and of the shadows cast over life by dark deeds. "Tantalizing!"—*New York Times Book Review*. (167856—$4.95)

- **BAD DESIRE by Gary Devon.** "A *very* good psychological thriller!"—Mary Higgins Clark. "More than a superb novel of suspense ... a deep and compelling story of the truly dark sides of love, and ferocity of passion."—Gerald A. Browne. (170989—$5.99)

- **WELL AND TRULY by Evelyn Wilde Mayerson.** Loss, redemption—and falling in love again ... "A fine novel that makes for compelling reading."—James Michener (169883—$5.50)

Prices slightly higher in Canada

Buy them at your local bookstore or use this convenient coupon for ordering.

NEW AMERICAN LIBRARY
P.O. Box 999, Bergenfield, New Jersey 07621

Please send me the books I have checked above.
I am enclosing $_____ (please add $2.00 to cover postage and handling).
Send check or money order (no cash or C.O.D.'s) or charge by Mastercard or VISA (with a $15.00 minimum). Prices and numbers are subject to change without notice.

Card #_____ Exp. Date _____
Signature_____
Name_____
Address_____
City _____ State _____ Zip Code _____

For faster service when ordering by credit card call **1-800-253-6476**

Allow a minimum of 4-6 weeks for delivery. This offer is subject to change without notice.

① SIGNET   **⊜ ONY**

AND JUSTICE FOR ALL . . .
(04!

- [ ] **BINO by A.W. Gray.** When his seediest client turns up dead, B suspects a whitewash of the dirtiest kind. What he finds links client's demise to a political assassination, and the bodies start pil up. Politics has always been the dirtiest game in town—and it's ab to become the deadliest. (401298—$3.

- [ ] **IN DEFENSE OF JUDGES by A.W. Gray.** ":Fast and furious ... rivet ... if you haven't met Bino Phillips, you've missed a real characte —*Washington Post*. "This is as good as it gets ... lurid, laid-ba and literate."—*Publishers Weekly* (402715—$5.

- [ ] **THE SUNSET BOMBER by D. Kincaid.** The hottest courtroom drama si *Reasonable Doubt*, this explosive novel spotlights a hard-driving attor in search of justice—no matter what the cost. (151267—$4.!

- [ ] **ICEMAN—A Jack Eichord Thriller by Rex Miller.** The Iceman's in to and as a toll of atrociously assaulted victims mounts, serial mur detective Jack Eichord vows to put this killer too savage for man-ma justice out of action. "Dynamite."—Stephen King (402235—$4.

- [ ] **SKELETONS by Eric Sauter.** "A searing slice of the underbelly o psychopath ... a macabre thriller ... swift and exciting!"—*Tren Times*. "A superb job of probing both the psyches of the hunter and hunted."—*The Orlando Sentinel* (402804—$4.`

Prices slightly higher in Canada

Buy them at your local bookstore or use this convenient coupon for ordering.

NEW AMERICAN LIBRARY
P.O. Box 999, Bergenfield, New Jersey 07621

Please send me the books I have checked above.
I am enclosing $_____ (please add $2.00 to cover postage and handli Send check or money order (no cash or C.O.D.'s) or charge by Mastercarc VISA (with a $15.00 minimum). Prices and numbers are subject to change with notice.

Card #_____ Exp. Date _____
Signature_____
Name_____
Address_____
City _____ State _____ Zip Code _____

For faster service when ordering by credit card call **1-800-253-6476**
Allow a minimum of 4-6 weeks for delivery. This offer is subject to change without not